Praise for the novels of

SHARON SALA

"Sala's characters are vivid and engaging."
—*Publishers Weekly* on *Cut Throat*

"Sharon Sala is not only a top romance novelist,
she is an inspiration for people everywhere
who wish to live their dreams."
—John St. Augustine, host,
Power! Talk Radio WDBC-AM, Michigan

"Veteran romance writer Sala lives up to
her reputation with this well-crafted thriller."
—*Publishers Weekly* on *Remember Me*

"[A] well-written, fast-paced ride."
—*Publishers Weekly* on *Nine Lives*

"Perfect entertainment for those looking for
a suspense novel with emotional intensity."
—*Publishers Weekly* on *Out of the Dark*

SHARON SALA

Blood Stains

MIRA®

Recycling programs
for this product may
not exist in your area.

ISBN-13: 978-0-7783-2941-1

BLOOD STAINS

Copyright © 2011 by Sharon Sala

For questions and comments about the quality of this book please contact us at
Customer_eCare@Harlequin.ca.

www.MIRABooks.com

Printed in U.S.A.

Secrets within a family are always a whisper away from a disaster, and the longer they are hidden, the more powerful they become, until the weight of knowledge becomes an unbearable burden.

Growing up, we are taught to tell the truth. But as we grow older, we soon learn there is a huge difference between the truth and the whole truth. Often, it becomes a matter of keeping peace in the family, even though the burden of keeping quiet becomes as stressful as keeping secrets.

I'm dedicating this book to the people who become caught between the secrets and lies. Remember—

The truth shall set you free.

One

The dark mound of dirt in the Slade family cemetery marked the final resting place of family patriarch Andrew Slade. Flowers that had been placed on the grave three days earlier were already shriveled from the chill Montana spring. He had been buried beside his loving wife, Hannah, on the Montana ranch that had been his solace, and no amount of weeping or praying could change the fact that he was dead. Although, if that had been possible, he would already have been resurrected.

His three daughters had been blindsided by his passing and were still dealing with the devastation.

The doctor called it an aneurysm.

His daughters called it a tragedy.

But they'd been raised to endure, and even though their hearts were broken, they were tending to business, just as they'd been taught.

At the age of twenty-four years, Maria Slade was not the oldest, but she'd always been the leader, and today she was doing her best to keep her sisters' emotions intact.

All three still lived on the property. Maria was the one who thrived outdoors, who had ridden the ranch with her father and their foreman, Bud, and was also her father's best friend. She came alive outdoors, could rope and ride as well as any hired hand, and had recently taken up training horses as her chosen profession.

Savannah was the youngest, but a whiz with math. She kept the books, both for the ranch and its horse and cattle breeding program, without a hitch.

Holly was the homemaker. When Hannah died, she'd stepped into the breach and kept the cupboards full and the house spotless, and had hosted their annual barbeque as if she'd been born to the job.

Within the hour, they would be going to Missoula for the reading of the will. It marked the finality of their father's passing, and for that reason alone, Andrew's daughters were dragging their heels.

Because Maria had always taken the lead, she was rushing to get ready, knowing it would be her responsibility to get everyone and everything in place so they could leave.

She glanced at herself in the mirror, giving her appearance one last appraisal. Dark hair brushed. Brown slacks, jade-colored blouse and suede jacket—subdued enough for the occasion but still comfortable for the chill of the day. Chocolate-brown boots in case of rain.

She squinted, testing to see if that would hide the fact that her eyes were still red from a morning bout of weeping, and then sighed. Why hide the fact that she was grieving? Everyone knew it. Taking a deep breath, she pivoted sharply on one heel and stalked out of the room.

As she was going down the hall, she heard the front door open, then close with a thud. That would be Bud coming to tell them he'd brought the car around. Bud's diligence over the past few days had helped them through many rough patches. She knew he was grieving for their father as deeply as they were. He and Andrew had been good friends long before Bud had come to work at the ranch, and working together all these years had only deepened the tie.

As she reached Savannah's door, she knocked sharply and called out, "Bud's here. We need to go."

"Coming," Savannah answered.

Maria moved down the hall to the last door and repeated the process.

"Holly! Bud's here."

The door opened immediately.

"I'm ready," Holly said, and fell into step beside her sister. A moment later, a door opened behind them and Savannah ran to catch up.

They entered the living room in tandem, their shoulders stiff, their chins raised as if bracing for another blow.

Bud was waiting for them. "The wind is sharp and it looks like rain. You might want to get some rain gear."

"We aren't made of sugar. We won't melt," Maria muttered.

Savannah stifled a sob and reached for Maria's hand.

Holly's chin quivered. "That's what Dad always said."

"Don't say I didn't warn you," Bud muttered, then spun on his heel and opened the door for them.

As the women grabbed their coats from the hall closet, they cast guilty glances at the firm set of his jaw. Maria reminded herself again that Bud was grieving, too.

"Sorry," she said, and gave him a quick kiss on the cheek as she walked past.

He hugged her back as an apology for his gruffness. "No need to apologize, sugar. We're all pretty raw."

Savannah laid her hand briefly on his forearm and gave it a squeeze.

Holly's gaze locked on his as she passed, then she blinked and turned away.

No one spoke as they got settled, and Bud put the car in gear and drove away from the ranch. It was too reminiscent of the feelings they'd had on the way to Andrew Slade's funeral. To add credence to Bud's warning, it began to rain before they got to the cattle guard at the end of the driveway.

Cattle stood in bunches with their heads down, their hindquarters turned toward the blowing rain. Andrew's quarter horse, Red, was tossing his head and neighing sharply as he circled the corral in a trot. He'd been acting up ever since Andrew's death. They had all been around animals long enough to know that the horse knew its master was gone and was as lost as the rest of them were.

Despite the rain that had begun to fall, the ranch hands who were fixing a break in the fence took off their hats as the car passed by them…honoring the family and the man who had been their boss. They were concerned, too, but for different reasons. They didn't know what would be happening to the Triple S. Would they still have jobs when this day was over?

A lone buzzard had perched on the crossbar over the entrance gate, waiting for a lull between gusts of the sharp north wind before taking flight. The intermittent sprinkle of accompanying moisture was more sleet than rain, a fitting reflection of the mood of the people inside the car as it passed beneath the buzzard's perch. The rattling sound of the car passing over the cattle guard sent the bird into the air, and as the car disappeared from sight, so did the ungainly scavenger.

Coleman Rice kept glancing at the clock and then back at the stack of paperwork on his desk as he paced his office. The Slade family was due to arrive at any moment, and he was dreading what was to come. In all his years as an attorney, Andrew Slade's will was certainly the most shocking he'd ever encountered. The information was so volatile that he had no idea how the women were going to react. He smoothed the hair down on both sides of his head and straightened his jacket just as he heard a commotion in the outer office.

They were here.

He took a deep breath and unconsciously threw back his shoulders, as if bracing for what was to come.

The door opened.

His secretary, Milly, announced unnecessarily, "The Slade family is here."

Coleman walked toward them, his hand extended.

"Ladies...Bud...I'm sorry to be seeing you under these circumstance. Please come in."

He had chairs arranged in a semicircle around the front of his desk, with a small, flat-screen TV on the bookshelf behind his chair.

"Take a seat," he said, gesturing toward the setting he'd arranged.

Bud seated the women, then took the last chair for himself. Once they had settled, Coleman got down to business.

"As you know...we're here today to read the last will and testament of Andrew Slade. It's brief and to the point, so I'll read it first. And then there's a video Andrew recorded for the four of you to see."

"Oh, no," Savannah muttered.

Maria took her hand. Holly took the other. The sisters sat quietly, bound by love and circumstance, while Bud looked as if he were wishing for this morning to be over.

"The dispersal of the property is straightforward,"

Coleman said, and proceeded to read through the where-ases and wherefores.

Maria began losing focus. Then she heard the lawyer clear his throat and tuned back in.

"The ranch will be left in equal parts to my daughters, Holly, Maria and Savannah, and to my treasured friend and foreman, Robert Tate."

Bud gasped. "No. That's not right. I didn't expect… he shouldn't have…it belongs to the—"

"Hush, Bud," Maria said sharply. "It *is* right. He did the exact right thing. We're family. All four of us—and we can't run the place without you."

Bud sat back, clearly stunned by the news.

Coleman held up his hand. "Let me finish."

The room got quiet.

"Besides the property and monies…there's the message Andrew left. Ladies, I will preface it by saying… it has nothing to do with what you've inherited—but it has everything to do with the rest of your lives."

The sisters glanced at each other, then at Bud.

He shrugged, as if to say he knew nothing about this. "Should I leave?" he asked.

Once again, Maria took charge. "No. You stay." Then she softened her voice as she added, "Please."

Bud nodded, then settled back in his seat, and they all watched as the lawyer slipped a disc into the player, hit a button, then left the room.

Andrew Slade's face appeared on the screen at the same time the door closed.

Breaths caught in unison, then they all exhaled softly as they braced themselves for whatever he had to say.

"Hello, my daughters. Obviously, if you're seeing this, I have passed on. Know that, while I am sorry to be leaving you behind, my faith in God and the knowledge that I will be with my beloved Hannah again is, for me, a cause to rejoice. However, what I have to say to you is something I've dreaded your entire lives, and I'm ashamed to say I chose the easy way out and left it for you to hear after my passing."

Unconsciously, the sisters leaned into each other. Maria noticed as Bud almost unconsciously slid an arm behind Holly's chair, as if bracing her against what was clearly going to be bad news. There was a muscle jerking at the side of Andrew's jaw as he faced the camera, which told her that her father had been under stress when he recorded his message. But she could not have imagined, in her wildest dreams, the words that came out of his mouth.

"My darling daughters…you need to know that I am not really your father. Hannah was not really your mother, nor were any of you ever legally adopted."

Shock spread across all three women's faces.

"What the hell?" Bud muttered, unable to believe what he was hearing.

"There is more," Andrew added. "You are not sisters."

Maria gasped. Holly moaned. Savannah began to weep.

Bud's arm tightened around Holly's shoulders.

The sisters looked at each other in mute disbelief, then Maria gently squeezed one of Savannah's hands as Holly did the same to the other.

"We *are* sisters—in every way that counts," Maria said sharply.

Andrew's voice drew their focus back to the screen.

"By now, I suspect your grief at my passing has turned to shock…even anger. I understand. But what you three need to understand is…I believed with every fiber of my being that, as I was following my calling as an evangelical preacher, God led me to each of you at a time when you needed me most. There are journals that I've left with Coleman, one for each of you. Everything I know about your past is in there, along with why your mothers put you in my care.

"Maria, you were the first one. You were born Mary Blake, in Tulsa, Oklahoma. Your mother had a hard life. She was, for lack of a better word, an escort at the time of her death. You were four years old when you witnessed her murder. As she lay dying, she begged me to take you and hide you. The details as to how it all happened are in your journal. To my knowledge, her murder was never solved.

"Savannah, you are actually Sarah Stewart from Miami, Florida, and the second child to be given to me. Your mother was dying of cancer and had come to my tent meetings to pray for healing. By then, Maria had been with me for nearly six months. You were barely two. You and Maria hit it off immediately when your mother came to hear me preach, and she saw the bond between you two. On the last night of the revival, she came to me in a panic. She and your father were not married, but he had never denied you, and he played an important role in your life. According to her, he was also a member of a very rich, powerful local family. When she learned she had inoperable cancer, he had stepped up and promised he would take you into the family, and he had informed them of his plans. The night she came to me, she was sobbing uncontrollably. Your father had been killed in a car accident early that morning, and already she had received a threat on your life. Aware that she had only weeks to live and no one else to whom she could turn, she begged me to take you and raise you with Maria. So I did. It was then that I began to understand I was being led down this path by a power greater than my own.

"Holly, you are my oldest, but you came to me last. You were born Harriet Mackey and were five when you and your mother showed up at a revival I was holding in St. Louis, Missouri. She seemed troubled, but I thought nothing of it. At one time or another, we are all troubled by something or someone. On the fourth and last night of the revival, I thought everyone was gone from the church. Maria and Savannah had gone to sleep in the pastor's office, and I was going to get them when your mother showed up at the door with you and a suitcase.

"Her story was staggering, but at that point, I didn't question God's plan. What you need to know is that she did not give you away. She was convinced that her husband, your father, was a serial killer the Missouri police had been hunting for nearly a year. She feared what the notoriety would do to your life when all was revealed, and that you would be branded as a killer's daughter. She was going to turn him in, and then come and get you and start over in a new place. Only she never came after you, and no one was ever arrested for the murders. I fear she paid for her bravery with her life.

"As I said before, Coleman has journals for each of you. I've written down everything I know. As to whether you go back to find your roots or not, that is your choice, but I caution each of you to remember, your lives were in danger then. They could be again."

The screen went dark.

It was only then that Maria realized she'd been holding her breath. She inhaled deeply as the room began to spin. Without thinking, she bent over and put her head between her knees.

Bud was out of his chair and at her side within seconds. "Maria…are you all right?"

"Breathe, Maria…keep breathing," Holly said, as she dropped on her knees in front of Maria's chair.

The office door opened as Coleman Rice hurried in. He'd heard the commotion and feared something like this might happen.

"What happened? Do I need to call an ambulance?" he asked.

"No," Bud said. "She's not sick. She's in shock. It will pass."

Maria's mind was in chaos. She'd been proud of being a Slade, but that had been a lie. She was the child of a prostitute. God only knew what kind of blood ran through her veins. She took a deep breath and stared at her sisters.

Savannah was in shock, probably unable to focus on anything except the fact that someone had wanted her dead.

Holly was shaking. Her father might be a serial killer who'd murdered her mother? What kind of a family had *she* been born into?

Bud stood. "Look at me," he said, his voice deep and demanding. "A name is nothing but a means of identification. You all still bleed red. You were raised by a good man—a man of God. You need to consider yourselves blessed that God spared each of you from what sounds like certain death."

Savannah nodded, gulping back tears. Holly was weeping quietly as she held tightly to Savannah's hand. But Maria's reaction was different. She was shocked and angry.

"My mother was a hooker! Who was my father? One of her…her tricks?"

Holly shuddered as she met Maria's gaze. "Trade you backgrounds. At least yours probably wasn't a serial killer."

Maria shuddered, then threw her arms around Holly's neck. "Sorry, sis. I wasn't thinking."

Savannah hugged the both of them. "We still have each other."

"And me," Bud added, and stuffed his hands in his pockets.

"Yes, Bud…and you," they echoed, drawing him into their circle.

Coleman had expected something like this. He'd argued for days with Andrew when he'd first heard their stories, saying how they would have questions that only he could answer and that he should tell them now, not after his death. But Andrew had been set on doing it his way. He'd handed Coleman the journals, explaining that everything he knew about each of them was written down. The rest they would have to learn for themselves.

"Hold on. All of you," Coleman said, as he approached the group. "Pointing fingers and attaching blame will not change anything." He picked up three envelopes from the corner of his desk. "These are the journals." He sorted through the names on the envelopes, then handed them out. "Andrew was diligent about putting down everything he knew. There are names and addresses in each, along with informational bits and pieces of your lives. Yes, things could have been handled differently, but there's no telling where you would have wound up if he'd turned those three women down. The best you could have hoped for was growing up in the state welfare system. The likelier possibility exists that none of you would have lived past the time it would have taken your mothers' enemies to find and kill you. Do you understand?"

It was the sharpness of his voice and the way in which he thrust the envelopes into their hands that brought them all back to their senses.

Savannah stared at her name, started to open the envelope, then changed her mind and slid it into her purse.

Holly shivered as she clutched hers to her stomach, as if it were a living, breathing entity that was going to change her life.

But it was Maria who, once again, was the first to regain control. She yanked the journal out of the envelope and opened it to the first page.

Your name is Mary Blake.

The skin on the back of her neck crawled as she remembered that she'd been a witness to her mother's murder. Her eyes narrowed.

"I'm going back," she said.

Coleman frowned. "I don't recommend any of you charging off without careful planning. Read your journals. Contact the proper authorities. Do not put yourselves in danger. It's the last thing Andrew would have wanted."

"No," Maria said. "You're wrong. This is exactly what he did want…and it's the reason he didn't tell us when we were kids. He knew we would be curious. He knew we would want to explore our pasts. He knew *us,* Mr. Rice."

"Do you two feel the same way?" Coleman asked, turning to the other women.

Savannah nodded. "I feel like I have to."

"Absolutely," Holly said.

"Then I'm going with you," Bud said.

Maria shook her head. "No. You're staying here and keeping the Triple S in one piece. I need to know that there's something here for me to come home to."

"Me, too," Savannah said. "I won't do anything to put myself in danger, but I want to meet my father's family."

"I did some checking. They're very wealthy," Coleman warned. "At the least, they'll look upon you as an upstart looking to lay claim to the Stewart estate."

Holly reached for Bud's arm. "Please…stay for us. The Triple S is home. We can't do what we have to do unless we have a safe place to come home to. We'll be okay. I promise I'll let the police handle my case."

"Fine," Bud agreed grudgingly. "But you have to keep me updated when you can. If you need me, I'll be on the first plane out."

Two

"Ladies and gentlemen, please stow your tray tables and return your seats to an upright position. We will be landing in Tulsa in about ten minutes."

The flight attendant's words barely registered as Maria glanced out the window of the airplane to the land below. It was green—so green, even though it was only April. Back in Montana, they still had the occasional chance of snowfall from a late spring storm. Below, the landscape looked like a blue-and-green crazy quilt, squares defined by a river and farmlands that ran right up to the outskirts of the large, sprawling city. All she knew about Tulsa, Oklahoma, was something she remembered from school, that at one time it had been considered the oil capital of the world.

It was strange to realize that she'd been born there—had lived the first four years of her life there—and yet had no memory of it at all.

The flight attendant was moving through the plane now, gathering up the last remnants of the snack they'd served. Maria wished her life could be collected in the same orderly manner. All the bad stuff discarded into the sack and gone, never to be seen again.

According to the journal her father had left her, the first four years of her life could not have been easy, but when she and Holly and Savannah had compared notes before they all departed to their own destinations, none of them had any memories of what their father had written.

In a way, it made sense that they would have forgotten. Witnessing a murder could be traumatic enough to cause hysterical amnesia. And Savannah had barely been two, so it was logical that she would have had no prior memories. But Holly had been five. School age. Didn't everyone remember their first day of school? Yet there was nothing of the story between the pages of her journal that had seemed remotely familiar to Holly.

Maria was still pondering the expanse of unanswered questions when she heard the landing gear going down. She glanced back out the window. The land was coming up at her at a rapid rate. For a few seconds she imagined she was being swallowed whole; then she shook off the fancy and began gathering her things.

Moments later, the wheels touched down, bumping slightly before leveling out into an uneventful landing.

Maria's grip on the armrests tightened as the plane taxied toward the gate. Her heart was hammering against her rib cage, and there was a panicked rhythm in her breathing. She had to calm down. It wasn't as if she were about to meet her unknown family at the gate.

She was walking into her past alone. In the journal, the only name Andrew mentioned other than hers and her mother's was Becky Thurman, the woman who'd helped him hide her—the woman who used to babysit her.

She shuddered.

What in hell was she getting herself into? She took a deep breath, remembering one of her father's favorite phrases. *With God, anything is possible.* A good reminder that she wasn't really alone—and that she had right on her side. It was time to stop the pity party.

Okay, Sally Blake…your daughter has come home to right a wrong. And if you have any pull with God, she's going to need all the help she can get.

After that, her focus shifted to recovering her bags and claiming her rental car. She'd booked a room online at the Doubletree Hotel in downtown Tulsa and had a map of the city in her purse. Even though she was anxious to get started, it was late in the day. Her best bet was to get settled in her room, get some food and rest and start early the next morning.

A brief conversation with the car rental agent to confirm her route revealed that she was only nine miles from her hotel. Pleased that at least one thing was turning out to be easier than she'd thought, she got her keys and made her way across the parking lot to the car, a white Chevrolet TrailBlazer.

Once out of the parking area, she merged onto the westbound lane of the Gilcrease Expressway and began keeping an eye out for Highway 75.

It was nearing five o'clock. Before long, the highways would be packed with people on their way home from work. She wanted to be checked in before the traffic got too bad. It would have been great to have her sisters for backup, but they were on their own quests for answers.

With one eye on the traffic and the other on the road signs, she slipped into the lane that took her onto Highway 75 southbound. At that point she began watching for 7th Street. Within a few minutes she exited west onto 7th. After that, it was no time at all until the seventeen-story hotel appeared on the horizon. That was when it hit her. Despite her earlier resolve, there was no escaping the fact that she'd flown halfway across the country to try to solve a murder.

The weight of responsibility kept getting heavier and heavier. By the time she pulled up in front of the hotel, her hands were sweating. She'd spent the last few days in a fever of anxiety, and now that she was finally here, exhaustion and nerves were about to take over. Anxious to get to her room before she crashed, she left her car at valet parking, grabbed her bag and headed inside.

The lobby was light and airy, with an underlying buzz of activity, but she couldn't focus on anything but the reception desk ahead. She had no memory of registering, but when she found herself in an elevator and headed for a room on the sixth floor with a key card in her hand, she had to accept that it had happened. Her stomach growled, reminding her that she hadn't eaten a real meal all day, but the thought of food made her ill. Tears were building at the back of her throat, and there was a knot in her belly that was growing by the minute.

Murder. I witnessed my mother's murder. Why don't I remember? Didn't I love her? If I loved her, wouldn't I have remembered what happened to her? What heinous life did I live that would make me block it all out?

Her hands were shaking as she reached Room 604. She thrust the key card into the slot and pushed her way inside, locking herself in as she went.

The quiet within the room was like a slap in the face. Now there was nothing to distract her from where she was or why she'd come. She pushed her bag against the wall, crawled on top of the bed and curled herself into a ball. By the time she closed her eyes, the room was spinning. Reaching over her head, she found a pillow, dragged it against her belly and buried her face as the tears began to fall. Sometime later, she fell into a long, exhausted sleep.

Maria was dreaming that her phone was ringing but she couldn't find the receiver to answer. After several rings, she finally woke up enough to realize it wasn't a dream. The loud jangle was a rude awakening from what had been a long, dreamless sleep. Still groggy, she reached for the receiver, fumbled it and then let it drop to the floor.

"Dang it," she muttered, before she finally picked it up. "Hello. Hello?"

"Good morning, Miss Slade. This is the front desk. We have a delivery for you. May we send it up?"

Maria glanced at the clock. Morning? She'd slept all night in her clothes? Then she realized what he was saying.

"A delivery? For me? Are you sure?"

"Yes, miss. Maria Slade."

"Okay…yes…send it up."

"Thank you," he said, and disconnected.

Maria began scrambling, smoothing down her hair and her clothes, then trying to find her purse for tip money. She hardly remembered coming into this room, let alone what she'd done with her things.

Finally she found the purse on the floor beside her suitcase and grabbed a couple of dollars just as a knock sounded on the door. After a quick look through the peephole to assure herself it was a hotel employee, she opened the door to a bellman carrying a bouquet of flowers.

"Just put them on the table," Maria said, then stood aside.

He paused on his way out the door. "Is there anything else I can do for you?"

"No, I'm fine, but thank you," Maria said, and handed him the money.

"You're welcome," he said, pocketing the bills as he left.

She locked the door behind him, then headed for the table and plucked the card from the flowers.

Remember, you're not alone. I'm only a phone call away.

Bud.

Maria's vision blurred as she clutched the note to her breast. Even though Bud Tate had been her father's friend and employee, to her, he was the brother she'd never had. There was a part of her that wanted to grab that bag she had yet to unpack and retreat to the safety of Montana. Being here was frightening in many ways, but Andrew Slade had not raised them to be cowards. Nor had he kept those journals without reason. She knew what she had to do. For twenty years someone had gotten away with murder. It was past time for justice.

She slipped the card into her purse, her eyes narrowing as she looked around her room. When her stomach suddenly growled, reminding her that she hadn't eaten a meal in nearly twenty-four hours, she knew it was time to get down to basics. After calling room service to order breakfast, she went to unpack. Within a couple of hours she had showered and changed and had a meal in her belly. Armed with a city map and her journal, she headed out the door.

Thanks to the help of the GPS in her rental car, Maria quickly found out that the address she was looking for was in what the locals called North Tulsa, which she was beginning to believe was the back side of hell. It was the most depressing area of a city she'd ever seen. Other than the occasional bondsman, pawnshop, or gas station, nothing was thriving. She'd seen only one grocery store, and it looked like it was on its last legs. There had been businesses here at one time, because the names and signs were still on the buildings, but the windows were boarded up and covered with graffiti. It was an area in its death throes, which she found horribly sad. She wondered if it had been this way when she'd lived here twenty years ago, or if this was something new.

The absence of commerce would have led one to assume that people would be hard to locate, but it was just the reverse. Traffic was moving swiftly along the streets, while people standing near alleys and on certain street corners seemed to be doing a brisk drive-by business.

Maria didn't want to think about what they were probably selling, but it was beginning to occur to her that coming down here alone had been a rash idea. Given the gang-related signs spray-painted on every flat surface, the people on street corners who watched her passing and the noise levels of the stereos in the cars that passed her, she would not have been shocked by the sound of gunfire.

She pulled to the curb in front of the address Andrew had given her and killed the engine, then looked around.

This was supposed to be the boardinghouse where she'd been living with her mother—the place where Andrew had first met them—only there were no hotels of any kind in sight. Just more empty, boarded-up build-

ings. Frustrated, she picked up the journal again and
leafed to the pages that recorded her mother's death.

Blood was bubbling from the corner of her lips.
I'd seen a man die from a punctured lung before. I
recognized the death rattle. Even though the ambulance had been called, I feared they would be
too late, and your mother, Sally, kept calling my
name.
I knelt at her side and took her hand. "I'm here,"
I told her. Her grip was surprisingly strong considering the fact that she was dying, yet she kept
repeating one phrase over and over. "You have
to hide Mary. Take her away with you." I looked
around and saw you standing in the shadows of
the hallway, your eyes wide and fixed on the blood
pooling beneath your mother's body. You weren't
moving. You weren't crying. You seemed to be in
shock. At that moment, Sally choked and her eyes
rolled back in her head. I thought she was gone.
Becky Thurman, the woman who lived across the
hall and the woman I learned was your babysitter, came running in. She screamed, then started
weeping, asking what happened. Sally gasped,
then started muttering, "She saw, she saw."
I was still trying to grasp the fact that she was
still alive when Becky asked, "Saw what?" Your
mother pointed to you. "Mary saw him shoot
me," she said. Then she looked straight into my
eyes. "You're a man of God. Hide her…without

me she'll have no one. If the cops know she saw, they'll drag her through the courts. He'll find her and kill her, just like he killed me."

I was horrified. I told her I couldn't possibly take you, but she was begging and begging. I saw her fading. I felt her terror. Finally I gave in and promised I would make sure you were safe. Then she died.

Becky was a lifesaver. She grabbed a small bag, packed it with your clothing and toiletries, handed you a stuffed rabbit and dashed across the hall with you just as the police were coming up the stairs.

She hid you in her room, while I stayed behind to meet the police, since I was the one who'd called. Later, after they were gone, she put you to bed at her place. I stayed over in Tulsa for two days to finish my revival. I prayed about you every night, and by the time I left town, I was convinced I was doing the right thing. You went with me without a word of complaint. Becky said you hadn't cried, hadn't spoken a word.

You wouldn't for nearly a month, and then, when you did, it was as if you'd been reborn after coming to me. You took everything I said and did at face value, and began your life over. I guess it was a coping mechanism.

Maria sighed. It was like reading a piece of fiction about someone else's life.

My God. How did I forget this?

She glanced around the neighborhood, eyeing the trio of men standing on the corner, then the storefronts. The problem was, with all these empty buildings, there was no one here she dared to question. As she started to drive away, she noticed a cross on a building a couple of blocks away, with a few people going in and out. A street mission. Ignoring her instincts to get out while the getting was good, she reached for the ignition and drove the two blocks down.

John 3:16 Mission.

The name said it all, Maria thought as she put the car in Park. The scent of cooking food was in the air as she emerged. According to a sign on the window, they were serving free lunch, which explained the number of people who kept going inside.

She hit the remote, locking the car as she walked toward the door. The car horn beeped to indicate success, and the sound caught the attention of a group of men standing near the entrance to a nearby alley. One of them whistled beneath his breath, then called out to her.

"Hey, bitch...you lose somethin'? I got what you need."

The others laughed as their friend grabbed his crotch.

Lord help me, Maria thought, and kept her head down and her eyes averted as she walked into the mission. The black-and-white floor tiles were cracked and stained, and the furniture was a mishmash of styles and colors.

But there was an air of comfort within as she paused near the door to get her bearings. Maybe it was the corn bread she could smell coming from the kitchen, and maybe it was the rich sound of gospel music coming from a CD player sitting on a shelf.

Humanity in an assortment of ages and sizes was already forming a line along one side of the room, waiting for the meal to be served. She took a deep breath and headed for the sound of human voices, trying not to react to the stares she was receiving. Being the only woman in the room amped up her anxiety. The fact that she was also the only Caucasian made her feel that much more vulnerable.

All of a sudden there was a voice behind her.

"Welcome to the house of the Lord."

Maria flinched, then turned abruptly to find herself face-to-face with a tall, skinny black man. He was wearing an African print shirt over a pair of faded blue jeans, with an ivory cross hanging from a thin strip of leather tied around his neck. Except for a halo of gray hair that stretched from ear to ear around the back of his head, he was bald. But his voice was soft and deep, and when Maria looked into his eyes, the tension she'd been feeling disappeared.

His gaze was rock-steady as he smiled.

Without thinking, she smiled back.

He eyed her clothes, the finely tooled leather of her purse, then arched an eyebrow.

"I'm guessing you're not in need of food, so how can I help you, miss? Are you lost?"

Maria's smile shifted. "In a manner of speaking…I guess I am."

"Did your car break down? Do you want me to call for a tow?"

"No, no…not that."

"Then how may I help you?"

Maria sighed. "I'm not sure how to start."

"At the beginning is usually best. So let's start over. My name is Henry."

"My name is Maria Slade."

"Then come and sit with me, Maria Slade."

He cupped her elbow, pausing to make sure she accepted the gesture, then motioned toward an empty table near the back of the dining room.

She nodded gratefully, her anxiety easing with every passing minute. As soon as they were seated, a young teenager appeared carrying two cups of steaming coffee. He placed them on the table near Henry's elbow, challenging Maria with a cold, angry stare, which upped her anxiety again.

"Thank you, Tyrell," Henry said.

The boy shrugged, then walked away with a swagger in every step.

Henry saw Maria's expression and felt obliged to add, "The boy's all right. Got a man-size chip on a kid-size shoulder. Gonna take him a few years of livin' on the right side of the Lord to get it off, but we're workin' on it…me and him."

Maria allowed herself a short moment of grief. Henry reminded her of her father, which made her stifle an urge to weep. But she hadn't come for comfort. She had questions that needed answers, and this Henry seemed amenable enough.

"Thank you for taking the time to talk to me."

"Certainly," he said. "As you were saying…I believe you were lost?"

Maria nodded. "My father died last week."

Henry's face softened into such an expression of empathy that it was once again all Maria could do not to cry. "I am sorry for your loss," he said.

"Thank you, but his death triggered a lot more than grief. After he died, I learned I was not his daughter by birth, and that, until the age of four, I lived with my mother in a boardinghouse called the Hampton Arms. Twenty years ago, it was a couple of blocks east of here. I flew into town to…I don't know…visit my past? Only the place isn't there anymore."

Henry's expression changed to one of curiosity.

"I remember that place. My, my…hadn't thought of it in years."

"What happened to it?" Maria asked.

"Time, mostly," Henry said. "Not much goin' on in this part of Tulsa anymore except trouble. For sure, the only thing thriving is bad business…not God's business."

"I understand," she said. "Time changes plenty. I don't suppose you know of anyone who used to live there…say twenty years ago?"

"Actually, I do. A man named Montrose. Used to work the desk there."

"How do I get in touch with him?" Maria asked.

"He comes here every day to eat. If you want to wait around, he'll likely show up." Then he added, "What was your mother's name?"

"Why?" Maria asked.

"I've lived here for nearly thirty years. I know there's gray in my hair, but my memory is still pretty good."

Maria couldn't believe her luck. "That's great," she said. "I don't know what my mother looked like but—"

He frowned. "Why don't you know what your own mama looked like?"

Maria shrugged. "I just don't. I have no memories at all of my life with her."

"That's a real shame," Henry said. "I'm thinking there's quite a story in that, but you didn't come to satisfy *my* curiosity. So, what was your mother's name?"

"Blake...Sally Blake."

Henry's eyes widened, and his lips went slack.

"Pretty brunette...nearly six feet tall. Had a real friendly way about her. Now that you mention it...you put me in mind of how I remember she looked."

Maria's heart skipped a beat. *Oh, my God. This is real.*

"I didn't put it together. She always called you Mary. I didn't know you were really a Maria." He reached across the table and laid his hand over hers. "It was a real tragedy what happened to her, but it explains why you don't remember. Losing your mama like that would be a terrible shock. Good thing you were across the hall at the babysitter's that night."

Maria's belly knotted, thinking of the deception her father and the babysitter had concocted to keep her alive.

"Yes…a good thing."

Three

Henry offered her a meal, and when he came back with the food he'd promised, Maria took her bowl of beans and chose a seat near a man in a wheelchair and across the table from a woman with no teeth. The smells emanating from their bodies were daunting, but she reminded herself that she was no better—only cleaner. She was the child of a prostitute, and if it hadn't been for Andrew Slade, this could have become her fate.

Bracing herself, she took a bite of beans and was surprised by the rich, meaty taste of the broth. The beans reminded her of roundup-day food and made her homesick for Montana, at which point she politely asked for someone to please pass the salt.

The salt slid toward her from somewhere upwind. She grabbed it on the fly, shook it over her bowl, then slid it back down without missing a beat.

Her presence was something of an anomaly to the hungry people at John 3:16 Mission, but not enough to sway them from free food. The meal progressed without conversation, and once she'd eaten her beans and corn bread, she got up and took her dirty dishes into the kitchen.

The room was small but orderly. Shelves had been added above a workstation against one wall next to an old four-burner stove. The industrial-size double sink was at the far end of the room next to a large drain board.

Henry was standing at the makeshift counter, serving the meal.

Tyrell, the teenager who'd given her a go-to-hell look, was at the sink, alternately washing, then drying, dishes in an effort to keep up with the need. It appeared to be a losing battle. The John 3:16 Mission was making do with odds and ends of assorted crockery. Spending money on paper plates and bowls obviously wasn't in the budget.

Maria sighed. She wasn't leaving until she got a chance to talk to the man Henry had mentioned, and she wasn't the kind of person to sit around and watch others work. So she slid her purse beneath a table, took off her jacket, rolled up her sleeves and moved into place at the sink beside Tyrell.

"I'll wash, you dry," she said.

He looked a little startled, then shrugged and handed her the dishrag, got a fresh towel and began drying the stack of bowls he'd just washed.

Henry caught the gesture and thought to himself that someone had raised her right, then turned his attention back to serving the line of hungry people.

Nearly an hour passed before Henry saw Montrose

Benton, the man Maria wanted to talk to, step up to the window for food.

"Hello, Montrose. How you been doin'?" Henry asked.

"Can't complain," Montrose said. "Heard about any work?"

"Not today," Henry said.

Even if he had, there wasn't a business owner in Tulsa who'd hire the old man in his current state. His clothes were filthy, and it was apparent he hadn't shaved in weeks. Henry didn't know what had gone wrong in this man's life and didn't have the ability to fix it even if he did. What Henry could do was feed Montrose's belly and hope something he said later might fill the man's soul.

"Eat up. And I hope you don't mind, but there's a lady here who'd like to talk to you," Henry said as he handed him the food. When the old man nodded, Henry added, "God bless you."

The old man smiled. "Thank you, Henry. Thank you."

Henry waited until Montrose found himself a seat and started eating before he went to get Maria. The woman was still at the sink. She'd surprised him by helping out like this. Despite the fact that she was in a better place financially than most people he saw, she seemed as lost as the old man with his beans.

He hoped Montrose could help her.

"Hey, Tyrell, stand in for me a minute, will you?"

Tyrell gratefully set aside his dish towel and headed for the food line.

"Not too much," Henry said softly. "It needs to go a long ways."

"I remember, Preacher Henry," the boy said, and deftly scooped a ladle of hot brown pinto beans into the next bowl, laid a square of corn bread on top and passed it along.

Satisfied that the boy had everything under control, Henry moved to the sink and tapped Maria's shoulder.

"The man I mentioned who used to work at the Hampton Arms is here."

Maria flinched, nearly dropping the pan she'd been scrubbing, then rinsed it off and set it aside before grabbing a towel to dry her hands.

"That's great," she said. "Will you introduce us? No one wants a stranger in their face when they're trying to eat a meal."

Again, Henry was taken by her manner. The man she wanted to talk to was a vagrant, and yet she was considering his feelings as much as her own desires.

"Yes, ma'am, I will, and I hope he has some answers for you."

"So do I," she said, then slung her purse over her shoulder. "I'm ready when you are."

Henry led the way out into the dining area with Maria close at his heels.

Henry suddenly stopped and bent down to speak to a tiny, wizened old man, and Maria eyed him carefully, wondering if seeing him would trigger any memories.

His cheeks were a washed-out red. She couldn't decide if it was from the broken blood vessels beneath his pale skin, or if they were chapped from living outside in all kinds of weather. Tufts of gray hair poked out the holes in the knitted cap on his head, matching a sparse assortment of gray, scraggly whiskers. A quick glance revealed that while he was dressed in several layers of clothing, he was nearly barefoot. The tennis shoes he was wearing were literally tied to his feet with some kind of grimy, frayed cording.

Just as she was about to feel sorry for him, he looked up. The smile on his face was unexpected in so many ways. How could a person still have joy in his heart while leading such a miserable existence?

"Montrose, this is the lady who wants to talk to you. Would that be all right?"

Montrose squinted as his gaze shifted to the woman standing beside Henry.

"Sure, I don't mind," he said. "Have a seat. I'll just finish my food while we talk."

Maria sat down in a chair across from him as Henry introduced them.

"Montrose, meet Maria Slade. Maria…Mr. Montrose Benton."

"Call me Montrose," he said. "Or Monty."

Maria smiled and nodded, but her heart was pounding. She didn't quite know where to start or how to explain her situation without giving too much away.

Since she wasn't talking, Monty wasn't interested in wasting time. He scooped more beans into his mouth, then chased it with a bite of corn bread as she took a notebook from her bag. He couldn't imagine what he had to say that would interest her, but it was a welcome change in his routine.

Maria glanced down at the notebook, then leaned across the table.

"Henry told me you used to work the desk at the Hampton Arms."

Monty's eyes widened. "You talkin' 'bout that old roomin' house that used to be down the street?"

"Yes."

"Yes, I did."

"How long did you work there?"

"Probably ten or fifteen years, but I lived there until it closed."

"Were you there twenty years ago?" Maria asked.

"Yeah, yeah…I would have been working the desk on the night shift around that time."

"Good," Maria said. "Can you tell me what you remember about the place?"

"I guess I remember a lot of things. I lived on the first floor near the back fire exit. Exactly what do you want to know?"

"Do you remember a woman named Sally Blake? She would have been living there at that time."

"Sally Blake…Sally Blake… I don't know if—"

All of a sudden, Maria saw recognition dawning.

"Oh, yeah, I remember her. Tall, curvy brunette with green eyes. Real looker, too."

His eyes narrowed. "You put me in mind of her," he muttered, then took another bite of beans.

A bean fell off his spoon and caught in his whiskers as he began to chew. Either he didn't know it or didn't care, but Maria couldn't think for watching the bean as it jiggled up and down in the precarious perch on which it had landed. She grabbed a couple of paper napkins that had been left on the table by an earlier diner and handed them over.

Montrose blinked, then grinned as he took the napkins and mopped at his beard.

"Sorry…when you live on the street, you lose company manners."

"About Sally Blake," Maria said, shifting the conversation.

Montrose nodded. "She lived on the third floor… her and her little girl. I reckon she lived there at least six years. I remember when she brought that baby home from the hospital. Cutest little bit of nothin' you ever saw. Had a whole lot of dark hair, just like her mama."

Maria's stomach lurched. He was talking about her. It was surreal to be sitting here, talking to a stranger who had more memories of her life with her mother than she did. It made her want to weep, but she hadn't come this far to screw up, and Montrose Benton was her first lead.

"To your knowledge, was the child's father ever in the picture?" she asked.

Monty hesitated. Maria was guessing he was hedging

his answers, pending how much she knew about Sally Blake's past.

"I know she was a prostitute," she said, not bothering to hide the distaste in her voice.

Monty's expression shifted slightly, but Maria couldn't tell what he was thinking.

"She did what she had to do to put food on the table and a roof over their heads," he said sharply.

"There are other jobs," Maria said before she thought.

"If you have the education to back them up, then yeah, there *are* other jobs. But you have to be able to read and write to get them, and the way I remember Sally Blake, she couldn't do either."

Maria was staggered. "You're kidding."

Monty's eyes narrowed thoughtfully. "Not hardly, miss. It's not the first time someone got passed through a school system without the proper skills," he said. "She had a good memory, so I guessed she faked her way through as far as she could. Who knows? Besides, it's not like she had anyone to speak up for her. She came up through the system."

"What do you mean, 'through the system'?"

"Welfare. She used to make jokes about the fact that the closest she'd ever come to Jesus was when she'd been found abandoned on the steps of a church."

Maria wanted to cry. Every judgmental thing she'd thought since learning about her mother's background had just made a one-eighty shift. Her mother had begun life as an abandoned baby and been shuffled through the welfare system, and never even learned to read and write. God. The more she learned, the more tragic the story became.

"What do you remember about her?" Maria asked. "Did you know her friends?"

Monty laid down his spoon and leaned back in his chair.

"Why all the interest in Sally Blake?"

Maria had never said the words aloud, but something told her that if she wanted answers from Monty, she was going to have to answer some of his questions, as well.

"I'm that little baby you remember her having. I just found out recently that she was my mother. I have no memory of her or of living at the Hampton Arms. I guess I'm just trying to get some answers about my past."

Her answer surprised him. She didn't look like someone who would have come from this side of town. Life was hard here, and had been for what seemed like forever. Most of the people who managed to get out didn't go any farther than a local cemetery.

"Well, I'll be," Montrose muttered, staring harder than ever at her. "I remember her baby girl. She doted on her…uh, on you…like nobody's business. Kept you dressed like a little doll…always tied your hair back with a ribbon to match your clothes."

Maria exhaled slowly. The words were balm to a very wounded psyche. She had been loved.

"And I remember the night she was killed like it was

yesterday," Monty added. "This area of the city wasn't high class, but it wasn't as derelict as it is now, either. Her murder shocked all of us. The worst of it was that nobody was ever arrested."

Maria's heart skipped a beat. Even though she didn't remember the event, she wasn't about to tell this man she'd come to rectify the fact that the killer had never been caught.

"I was really hoping to talk to some of her friends. Would you happen to remember any of their names… maybe someone who also lived in the hotel when she did?"

The old man scratched at the side of his jaw, then picked up a crumb of corn bread and popped it in his mouth, chewing as he thought. "Hmmm, I can't rightly say as to who her friends were, but I remember Tank Vincent."

Maria quickly jotted down the name. "Who was Tank Vincent?"

"Her pimp."

"Oh. Right," Maria said, then sighed. "I don't suppose you'd know if he still lives in the area?"

"Naw…haven't seen hide nor hair of the man in ages. Sorry."

Maria nodded absently. It was nothing she hadn't expected, but she hated to give up.

"Is there anything else you can remember? Anything at all?"

"Only that she didn't deserve what happened to her. I'm real sorry I can't be of more help."

"No...no...you've helped a lot," Maria said. "Sorry I bothered you, but I really appreciate you taking the time to talk to me."

"I'm real sorry you had to grow up without your mama," he said softly.

"I was lucky," she said, thinking of Andrew and Hannah. "I had really good people in my life."

"That's good...real good," he said as Maria stood up.

She reached across the table with her hand extended.

"It's been good to meet you."

It had been a long time since someone had wanted to shake his hand. Monty stood abruptly, his shoulders straightening unconsciously as their hands met.

Moments later she was walking away and he was unfolding the wad of twenties she'd left in his palm. One hundred dollars. He couldn't remember the last time he'd had that much money. He looked down at the shoes tied on his feet and shoved the money in his pocket. No need advertising his good fortune. After waving goodbye to Henry, he shuffled out of the mission only moments behind Maria as she pulled away from the curb.

He went in one direction as she went in the other.

Both had gotten far more out of the conversation than they had expected.

It was nearly four o'clock before Maria got back to her hotel room. She kicked off her shoes, then crawled up on the bed and pulled her journal out of her bag. She couldn't remember reading anything in it about Tank Vincent but wanted to double-check, and she quickly fell back into Andrew Slade's story.

I'd driven into Tulsa from Arkansas and had a five-day revival ahead of me. I'd just rented a room at the Hampton Arms on the north side of town near the church where I would be preaching. I met your mother on the hotel stairs. I was going up as she was coming down. I remember thinking how tall she was because when we passed, we were nearly eye-to-eye.

I said hello. She grinned and waved and kept on moving, taking the steps down two at a time. When I reached the third floor, I saw a little girl and a woman going into the room that wound up being next to mine. Later I would learn that was you and your babysitter, Becky Thurman. She kept you every time your mother had what she referred to as a "date."

The next time I saw your mother, which was a couple of days later, she was sitting on the stairs outside our rooms, and you were with her. I was leaving the hotel for the evening services at the church. For some reason I got the impression that she was waiting for me, but she didn't say so. She had found out I was a preacher...don't know how, but she had, and she was asking all kinds of questions about hell and sin and forgiveness. You were playing with a doll, taking the clothes off it and putting them back on it, over and over. Every so often she would touch your head or pat your back—gentle, motherly touches just to reassure you she was there. I offered to take her to church for the evening meeting. She seemed startled by the offer, but to my surprise, she went, bringing you with us.

I will say, you were very good. In spite of the spirit-rousing sermon and gospel songs, you fell asleep in your mother's lap. Every so often I would catch a glimpse of her face as I was preaching. It made me think of a kid looking through a candy-store window, longing for something she was never going to get.

She didn't say much on the way back to the hotel, other than to question me about my personal life. I kept thinking she was going to make a move on me…. You know…hit me up for a "date," but it was just the reverse. Looking back, her questions were more like an interview, as if she was checking out my credentials to see if I was good enough to take care of you, even though she had no way of knowing there would be a need. She refused any further invitations to attend the revival, but whenever I saw her, she called me Preacher Man.

Within two days, she was dead and you were orphaned. What you need to know is that she loved you very much.

Maria's vision blurred as she continued to scan the

journal for a mention of Tank Vincent, but there was none. Still, the day hadn't been a disappointment. She had her first solid lead, though no way yet of following it up. It was time to go to the police.

The next morning dawned on a cloudy note, with a promise of thunderstorms in the afternoon. Maria dressed for the weather in brown slacks, a long-sleeved top in butter yellow, with a darker brown gabardine jacket and a pair of oxblood-colored Justin ropers. Wearing the boots gave her a connection with home, which she needed to get through the day ahead of her.

She'd been pleased to learn that the Tulsa Police Department headquarters was just a few blocks from her hotel. After a quick breakfast in the coffee shop downstairs, she picked up her car from the valet parking attendant and drove away, armed with her map of the city and Andrew's journal.

There was a knot in Bodie Scott's stomach that wasn't going to go away anytime soon. He'd been a homicide detective with the Tulsa P.D. for nearly ten years, but he was never going to get used to notifying a family of a loved one's death. It was the worst part of his job. Getting the guilty party behind bars was all he could do to bring closure to a family's grief. After that, it was out of his hands.

The case they'd just closed had been a rough one. An eleven-year-old girl had gone missing on her way home from school. It had taken two days for her body to be found, and then countless hours of police work before they'd had enough evidence to make an arrest. Telling the parents that the killer had not only confessed but was also behind bars had been almost as difficult as the day he'd gone to tell them she was dead.

He wasn't a drinking man, but right now he could use something to shift focus and get his mind off the sound of the mother's weeping in the house he'd just exited.

He headed back to the precinct, hoping that the rest of the day would be calm. What he hadn't counted on was anyone knowing that today was his birthday. When he walked back into the office, the last thing he expected were the balloons tied to the back of his chair and the cake in the middle of his desk. The minute they saw him walk in, someone yelled, "Cake!" and someone else said, "About time." There was a lot of back thumping and happy birthday wishes as everyone crowded around his desk for a piece of cake.

Bodie exhaled on a sigh, then grinned. It wasn't what he'd expected, but now that he thought about it, it was a great change of pace.

"Thanks, everyone. This is great." He stuck a finger in the icing and then licked it off as he reached for the plastic knife beside the cake. "What kind of cake is it?"

His sometime partner, Dave Booker, picked up a paper plate and a plastic fork. "Birthday cake," he said. "Me first."

"Hell no," Bodie said. "It's my birthday. I get the first piece."

He cut a piece from the corner, slid it onto a plate, then stepped back.

"Have at it. I've got mine," he said, and forked a big bite into his mouth as he turned around.

A tall brunette was coming through the doorway, escorted by a uniformed officer, who hailed him with a wave. Her stride was sure, her shoulders straight. There was an expression on her face that said she meant business.

He chewed and swallowed as fast as he could, then set his cake aside as they approached.

"Hey, Scott, the lady asked to speak to a homicide detective. You got a minute?" the uniform asked.

"Absolutely," Bodie said, and promptly shook her hand. "Ma'am...I'm Detective Scott. Bodie Scott."

"Maria Slade," she said, shivering slightly as his fingers curled around her hand. This man didn't know it yet, but he was going to help her solve a murder.

Bodie grinned. "Sorry about the hoo-rah. We were just havin' a little birthday cake. Let me get my notebook and we'll find a better place to talk."

Maria eyed the cake and the other detectives, nodding to the ones who met her gaze, but inside she was a bundle of nerves. Today she was officially opening the proverbial can of worms.

"This way," Bodie said, and headed for an interview room with Maria beside him. He opened a door, then stepped aside.

"In here, Ms. Slade."

"Thank you," she said, and quickly took a seat at the table.

Bodie sat down across from her, then slid his notebook onto the table.

"So, how can I help you?"

"I need you to help me solve a murder."

Four

Bodie's eyes narrowed. His instincts had been right about this woman. She'd definitely come with a purpose. Their conversation had just turned into an interview.

"A murder? Who was killed, and how are you involved?"

Maria's fingers trembled slightly as she laid down the journal.

"This is a long, complicated story, but I'll make it as brief as I can. For all intents and purposes, I grew up the much-loved middle daughter of a Montana cattle rancher, Andrew Slade. Last week Dad died. My two sisters and I went to the lawyer for a reading of the will and…and…"

When her eyes filled with tears, Bodie leaned forward.

"Losing a parent is devastating, no matter how old we are. I know. Just take your time."

Maria focused on the gentleness in his voice as she

took a tissue from her purse, wiped her eyes and blew her nose, then took a deep breath.

"Sorry. There are no words to explain how we felt after the reading began. On that day we learned he wasn't really our father, and that none of the three of us are even related to each other."

Bodie couldn't imagine what a shock that must have been. Then the legal aspects of that began to sink in.

"Wait! What are you saying…that you were all kidnapped?"

"No, no." She sighed. "I told you it was complicated. At the time our father—Andrew—came to care for us, he was an evangelical minister, traveling all over the country. All three of us have a different story, but mine started with a murder here in your city. Twenty years ago, a prostitute named Sally Blake was murdered at the Hampton Arms in North Tulsa. No one was ever arrested, and the case went cold."

Bodie leaned back in his chair. "You're wanting me to open a cold case."

She nodded.

"With what evidence?"

"Right now, I don't have any…but with your help, I'll find it."

Bodie sighed. "Look, Ms. Slade, this isn't how investigations work. Unless you have something new to add to what's in the file, that isn't going to happen."

Maria shoved a hand through her hair in frustration. No matter how many times she said it, it still didn't seem possible.

"I do have something...I just don't remember it."

Bodie frowned. "You don't remember it?"

"No."

"How would you have information relating to a twenty-year-old murder case? You couldn't have been much more than a toddler then. What could you possibly know that—"

"I was four. Sally Blake was my mother, and according to the journal Dad left me, I saw the murder happen."

Bodie's heart skipped a beat. "You witnessed her murder?"

Maria nodded.

"Why didn't you say so at the time of the investigation?"

"It's all in the journal, but the bottom line was, as Sally Blake lay dying, she begged him to take me and hide me. She kept saying...that if he knew I'd seen it happen, he would find me and kill me, too."

The hair stood up on the back of Bodie's neck. "Holy... He? He who?"

"That's the problem," Maria said. "Sally died before she could name the man. And supposedly I was in shock. They whisked me away, hiding me before the police arrived at the hotel. I didn't speak a word for a month. Then, when I did, it was as if the first four years of my life had never happened. I never asked about my mother or where she was. I never behaved as if I was suddenly living with strangers. I just woke up one morning as if I'd decided to come back to the land of the living, accepting where I was, and who I was with, without question."

"You said *they*.... Who helped Andrew hide you?"

"A woman named Becky Thurman. She was my babysitter when my mother went out on her 'dates.' She lived across the hall from us. I googled her name in the Tulsa phonebook before I left Montana, but I didn't get a hit."

"That's quite a story," Bodie said.

Maria shrugged. "So are you going to help me?"

He sighed. "I'm not sure where we can go with this if you can't remember anything, but I will pull the case files and see what we're looking at, okay? Is there anything else you can tell me?"

Relief flooded her body, leaving her slightly light-headed. She smiled.

Bodie stifled a grunt. Her smile had hit him like a fist to the gut.

"Yesterday I went looking for the hotel. You know, thinking if I saw it I might remember something. But it's not there anymore."

"Yeah, North Tulsa has its share of problems," Bodie said.

"After I realized it was gone, I went a couple of blocks farther to a place called John 3:16 Mission. I spoke to a man named Henry, the preacher who's running it."

Bodie couldn't believe what he was hearing. "You went into that neighborhood investigating on your own?"

"Yes? What's the big deal?"

"It's a tough part of the city, and going around asking questions about a murder, even if it's an old one, can get you killed. That's the big deal."

Maria leaned forward, tapping the table with her finger to punctuate her words.

"No. Facing a freak blizzard on a horse and being five miles from home is a big deal. Yesterday was nothing. It was a bright and sunny day. I drove to the mission, got out and went in. The end."

Bodie couldn't quit staring. From the onset he'd been taken by her determination, and during their interview he couldn't help but notice her beauty. But it was becoming apparent that this woman was tough in ways he had not expected.

"Okay, so you talked to this Henry. About what?"

"The Hampton Arms. He told me that one of the regulars at the mission used to work the night shift there."

"So you talked to him?"

"Not for a while. I was washing dishes when he finally showed up and—"

Once again, her story was going all over the place and he was having a difficult time following.

"You washed dishes at the mission?"

Maria frowned. "Yes. After I ate with them. Are you hard of hearing?"

The sarcasm in her voice was impossible to miss. Bodie stifled the urge to grin and just shook his head.

"No, ma'am."

"Then stop interrupting me or I'm never gonna get this told."

"Sorry."

"As I was saying…after this man, Montrose Benton, showed up, we talked for a while. He remembered Sally Blake and her daughter. He remembered the night Sally was murdered, and that the crime was never solved. What he did tell me was something that wasn't in the journal Dad left. It was the name of the man who used to be her pimp."

Bodie's interest spiked as he grabbed his notebook. "What's his name?"

"Tank Vincent. I'm sure he has a different first name, but that's all he knew."

"I'll run the name and see what comes up."

That was exactly what she needed to hear. "Thank you. Thank you so much."

"Don't thank me yet," Bodie said, then glanced at the clock. "Why don't you come back tomorrow morning? That will give me time to locate the case file and run a background check on the pimp. It's doubtful he would still be in the area. After this many years, he could easily be dead." He glanced down at his notes. "Tank Vincent, right?"

"Right."

"Where are you staying?"

"The Doubletree in downtown Tulsa. I'm in Room 604. This is my cell number." She slid a card across the table.

Bodie glanced at it.

Maria Slade
Horse trainer
Triple S Ranch
Missoula, Montana

There were also home and cell phone numbers.

"You train horses?"

"Among other things," Maria said.

He slipped the card in his pocket.

Maria gathered her things and followed him out. It wasn't until he was walking her to the elevator that she finally noticed how tall he was and how wide his shoulders were beneath his jacket. Before she could follow the thought any further, the elevator doors opened. She walked in, then turned around. The last thing she saw was the intent expression on his face.

Bodie waited until the elevator started down, and then shoved his hands in his pockets and headed back to his desk. The only cake left was the piece he'd started eating earlier. He polished it off, dumped the remnants of the makeshift party into the trash and got on his computer. Her story had been nothing short of amazing, and he already had an itch to know more—about the case… and the woman herself.

Still full of nervous energy, Maria didn't know what to do next. She craved answers and action, which was understandable. While this was all news to her, twenty years had come and gone. Whatever clues might have been followed, and whatever witnesses could have come forward, were obviously absent. There were no easy answers to be had. All she could do was wait and see what Detective Bodie Scott came up with. She slid behind the wheel, started the car and drove away.

She was on her way back to the hotel when she realized she'd missed her turn and was on 6th Street instead of 7th.

"Dang it," she muttered, and began looking for a place to turn around. She pulled off into a parking lot, made a quick U-turn and started to backtrack when a building sign across the street caught her attention. The business sold restaurant equipment, including some from restaurants that had been liquidated. Immediately she thought of the mission, and the tiny stove and refrigerator that Henry was using to feed so many people. Before she could talk herself out of it, she began looking for a place to park.

The CD player was stuck on "Washed in the Blood of Jesus." The phrase "oh, Lord, oh, Lord, oh, Lord" kept repeating. Henry sighed. It was exactly what he felt like saying today.

But feeling sorry for himself wasn't going to solve a thing, even though everything here was wearing out, including the music. The only thing truly alive in this place was the Spirit of the Lord, and sometimes even Henry had a hard time finding it.

Suddenly the ladle scraped against the bottom of the soup pot. He sighed. Now the soup was all gone. All he could do was apologize to the next hungry person who was going to go without.

"I'm sorry…that's all for today. The soup's gone," he said gently.

The disgruntled murmurs were understandable. He'd been hungry plenty of times in his life. It hurt him to have to turn away hungry people, but he could only do so much, and there had been slim pickings in the pantry today. He was going to have to start making some calls this afternoon to a few of the charities he knew that might make donations. If they didn't come through, he didn't know what was going to happen tomorrow or in the days to come. His steps were slow as he carried the last empty soup pot over to the sink.

Tyrell was at his usual station, washing dishes. He heard the regret in Preacher Henry's voice as he handed over the pot and knew the old man was worried. Short of holding up a liquor store, which wasn't on his list of things to do to get him out of this neighborhood, he was at a loss as to how to help.

Then someone knocked behind them. They turned to see a man standing in the doorway with a clipboard in his hand.

"Excuse me, I'm looking for Preacher Henry."

"That would be me," Henry said.

The man gave the kitchen a quick glance and then tapped his clipboard.

"I have a delivery for you at this address. I'm assuming you'll want it all set up in here."

Henry frowned. "I'm sorry. We didn't order anything."

Then he thought of their food shortage, and wondered if God had worked a blessing and someone was donating some food. "Exactly what is it that you're delivering?"

The man checked the clipboard. "I have a commercial-grade cookstove, a double-wide refrigerator, a Deep-freeze and some dishes to unload. Where do you want them?"

Henry frowned. "That's definitely a mistake. We didn't order any—"

"Oh, sorry. I didn't make myself clear. The items are a gift. I was supposed to give you this letter, as well. So...do you want to keep that little stove and fridge, or do you want us to haul them off for you?"

Henry didn't know what to say. "Just a minute," he said. "Let me read the letter."

Curious, he opened it. As he read, shock spread throughout his body.

> Preacher Henry, please accept these items as a gesture of appreciation for the kindness you showed to a stranger. At one time in his life, my father, Andrew Slàde, was a preacher. He would have been amazed at all you accomplish. I'm donating these things to the mission in his name. You are an amazing and generous-hearted man, and I know you will put them to good use.
>
> Please give my best to Tyrell.
>
> Maria Slade

A check for five hundred dollars fell from the letter into his hands.

"Praise the Lord," Henry said, and slid the check in his pocket as he turned to the delivery man. "Bring in the appliances. I'll figure out how to hook them up later."

"No worries there, Preacher. We'll be hooking everything up. It's already in the orders."

Henry broke into a smile. "Hallelujah!! Bring them in, bring them in."

Tyrell could tell something big was happening.

"Hey, Preacher Henry. What's goin' on?"

"You remember your dishwashing partner from yesterday?"

Tyrell frowned. "You mean that skinny white woman?"

Henry grinned. "She was hardly skinny...just tall. Taller than you," he added.

Tyrell frowned. "Man...like it matters. I'm still growin'."

"Yes, well, that skinny white woman just gave us a commercial-grade cookstove, a double-wide refrigerator, a Deepfreeze and some dishes, plus money to buy more food."

Tyrell's mouth dropped. "Why you reckon she went and did something like that?"

Henry laid a hand on Tyrell's shoulder as his voice softened.

"'Cause she has a good heart, boy, and despite the

way she looks, she's about as lost as those people we feed every day."

At that point the first of the appliances was wheeled in on a dolly. Within a couple of hours, the old cookstove was gone and the new one set in its place. The double-wide refrigerator was humming as it began to cool down, and a chest-style Deepfreeze was doing the same. The last of the delivery turned out to be three large boxes of restaurant-style crockery and pans.

"Wow," Tyrell whispered, as he looked around at the gleaming appliances. "This place looks like a real restaurant now."

"Wow is right," Henry said, as his eyes filled with tears. "So…what are you doing for the next couple of hours, Tyrell?"

"I don't know. Why?"

"I'm going to Sam's Wholesale for some groceries. I might need me a helper to carry the stuff."

It was Tyrell's habit not to show his true emotions, so he shrugged, stifling a grin.

"I reckon I got time for that."

Henry clapped him on the shoulder. "That's what I like to hear. Let's get crackin'."

Maria would have liked to have seen the expression on Preacher Henry's face when the appliances were delivered, but if she had, he would have felt obligated to praise her, and she hadn't done it for the praise. She'd done it for Andrew for taking her out of danger—for not walking away and leaving her behind.

Armed with her map, she continued to drive around the neighborhood, hoping there would be something in the area where the Hampton Arms had been located that would seem familiar.

Bodie was at his desk running names through the computer. Without a physical description, it was difficult to pin down who Tank Vincent really was. There were a large number of perps with the last name Vincent, but Bodie couldn't get a link between them and pimping, and had been unable to get a hit off the street name Tank. He sighed. Twenty years was a long time ago. The info he was looking for probably hadn't even been entered into a database—or the man from the mission who'd given Maria Slade the information had been wrong.

Now what?

"Hey, Bodie…someone from records sent this up."

A file slid across his desk.

"Thanks," Bodie muttered.

He fingered the tab. Sally Blake.

Immediately his thoughts turned to Maria Slade. There was a real strong possibility that nothing would come of this, but for her sake, he hoped he could help. Now that the file was in his hand, the task he'd set for himself had become real. It was time to let Lieutenant Carver know what was happening. He kept hold of the file, shoved his chair away from the desk and headed for his boss's office.

* * *

On most days Phil Carver liked his job. He was proud of having made lieutenant five years ago, and had an eye on the captain's job, but that was down the road. However, there were days like today when he would have liked a do-over.

The morning had begun with a blowout on the way to work. By the grace of God, he'd managed to avert an accident and pulled off to the side of the road. By the time he got a tow and had a police cruiser come pick him up at the garage, he was an hour and a half late getting in to work. There were a handful of messages on his desk from the captain, and one from a councilman he went to church with, which meant the councilman's teenage son had most likely been arrested again. It wasn't the first time he'd been called to intercede, even though he'd firmly explained months ago that since the incidents were no longer the boy's first offense, he was going to go through the system like everyone else.

There was a knock at his door. He looked up to see Bodie Scott at the door and waved him in.

"Morning, Lieutenant. Got a minute?"

Phil shoved the stack of paperwork to the side. "Yeah, sure, what's up?"

Bodie handed over the file. "This. Thought I'd give you a heads-up before I got into this too deep."

Carver began frowning as he flipped through the file. "It's a cold case. Why did you dig this up?"

"I had a woman come in today who claimed to be

the daughter of the deceased. She also claimed she'd witnessed the murder."

"Then what's the problem? Find the person she's accusing and we'll go from there."

"There's a slight problem. The trauma of seeing her mother murdered caused amnesia. She's forgotten the first four years of her life."

Lieutenant Carver rolled his eyes. "What the hell? It's not even summer yet, and they're already coming out of the woodwork. So she's claiming to have witnessed a murder but doesn't remember there *was* a murder. How does that work?"

Bodie began to explain. By the time he was through, Carver was beginning to understand what was at stake.

"Did you get a hit on this pimp?"

Bodie shook his head. "Not yet."

"Twenty years is a long time. If he's dead, then you've got nothing."

Bodie kept remembering the tears in Maria Slade's eyes and the determination in her voice.

"We just got started. I've got the woman, and maybe being back here will trigger some memories."

"She was four. How much of your life do you remember from that age?"

"It's not the same thing. I didn't see my mother get murdered. Besides, I've got a feeling about this."

Carver grinned. "You and your hunches."

Bodie shrugged. He'd been teased about them before. "So…we good to go on this?"

Carver frowned, then nodded. "For now. See what you can find out. Keep me updated." Just as he was about to close the file and hand the file back, he noticed a name that set his nerves on edge. "Son of a bitch," he muttered.

Bodie frowned. The lieutenant wasn't in the habit of cursing. "What is it?"

Carver pointed to a name on the paperwork. "See this? Frank McCall was the lead on the case."

"Yes, sir. How does that matter?"

Carver sighed as he handed the file back. "He's in the pen at McAlester doing twenty-five to life."

"Seriously? What for?"

"Dirty cop. Suppressing evidence, planting evidence. You name it. He got caught planting evidence, but by the time it all unwound, there were dead informants and some drug runners in the mix. Long story short—one bad cop makes everyone else look dirty. We spent years overcoming that black mark."

All of a sudden the file in Bodie's hands felt somehow heavier—explaining why so little info was actually in there.

"Were all his cases compromised?"

Carver shrugged. "It was hard to tell."

Bodie fingered the edges of the file. "Are you afraid that opening this case will bring up the old dirt?"

"Who knows, but it doesn't matter. If he suppressed evidence in this one, as well, we'll eventually find out."

"As will the media," Bodie said.

"You let me worry about the media," Carver said. "You're gonna need all you've got and then some to solve this, when all you've got is a witness with amnesia and a missing pimp who's had twenty years to get good and lost. And FYI…if we have something big break, just know your cold case will have to take second place."

"Yes, sir."

"Now go do your thing," Carver said.

"Yes, sir."

"And close the door when you leave. I've got a handful of phone calls to return and not nearly enough patience."

Bodie left, quietly closing the door behind him. He liked his job, but he had no aspirations to move higher up the food chain.

Five

Bodie had been at his desk for what felt like hours, going through the cold case file, making notes and phone calls. He'd run another search through their database for Tank Vincent, without success, and had given the task of trying to find the man to a rookie whose partner was out sick. He'd just put the file aside, knowing he'd done all he could do from his desk until he got confirmation on the requests he'd put out, when his partner, Dave Booker, showed up.

"Hey, Bodie, we caught a murder-suicide. Grab your hat."

Bodie picked up his Stetson and settled it firmly on his head.

"I have my hat. You got that fancy gold pen?"

Dave grinned. "You know my wife gave that to me for my birthday. I have to use it. Otherwise it would hurt her feelings."

"That's bull," Bodie said, grinning back. "Your pen cost more than my hat. I'm driving."

Dave shrugged. "Whatever."

"Fill me in on the way," Bodie said, as they headed for the parking lot.

It didn't take long for Dave to relate the tale.

A distraught daughter had found her aging parents dead, along with a suicide note.

As Bodie arrived at the address, they realized the media had already descended on the upscale neighborhood.

"Son of a bitch," Dave muttered, as Bodie maneuvered their car around a news van. A uniformed officer waved them forward. Bodie parked beside a van from the crime lab.

"Do we have the daughter's name?" Bodie asked, as they headed for the house.

Dave checked his notes. "Terri Ray."

Bodie nodded. When they entered the house, the medical examiner was still there, and the forensic team was still gathering info. It was up to the detectives to piece together the last twenty-four hours of Robert and Julia Baker's lives. After a scan of the murder scene and a few questions to the M.E., Bodie found the responding officer and took his statement.

The officer ran through his facts, including the daughter's story. According to her, Robert had left a note explaining how he'd emptied an entire bottle of sleeping pills into Julia's glass of warm milk, then watched her fall asleep as they lay on their bed watching home movies. In the suicide note, Robert stated that he was waiting for the moment when Julia would take her last breath, at which time he planned to put a gun to his head, because he didn't want a life without her.

It was a tragic story, but for their daughter, it was nothing short of devastating. When Dave and Bodie found her, she was in the living room, still trembling from the trauma of her discovery, seemingly unaware of the tears that kept running down her cheeks. Her eyes were wide and fixed as she watched the police tramping through the rooms of her childhood home. She appeared on the verge of hysterics. The sooner they got her statement and got her out of there, the better.

"I've got the neighbors. You get the daughter," Dave said.

Bodie moved toward the sofa.

"Ms. Ray...I'm Detective Scott from Homicide. I just have a few questions."

She quickly swiped at her eyes and blew her nose as he sat beside her.

The shock of what she'd found was still evident in her eyes. The pupils were dilated, her eyelids red and swollen. When they shook hands, he could tell by the cold, clammy feel of her skin that she was close to passing out.

Bodie clicked his pen. "Your parents' names are Robert and Julia Baker. Is that correct?"

She nodded.

"What alerted you to the fact that something might be wrong?" he asked.

"I was supposed to run errands for Dad today. He made lists. I filled them. You know...buying groceries, dropping off clothes at the cleaners or picking them up. Whatever they needed, I shopped for, or else I stayed with Mother while he shopped. This morning he didn't answer either their home phone or his cell. I came over because I was worried."

"So you found them. I understand there was a suicide note."

"Yes."

"Did you touch it?"

She closed her eyes. Bodie imagined she was reliving the moment of discovery. Her voice started to shake as she spoke.

"Yes, I picked it up and read it after I found them like…like that. Then I laid it back down and called the police."

"How long had it been since you'd heard from your parents?"

"I talked to Dad last night. I always call and check on them before I go to bed. They are…were…both in their late eighties."

"Did he seem despondent?"

She nodded. "Yes, but it was nothing new. Mother has…had Alzheimer's. Up until last Sunday he'd been coping."

Shit. Alzheimer's. The same ugly disease Grandma Scott had died from. The scene was beginning to add up.

"What happened last Sunday?"

"That morning, when Mother woke up, Dad said she didn't know him. She got scared and started crying, telling him to get out of her house. It nearly killed him. He called me, sobbing, saying that she was afraid of him and asking what did I think he should do. Of course I came right over. By the time I got here, Mother had calmed down. I suggested the possibility of putting her into a nursing home."

"I take it he refused," Bodie said.

Terri nodded. "He got very angry with me for even suggesting it. I stayed for a while longer, and as time passed, they slid back into their little routine. I thought that the crisis had passed. Obviously I was wrong."

Her face crumpled as a fresh set of tears began to fall.

Bodie sighed. The whole thing was a tragedy.

"Is there someone you can call? A family member... a friend?"

Terri ran a shaky hand through her tousled hair. "My husband is in Iraq. Our son is away at college. I called our priest. He'll be here shortly."

No sooner had she said the words than the doorbell rang.

"That's probably him," Terri said. "Do you need me anymore?"

Bodie nodded. "No, ma'am." Then he handed her his card. "If there's anything I can do, feel free to call."

She slipped the card into her pocket and walked out of the room with Bodie right behind her.

He caught a glimpse of a man in dark clothing with the expected flash of a white clerical collar. There was a cluster of mumbled words, followed by a fresh set of harsh, agonizing sobs as the priest took Terri Ray into his arms.

Bodie paused on the way out the door.

"Excuse me, Father. I'm Detective Scott. She has my card," he said, then felt obliged to add, "and my sympathies."

The priest nodded. "I'm Mrs. Ray's priest from St. Mary's. I'm going to take her home."

Even though the incident appeared to be an open-and-shut case, protocol demanded the investigation proceed until the evidence proved cause of death, which was now in the hands of the crime lab. By the time Bodie and Dave headed back to the department, it was already evening.

"That was a tough one," Dave muttered, as Bodie braked for a red light.

Bodie nodded.

"Would you do that?" Dave asked.

"Do what?" Bodie asked.

"What that man did…to himself and his wife."

Bodie frowned. "My gut reaction would be no, but as my Dad used to say, 'Don't judge a man until you've walked a mile in his shoes,' so I guess my answer should be…I don't know."

"Yeah. Me, neither," Dave said.

The light turned green. Bodie accelerated, and they moved through the intersection. By the time they got back to the precinct, it was nearing 6:00 p.m. Bodie checked his messages and found one from Shorty Carroll, a retired detective from the vice squad. He'd called

Shorty earlier about the cold case, but the man hadn't been home, so he'd left a message for him to call. Now they were playing phone tag. Bodie hoped Shorty would still be there when he called back. If anyone knew about hookers and pimps from twenty years ago, it would be Shorty.

Bodie took a seat and quickly returned the call.

The call was answered on the third ring.

"Hello."

Bodie leaned back in his chair. "Hey, Shorty. This is Bodie Scott from Homicide. We met back at Carl Finley's retirement party a couple of years ago."

"Yeah, yeah, I remember you," Shorty said. "The cowboy."

Bodie grinned. His penchant for boots and Stetsons had quickly earned him the nickname.

"Yeah, thanks for getting back to me so quickly."

"No problem. What's up?"

"I'm working a cold case. It's a homicide from twenty years ago, when you were still with the department, but there's not much in the file to go on."

"So what's the name of the vic?"

"Sally Blake. She was a twentysomething hooker who was murdered in her room at the Hampton Arms."

"That old hotel used to be over on the north side?"

"Yes."

"Sorry, the name doesn't ring a bell," Shorty said.

"I wasn't calling you about the vic. I'm running down leads, and a name popped up that I thought you might know. It was the name of her pimp. A man named Tank Vincent."

"Vincent…Tank Vincent? I don't think… Oh! Wait. I do remember him. Great big good-looking guy at the time. Think a young Nick Nolte and you got the gist. Had his hair bleached blond, and wore it straight and long, like a woman's. Hung way below his shoulders. Yeah, I remember Tank. He came by the name honestly. Had the upper body strength of a weight lifter."

Bodie's pulse kicked up a notch. Bingo.

"In that case, I don't suppose you know what he's up to now? He isn't coming up on any of our databases, and I was afraid he might be dead."

"Oddly enough, I ran into him about five years ago when I was fishing down at Lake Eufaula. He was running a bait shop. Couldn't believe my eyes when I walked in to buy some stink bait. I almost didn't rec-ognize him. The young Nolte had morphed into a bad version of the older one. We had a beer and a couple of laughs. But after I hurt my back in 2008 I haven't been able to make the drive anymore. Don't know whether he's still there or not."

Bodie was taking notes. The thrill of the hunt was kicking in.

"I don't suppose you remember the name of that bait shop?"

Shorty laughed. "Yeah. It was one of those real mem-orable names. Bait and Beer."

Bodie grinned. "Thanks, Shorty. Take care."

"You, too," Shorty said, and disconnected.

Bodie hung up the phone, then turned to his computer, pulled up the phone records for Eufaula and began scanning the yellow pages for a bait shop called Bait and Beer. He found one, then began looking for the owner by cross-checking against a list of businesses with liquor licenses, which the owner would have needed to sell beer. When the name Samuel Gene Vincent popped up as having a liquor license for Bait and Beer, he printed out the info. Then he tapped into the Oklahoma Department of Motor Vehicles, found a corresponding name with an accompanying photo and printed that out, as well. Now he had a picture and an address. Shorty was right. Vincent did bear a striking resemblance to present-day Nick Nolte.

He slid the info into the cold case file, along with his notes, and headed for the parking lot. He planned to contact Maria Slade tomorrow, but he was too hyped to go home. He wanted to show her the DMV photo and see if it rang any bells. He pulled the card she'd given him out of his pocket, dialed her cell phone and waited for her to answer.

Maria was just about to go downstairs to the hotel restaurant when her cell phone rang. The caller ID came up as the Tulsa Police Department. Suddenly there was a knot in her stomach. She answered quickly.

"Hello?"

"Ms. Slade. This is Detective Scott."

Maria sat down on the side of the bed. "Yes? Is something wrong?"

"No. Nothing like that."

She sighed. "Oh, okay, it's just that I didn't expect to hear from you tonight, so of course the first thing I thought was that you'd changed your mind. Sorry. That's how my brain's been working these days."

"No problem. Say, listen…would it be all right if I came by? I have a couple of things I want to show you."

"Yes, of course." She glanced at the clock. "It's after seven. I was about to go downstairs to dinner."

"I haven't eaten since breakfast…except for some cake."

Maria grinned. "You're welcome to join me, but won't your family be expecting you at home?"

"No wife. No kids. No dog. And remember that cake all over my desk when you came in?"

"I guess," Maria said, unwilling to admit she'd been so nervous she hadn't seen anything but his face.

"Today's my birthday. I would appreciate a little company tonight."

She refused to acknowledge the spurt of interest following that news—not to mention the news that he was single.

"In that case, happy birthday, Detective, and I'd be happy if you would join me. I hate to eat alone."

"Me, too. How about I meet you in the bar and we'll go from there?"

"All right," Maria said.

"See you in a few," Bodie said.

"Yes, see you soon," she said, then dropped her cell

phone in her purse and told herself the reason for the skip in her heart had nothing to do with the fact that she would be dining with a very handsome man. He was only doing his job and being kind. Still, she found herself hurrying as she headed for the elevator.

In the grand scheme of life, fate often has a way of evening the odds, which was certainly the case for hotshot lawyer Franklin Sheets. The last thing he expected to see in the lobby of the Doubletree Hotel was a ghost.

He had just taken a table in the bar and was waiting to meet a client for cocktails when he saw it appear. She was dressed in contemporary clothing and her hair was longer than he'd remembered, but as he lived and breathed, it was the ghost of Sally Blake.

Twenty years ago he might not have been so shocked, but after all this time, he would have assumed she'd moved on, or gone into the light or wherever it was spirits were supposed to go. Obviously hers had not.

Panic hit, followed by a nausea so strong he thought he would throw up. She paused in the lobby, looking around as if to get her bearings, then turned toward the bar, locked on to his presence and started walking toward him. He wondered if anyone else could see her and wondered if she'd come to take him to hell.

His legs went weak, and his hands started to shake. The closer she came, the faster his pulse raced. She was coming closer—moving with that slow, lanky stride he remembered so well, with her arms swinging freely, her head back and her chin up. He stood abruptly, fully intending to run, but his legs wouldn't work. His heart was thundering so hard, he wondered if it could explode from fright. A few more steps and he would find out.

God…God…no, please, no…don't let her—

Their gazes met. He could smell the faint scent of her perfume, and then she was right in front of him. He opened his mouth to beg for mercy—then she passed him by.

He spun abruptly, watching in disbelief as the ghost took a seat a few tables over. When she ordered a beer, he fell backward into his chair, trying to understand what had just happened.

She was talking to the waiter, then taking a cell phone out of her purse and reading a text.

Holy shit. That wasn't a ghost! It was a living, breathing woman.

His mind began to race. He'd always heard that everyone had a twin, but this was crazy. This woman looked like Sally had looked twenty years ago. How could she…?

The kid. Son of a bitch…this had to be the kid.

He swiped a shaky hand across his face and tried to laugh. Ghosts. How stupid could he be? The kid had grown up, that was all. He'd never expected to see her again, but now that he had…no big deal. She didn't know him. One thing about Sally. She would never take her dates to her room. And even if the kid remembered the few times he'd seen them out and about, there was no way she could connect him to her mother. Even though he was still slim and fit, he looked nothing like the man he'd been then, mimicking wealth with a ten-year-old Corvette, his JCPenney suits and fake gold jewelry. But he'd had plans and dreams, and by God, he'd made them happen. His suits were Armani now, and his watch *was* gold, as in Rolex. And the car he drove these days was a baby blue Mercedes with matching leather seats—his dream car.

Convinced that he'd made a big deal out of nothing, he waved at his waiter and ordered a second glass of wine, then glanced at his watch. Where the hell was his client? Didn't the little bastard know his time was valuable? He would give him ten more minutes, and then he was out of here.

His second drink arrived at the same time that a man walked into the bar. Franklin eyed him, thinking to himself that he knew the guy from somewhere. As the man passed, he caught a glimpse of a badge clipped to his waist and the bulge of a shoulder holster, and thought cop. *That's it. The guy's a cop.*

Out of curiosity, he turned to see where the man was headed, and once again, his stomach rolled. That woman—the Sally Blake look-alike. The cop was going to her table.

"So what?" Franklin muttered, unaware he was talking aloud. "So she's talking to a cop. So what? It's still nothing to do with me."

"Mr. Sheets. Sorry I'm late."

Franklin jumped, then turned around. The missing client had arrived. He glared at the pasty-faced accountant who was having trouble with the IRS and thought about telling him he wasn't going to take the case. Then he remembered the hefty retainer he'd already accepted and made himself focus.

Maria saw Bodie enter the bar and lifted her hand. Immediately he saw her and headed her way, moving with a slow, easy stride that reminded her of the cowboys on the Triple S. She hadn't known he wore a Stetson, but she had seen his boots. Even though it wasn't how she'd imagined a detective would dress, she thought little of it. This was Oklahoma, after all. Plenty of cowboys here.

Now, watching him wend his way through the maze of small tables, she had to admit that he was very easy on the eyes.

"Thanks for agreeing to talk to me," Bodie said, as he took a seat at the table beside her and laid his hat on an empty chair.

"No problem," Maria said. "You're the one doing me a favor. It's why I came here, remember?"

The waiter stopped by the table to get his order. Bodie noticed the brown long-neck bottle in front of Maria and stifled a grin. A woman after his own heart.

"I'll have what she's having."

As Maria's focus shifted, she realized the detective was watching her. They locked gazes, and she was the first to look away. Suddenly the condensation dripping down the side of the bottle became an irresistible point of interest.

Bodie could tell she was nervous. He didn't know whether it had to do with him, the case, or both.

The case he and Dave had just worked was still weighing on his mind. He would like for this one to have a better resolution. If he was to believe everything Maria had told him, then all he had to do was find a way to help her unlock her memory.

The waiter came back with his beer.

"Thanks," Bodie said, then eyed Maria. "Did you make reservations in the restaurant?"

"No, I was just going to take my chances," she said.

"Grab your drink and let's head that way. My belly's rubbing against my backbone."

Maria grinned. "That's pretty hungry."

Bodie grabbed his hat, settled it on his head, then picked up his beer.

"When it comes to food, I don't mess around. After you, ma'am."

Maria walked out of the bar, thinking only of the detective behind her, and she didn't even notice that another set of eyes was following her every move.

Six

Bodie waited until after he and Maria had ordered their food before taking the DMV photo of Tank Vincent out of his jacket pocket.

"This is what I wanted to show you," he said, and slid it across the table.

Maria picked up the sheet of paper. The moment she saw the name Samuel Gene Vincent, her skin crawled.

"Is this Tank?"

Bodie nodded. "Does he look familiar?"

She looked again, studying the face intently. His features were strong, his face a little square. His hair was gray and somewhat bushy. His nose sat slightly sideways on his face, as if he'd run into a wall. She saw the birth date and did a little math in her head. He was sixty-four, which meant he would have been forty-four when her mother died. But no matter how long she looked, it was like looking at a total stranger.

Finally she handed the photo back to Bodie.

"I'm sorry, but I don't remember ever seeing this man."

Bodie shrugged. "It's not surprising. It's been twenty years. According to my source, in his day, Tank Vincent was a big body-builder type with long bleached-blond hair."

An image flashed through Maria's mind of a great big man with long yellow hair and a gold-capped tooth.

Bodie saw the expression on her face and realized something had just clicked.

"What?" he asked.

"I don't know… It was when you mentioned the hair that I flashed on a giant of a man with long blond hair and a gold-capped tooth."

"Really?" Bodie asked. "Well, that's something I can check out when I head down to the lake tomorrow."

"Lake? What lake?" Maria asked.

"Lake Eufaula. That's where Tank Vincent lives these days, running a bait and beer shop."

Maria leaned forward. "I want to go with you."

Bodie frowned. "Look, we're opening a cold case here, which means for the last twenty years, someone believes he's gotten away with murder. If anyone gets wind of the fact that the case has been activated because you witnessed that murder, it won't matter whether you can remember right now or not. They *will* try to get rid of you."

"I'm not stupid. I'm well aware of that," Maria snapped. "But this was my mother. With her dying breath she was thinking of me to make sure I stayed safe. I'll do whatever it takes to get justice for her."

Bodie frowned. He had a feeling if he didn't give in, she would be off on her own.

"I'll pick you up around eight in the morning. It's a bit of a drive."

"Thank you," she said.

"Don't thank me yet. We don't have much to go on, and if Tank Vincent doesn't come up with something and you don't remember anything further, this investigation might end before it gets started."

"I have faith that's not going to happen," she said.

He sighed. "Maybe if I hang out with you long enough, some of that sunny expectation will rub off on me."

Maria caught the vibes of his dejection.

"Bad day?"

"Yeah. It happens."

"I'm sorry," she said. "Here I am all gung ho about a twenty-year-old murder, and you're dealing with this every day."

"That's okay. Each case matters the same to the people who are left behind."

"What made you want to be a cop?"

"I like puzzles and I don't like crooks. Once I figured out there was a job that encompassed both, it was a simple choice."

Maria was caught. From the intensity of his gaze to the way the left corner of his mouth tilted slightly as he spoke, he was a very sexy man. His eyes were such a clear blue that they made her think of Montana skies, which made her think of home. She wondered where he'd grown up, then decided the best way to find out was to ask.

"Where did you grow up?"

"A cattle ranch near Claremore. That's a little northeast of here."

Maria nodded. "So your parents are ranchers. Any siblings?"

"Two brothers, both younger. One works with Dad at the ranch, the other is a football coach at a high school in Claremore. Between them, Mom and Dad have five grandkids. How about you?"

Maria plopped her elbows on the table and began running the tip of her finger around the lip of her beer bottle.

"There are three of us girls. None of us are married, although Savannah has a boyfriend who owns a ranch near ours. We all still live at home, which might seem strange to some, but we're all involved in running the ranch. Dad brought us up that way and it stuck."

"So Savannah is one of your sisters," he said. "Who's the third?"

Her face lit up. It was the first time he'd seen her so animated.

"Savannah's the baby. Holly is the oldest. I'm the middle child. Oh, and there's Bud. I don't know what we would have done the last few days if it hadn't been for him. But that's the way it's always been."

Bodie frowned. Bud? This was the first time she'd

mentioned a man in her life, and that wasn't what he wanted to hear.

"So who's Bud?"

"Dad's foreman, and even though he was quite a bit younger, he was also his best friend. He taught me to ride and everything I know about training horses. Hannah, our mother, died when Holly was in junior high school. Bud became the shoulder I cried on when something happened at school. You know all the drama that comes with growing up...facts of life, boys, the whole bit. Dad was the backbone of the ranch, but Bud is its heart. He loves the place as much as Dad did and put up with all three of us, no matter what. He never backed off from a question I asked, even when his ears turned red from embarrassment. I don't know what I'd do without him."

Bodie nodded, but his mind was racing. Was she saying he was like a brother...or a lover? Although it was none of his business and she was too much of a stranger for it to matter, it still did. He was beginning to realize he didn't want Maria Slade to be otherwise engaged, so to speak.

Before he could press her for more information, their meal arrived. After that, the conversation turned to intermittent comments about the food, the service and how far it was to Lake Eufaula.

Franklin Sheets had finished his business nearly an hour ago, and still he lingered in the hotel lobby, having taken a seat behind a potted plant near the entrance to the restaurant. There was absolutely no reason to believe their meeting was anything but personal, but his guilty conscience and a healthy dose of fear kept him from leaving.

Just when he thought they would never leave, they appeared in the doorway. The cop had his hand at her back, and she was talking as they walked. He wished he could hear what they were saying, but they weren't coming in his direction, and with all the open space between them, he could hardly get up and move closer without calling attention to himself.

They paused in the middle of the lobby. Franklin watched the cop hand her a card. She dropped it into her purse, then looked up at him and smiled.

Franklin's gut knotted. He wondered if she was in the same business as Sally had been. It was eerie to watch her. Like Sally Blake come to life again. He shifted slightly, watching as the cop frowned, then pulled out his phone. Obviously he'd gotten a call. Whatever it was about, it put an end to their meeting. With a few short words and a hand on her arm, the cop was out the door, leaving the woman alone in the lobby.

Franklin couldn't read the expression on her face. He couldn't tell if she was into the guy, which could have meant that their dinner had been a personal affair, or if their meeting was strictly business. However, he was certain that whatever the reason for her presence, it had nothing to do with him.

When she headed for the elevator, he started to leave. Then, before he knew it, he was following her across the lobby. When the doors opened, he was one of seven others who boarded with her. Confident he would not stand out in a crowd, he took out his cell phone and pretended to be checking messages. She never looked back, but when she got off the elevator on the sixth floor, he got out behind her. Careful to leave a good distance between them, he followed. When he saw her go into Room 604, he had all the information he needed. He turned around and headed back to the elevators, rode down, then went out front to pick up his car. Franklin was a man who did not like surprises. He didn't know her name, but he knew where she was staying. He wasn't expecting to need that info, but he believed in being prepared.

Traffic was busy, as usual, as he headed home, his thoughts turning to the tasks at hand. He had to be in court at 9:00 a.m. and he still needed to polish up his summation. The district attorney's job was coming open, and when election year rolled around, he wanted his name on that ticket.

Maria showered quickly and got ready for bed. But when she crawled between the sheets, she realized she was still too hyper from her dinner with Bodie Scott to settle down. She reached for her journal. She was homesick and tired, and still grieving for her father. Just seeing his handwriting was enough to make her cry. But there had to be something in those pages that would trigger her memory. She needed to remember—and to remember everything—in the very worst way.

She flipped the journal open, scanned through several pages, then stopped on a date.

July 3rd—her birthday.

You turned eight today, but you didn't want a birthday cake. You wanted pie. Lemon pie. So your mother made pie. We put candles in the meringue and everything. Sang "Happy Birthday" to you, and when you leaned forward to blow them out, all of a sudden your expression went blank. You didn't move. You didn't even try to blow out the candles. I spoke your name…. "Maria…Maria…what's wrong?" I said. You looked up at me with this strange expression and said, "Mommy doesn't like lemon." Hannah patted your back and said, "Yes I do, honey. It's one of my favorites, remember?"

You shuddered, then blinked, and the moment passed in the commotion of blowing out the candles, then cutting the pie. But I knew what had happened. A piece of your past had emerged. I waited and waited for a sign from you that you were regaining your memory…that you might want to talk about what you'd seen. But the time never came. Whatever had slipped into your thoughts had slipped out again as fast as it had come.

Maria's vision blurred as she laid the journal aside. So much pressure to remember. How was she going to find the switch to make it happen when she'd spent twenty years subconsciously suppressing everything about her past?

Frustrated and a little overwhelmed, she rolled over onto her side, closed her eyes and cried herself to sleep.

Bodie was still thrown by the call he had received at the hotel. Dave and his wife, Patty, had been out to dinner and were on their way home when they were sideswiped by a drunk driver. They weren't badly injured, but their car was totaled and they were both getting patched up in the E.R. Dave was missing his wallet, and Patty's purse was in shreds all over Peoria Avenue. By the time they'd located it, someone had taken the cash. Patty had consoled herself with the fact that she'd retrieved all her credit cards and her driver's license. Dave was hoping his wallet was still in the car, but that meant he was minus money for cab fare, so he'd called Bodie.

Bodie had come through for them in record time. He'd been properly horrified by their stitches and bruises, and loaded them into his car and took them home. By the time they pulled up in front, it was after eleven and Patty was in tears.

"I'm sorry, I'm sorry," she kept muttering. "I don't know why I keep crying."

"It's just shock, honey," Dave said. "I feel a little like crying myself."

"Wait a minute," Bodie said, and quickly got out of his car, then helped her out. He steadied her on one side as Dave took the other. Together, they got her inside the house and into the bedroom. At that point, Bodie knew it was time for him to disappear.

"Is there anything else I can do for you guys?" he asked. "Do you need some water…some ice packs… anything?"

Dave shook his head, then winced.

"No. We'll be all right. Just slow and sore. I guess I don't need to tell you I won't be in tomorrow."

"I won't, either," Bodie said. "I'm heading to Lake Eufaula in the morning to run down a lead."

Dave frowned. "For what case? What don't I know?"

Bodie hesitated, then shrugged. "You remember that woman who came in this morning while everyone was eating my cake?"

Dave's eyes widened. "That real tall one with long dark hair?"

"Yeah."

"What about her?"

"She claims to be a witness to her mother's murder, which turned out to be one of our unsolved cases from twenty years back. It's a long story, and I'll tell you more about it when you're feeling better."

Dave sighed. Right now he felt like shit and couldn't work up enough interest in something that had happened twenty years ago to push for more answers.

"Thanks again, buddy," he said.

"That's what partners are for," Bodie said. "I'll let myself out. You guys get some rest."

It was close to 1:00 a.m. by the time Bodie got home. He dropped his keys on the hall table and headed for the kitchen. Out of habit, he checked his messages, then smiled as he listened. Both his brothers had called with birthday greetings, and there was a call from his parents, as well, wishing him happy birthday, then asking when he was coming home for a visit. It was too late to call them back, so he headed for the bedroom. It was already tomorrow, and he needed to get some rest. After a quick shower, he crawled into bed and wearily closed his eyes.

"Dance with me, Frankie. You know how I like to dance."

The music swelled as the tall, leggy brunette, wearing nothing but a red teddy and high heels, began moving and swaying to the rhythm.

"Stop it, Sally. I don't want to dance. I want to fuck."

Sally frowned. She stopped, turned off the music and then stripped abruptly before she turned to face him.

"Fine. If we're all business, that'll be fifty dollars."

Frankie tossed a handful of bills across the bed. She picked them up and counted them slowly, struggling to keep track of the amount in her head.

He frowned. "Hurry up. I don't have all night."

She stuffed the money into her purse, then turned and all but strutted toward the bed.

Frankie shuddered. Despite the fact that she was

nothing but a whore, he couldn't get her out of his mind. Sometimes he treated her badly, just to remind himself that he was the one in charge and she meant nothing but a good fuck. Sometimes it worked. Sometimes it didn't. Tonight it didn't. He wanted her bad and hated himself for his weakness.

She was an Amazon, girded with nothing but her sex appeal and those black high heels.

"So how do you want it, Frankie? Blow job or all the way?"

"All the way."

She took a condom from the bedside table.

Frankie frowned. "I'm not wearing a condom. I don't like the way it feels."

"It's the condom or a blow job."

"Hell, no," he said. "I paid you. I get what I paid for."

She stopped. He couldn't read the look on her face, but when she turned around and walked back to her clothes and took the money he'd just given her out of her purse, he couldn't believe it. But it wasn't until she tossed the bills on the bed and reached for her clothes to get dressed that he lost it.

He came off the bed in a rage, grabbed her by the arms and threw her down onto the floor, on top of the dress she'd been about to put on. Before she could scream, he was on top of her, then in her. The violence of what was happening was a turn-on he hadn't expected. He knew she was screaming now, and trying to kick him off, but he didn't care. He rode through the rape on a high like nothing he'd known. When it was over, he got up and started dressing, but she didn't move.

"Get up," he muttered, then took the money and threw it toward her.

Quiet tears were running down her cheeks as she rolled over onto her side, curling up into a fetal position.

"Get up, dammit!"

Sally was shivering, but her voice was firm. "You got what you wanted. Get out. Get out, and don't ever call me again."

"I'll call anytime I want," he yelled. "You're the one who's for sale, remember?"

All of a sudden she was on her feet. Blood was dripping from a cut on her bottom lip, and there was the beginning of a bruise already taking shape beneath the skin on her cheek. She should have been submissive. Instead, he knew a moment of fear when she walked toward him, then stabbed a finger in his chest.

"You will be sorry for this," she said softly. "One day, you will be paying for more than a fuck."

Frankie cursed, but standing toe-to-toe, he didn't have the guts to hit her. Instead, he glanced around the room, making sure he wasn't leaving anything behind, and slammed the door as he left.

You will be sorry...you will be sorry...will be sorry... sorry...sorry....

Franklin gasped and sat up with a jerk. His sheets

were drenched in sweat, and his heart was pounding so hard he thought he might be having a heart attack.

"Oh, God, oh, God, oh, God," he whispered, as he laid the flat of his hand against his chest. "I'm okay. I'm okay. That was just a dream brought on by seeing that woman. It means nothing. Nothing."

Slowly, his heartbeat returned to a normal rhythm. He glanced at the clock. It was almost 6:00 a.m. That was one hell of a way to start off a day.

Frowning, he threw off the covers, strode into his bathroom and began getting ready for work.

He splashed his face with water, then reached for the shaving cream, pausing for a moment to appreciate his features.

He looked good for fifty-seven, and he knew it. He wasn't a big man, but he was fit. His features were even, his hazel eyes revealing his intelligence and charm. But it was the cleft in his chin that he liked the most. It gave him a certain memorable distinction.

He slathered the shaving cream on his face, then reached for the razor. Almost instantly, his thoughts shifted to last night and the coincidence of seeing Sally's daughter after all these years. The more he thought about it, the more he felt the need to cover his tracks.

Just before he was ready to walk out the door, he slipped into his office and grabbed the Rolodex from his desk. There was only one name behind the *U* tab. He punched in the numbers and waited for it to ring. When the caller finally picked up, Franklin could tell he'd woken him up.

"Yeah?"

Franklin grinned. "Good morning, Ed. It's me, Franklin Sheets. Sounds like the sleep fairy missed your house last night."

"I've been working a case. I haven't been in bed but a couple of hours."

"That's why I called," Franklin said. "A case."

The man sighed. "Can you call back this afternoon?"

"No, I'll be in court, so wake up, Ed Underwood. Get your pen and paper, and pay attention. You're supposed to be the best private investigator in Tulsa."

"This is gonna cost you," Ed muttered.

"It always does," Franklin said. "Now listen up. I don't have much time, but I need you to tail a woman for me for a while."

Ed snorted, not bothering to hide his glee. "What's up, buddy? Someone two-timing you?"

"No. Nothing like that. I told you. It has to do with a case," Franklin said, anxious not to make his friend curious.

"Okay. What's her name?" Ed asked.

"I don't know," Franklin said. "But she's staying in Room 604 at the Doubletree Hotel downtown."

"Crap. How do you expect me to—"

"You're the P.I. Figure it out," Franklin muttered. "Call me tonight with an update."

"Yeah, yeah, all right," Ed said. "Now get off the phone so I can get dressed and get to the hotel before the morning traffic gets bad."

* * *

Maria was in the shower, getting ready to meet Bodie Scott. She didn't know what today would bring toward solving her mother's murder. She did know that her anxiety over what to wear had nothing to do with looking up an old pimp and everything to do with spending the day with one good-looking cop.

Seven

Ed Underwood wheeled into the parking garage of the downtown Doubletree at straight-up seven o'clock. He didn't know nearly enough about the woman he was going to tail to make this job easy, which meant some money would have to change hands.

Mentally marking his parking space, he dropped his keys in his pocket and headed for the main entrance. He'd been a cop before he'd become a private investigator, and he'd had a lifetime to accumulate a list of snitches from all over the place. It had been at least a year since he'd been in this hotel, but he knew a bellman who'd helped him out before. He just hoped the man still worked here and was on duty today.

He walked past several shuttle buses and a long line of cabs waiting for fares, which meant some big convention group was either checking out or checking in. As he entered the lobby, he paused in the doorway for a moment to get his bearings. The lobby was full of luggage and guests. Bellmen were all over, many coming out of elevators carrying bags, which meant the convention must be leaving. He glanced at his watch, then hailed a bellman coming toward him pushing a loaded luggage cart.

"Hey, buddy, is DeMarco Louis still working here?"

"Who's asking?"

"Oh. Sorry," Ed said, and whipped out his P.I. identification.

The bellman shrugged, then pointed over his shoulder.

"I rode up in the elevator with him. He should be coming down soon."

"Thanks," Ed said, and slipped the man a couple of bucks before heading toward the elevators.

Intent on keeping a low profile, he kept his head tilted in a slight downward position and made a point of hiding among the guests who were checking in and out, anxious not to call attention to himself. Once he reached the bank of elevators, he stepped off to the side and took out his cell phone, pretending to be checking messages, but his focus was entirely on who was coming out of the elevators. Several cars emptied before he saw his snitch.

DeMarco Louis was a skinny little black guy in his late forties who played up his resemblance to comedian Chris Rock by always being ready with a joke and a laugh. He was pushing a luggage cart for a contingent of women who were laughing and talking as they followed him, and he was giving them sassy feedback as they walked, keeping them all in stitches.

Staying a few feet behind, Ed walked outside with the others, then waited until the women were gone and DeMarco was about to go back inside.

Ed stepped out behind him and clapped him on the shoulder.

"Hey, buddy. Long time no see."

The smile was still on DeMarco's lips as he turned around. When he saw who it was, his eyes narrowed.

"Yeah, it's been a while. What do you want?"

Ed made a face. "Hey, man…I might just be saying hi."

"Hi," DeMarco said. "I'm busy. Gotta go."

"So, I need a little info," Ed said.

DeMarco rolled his eyes.

"Why you white guys always have to play around with bein' all polite and stuff? Why can't you just say what you came to say and not waste my time?" Then he frowned. "How do you know I have the answers you need?"

"Because I need some info about one of the hotel guests."

DeMarco frowned. "That kind of info can get a person fired. I like my job."

"It's nothing big. I just need the name of the woman who's staying in Room 604. That's all."

"Ain't nothin' in the world for free," DeMarco said.

Ed nodded. "I know, I know. I got you covered, buddy. Just get me a name."

DeMarco held out his hand.

Ed dropped a fifty-dollar bill into his palm.

DeMarco frowned, but didn't move.

Ed sighed. "Come on, man…it's just a name."

"It's my freakin' job, man."

Ed doubled the offer.

DeMarco palmed the money and slipped it into his pocket.

"Wait here," he said.

"Thanks, man," Ed said.

"Don't thank me yet," DeMarco said, and walked away, pushing the luggage cart ahead of him.

Ed stifled the urge to rub his hands together. He loved it when a plan came together.

A few minutes later DeMarco came back out, pushing another cart full of luggage. Once he got the departing group into a shuttle and on the way to the airport, he headed back inside, pausing momentarily to slip a piece of paper into Ed's hand.

Ed glanced at the paper.

Maria Slade—Missoula, Montana.

Ed pocketed the info, and then slipped back into the hotel and headed for an elevator. He needed to get his eyes on the woman in 604.

Maria had already figured out that Oklahoma heat wasn't just hot. The humidity often turned the weather into a sauna. Since they were driving to a lake, she'd chosen a loose cotton shirt to wear with her jeans, and put her hair up off the back of her neck.

She sat down on the side of the bed and was reaching for her boots when there was a knock at her door. Frowning, she glanced at the clock. It was too early for Bodie. Still, he was the only person who would be knocking. Housekeeping wouldn't be around for a little while yet.

She moved to the door, then glanced through the peephole and saw the uniform of a hotel employee. Without thinking, she opened the door.

"Yes?"

"You called to have your food tray picked up?"

Maria frowned. "No, I'm sorry. I didn't order room service."

The man glanced at a note in his pocket, then looked embarrassed as he quickly backed up.

"My apologies. I must have written down the wrong room number. Sorry."

"No problem," Maria said. "You have a nice day."

She shut the door and went back to put on her boots. Now that food had been mentioned, she realized she was hungry, and if she hurried, she had just enough time to grab something at the coffee shop before Bodie Scott arrived.

Ed couldn't help but be curious as to why Franklin Sheets wanted to know this woman's movements, then shrugged off the thought. Even though she was damn pretty with a kick-ass smile, he got paid for information, not curiosity. He headed for the service entrance, unbuttoning the uniform he'd filched as he went. He dropped it on top of a stack of boxes and then headed for the stairwell. He wasn't looking forward to walking six floors down, but he'd overheard two employees talking about the security cameras in the east stairwell being on the fritz, and he lived by the motto of better safe than sorry.

Within minutes, he was out of the hotel. He got back in his car and drove a short distance away, then parked where he could keep an eye on the hotel entrance. If that leggy brunette left the hotel, he would be ready.

Bodie found himself looking forward to the day as he showered and dressed. He told himself it was because he liked Lake Eufaula and would enjoy the drive, but if he was being honest, Maria Slade played into the equation more than she should. He glanced in the mirror as he buckled his belt, eyeing the overall look, then rolled his eyes.

"Damn, Bodie. When was the last time you cared what you looked like when you went to work?" he muttered. "She's part of a case, therefore she's off-limits."

He poured himself a cup of coffee to go, grabbed a sweet roll from a covered cake stand on the cabinet and headed out the door. It was time to get this day in gear.

Maria was at a table in the coffee shop, licking sugar off her fingers, when her cell phone rang. She glanced at the caller ID and then sighed. Bud. She should have called last night.

"Hey, Bud."

"You didn't call."

"I know…I know. I'm sorry, but yesterday was really busy *and* somewhat productive."

"You're not putting yourself in danger?"

"No."

"Have you gone to the police?"

"Yes. I'm waiting for a detective right now."

"Oh, yeah…so what's up?"

Maria could tell from his voice that he already felt less tense.

"We think we've located the man who was my mother's pimp. We're going to drive out this morning and talk to him."

"Yeah, okay," Bud said. "Stay safe. Don't do anything stupid—and remember to call me."

Maria grinned. "Yes, sir."

Bud snorted softly. "Don't be a smart-ass. You know what I mean."

The concern in his voice was her undoing. Tears suddenly blurred her vision. She had to end this conversation before she made a fool of herself. When she saw a tall cowboy entering the lobby and realized it was her detective, she stood up from the table and grabbed her purse.

"Uh…hey, Bud, my ride's here. Gotta go."

"Okay, honey. Love you."

"Love you, too," Maria said, and dropped her phone back in her purse as she hurried across the lobby.

* * *

Bodie was scanning the lobby when the hair rose on the back of his neck. He turned around just as Maria walked out of the coffee shop. He didn't question the instinct that had made him look—only that his radar was definitely tuned to her.

He lifted his hand and waved as she came toward him. The smile that broke across her face was unsettling, and even more so when she got close enough that he could see she'd been crying.

"Is everything okay?" he asked.

She nodded. "I was just talking to Bud. Made me a little teary."

"Oh, yeah, the foreman. I suppose he's pretty attached to all of you." Then he held his breath, waiting to see how she answered.

"He's the brother we never had."

Bodie's pulse kicked as he resisted the urge to grin.

"That's great," he said. "Never can have too much family. So…are you ready for this trip?"

"Yes," she said. "The sooner this case is solved, the faster I can get home."

"So let's get this started and see what we can do to help make that happen," he said, and refused to acknowledge the spurt of disappointment he'd felt when she mentioned going home.

They exited the hotel, and within minutes were out in traffic and heading south.

* * *

Outside, Ed sat up and took notice when he saw Maria Slade come out of the hotel, but when he saw who she was leaving with, he frowned. He knew Bodie Scott. Even worse, Bodie Scott knew him. He was going to have to be careful that Bodie didn't spot the tail.

Maria eyed the Tulsa skyline as Bodie skillfully maneuvered through city traffic, hit the Muskogee Turnpike and headed southeast. Country music was playing softly in the background, a good accompaniment to his boots and hat. She felt comfortable in his presence, as if she'd known him for years, which was unusual for her. She'd never been the kind to make friends quickly, and given what she'd just learned about her past, that bit of her personality finally made sense.

The silence between them was noticeable, but not uncomfortable. Maria kept thinking she should say something, but Bodie beat her to it.

"You said you have two sisters. Tell me about them."

The subject was a favorite. She didn't have to be asked twice.

"I think I mentioned before that Savannah is the youngest. She's a little bitty blonde who looks like she quit growing too soon. Holly is the oldest. She's average height, but gorgeous. Built like a Hooters waitress, to her embarrassment."

Bodie grinned. "I can't say as either one of those descriptions would be the kind to put a man off."

"And you'd be right," Maria said. "Savannah's been sort of in love with our nearest neighbor ever since junior high. Someday they'll get married. Sooner than later, if he has his way. Holly…well, Holly isn't seeing anyone, but I keep thinking there's something between her and Bud. They might not know it yet, but I think it's real."

This was even better news to Bodie. Not only was Bud like a brother to her, but he also had the hots for another sister. As long as it wasn't this one, he was fine.

The moment he thought that, he shifted uncomfortably. *What the hell is wrong with me? I just met this woman yesterday. She's a total stranger who's involved in a great big mess. Get over yourself, Bodie, and remember you have a job to do.*

Deciding it was time to change the subject, he tossed out the first thing that came to mind.

"So what's your favorite meal?"

Maria grinned. "You saw it last night."

"Ahh, a steak-and-potatoes girl."

"What's yours?" she asked.

"Baby back ribs and a butt-load of fries."

Maria laughed. "If I ate that, my butt is exactly where those fries would go."

Bodie gave her a quick glance, then refocused on the road, but his heart was pounding in a crazy, scary way.

Damn, damn, damn. I'm really liking this woman.

"You look pretty good just the way you are," he said softly.

Maria shifted nervously. That almost felt like a pickup

line. She turned sideways in the seat, eyeing the jut of his chin and the way his eyes crinkled at the edges when he smiled.

He caught her staring, arched an eyebrow and played innocent.

"What?"

"Is that your usual pickup line?" she asked.

So she was reticent. It figured. She'd just lost her father—found out she was actually an orphan and a witness to a murder—and he'd come across like a dumb-ass on the prowl.

"My bad," he said. "Didn't mean to insult you. I was just stating the obvious. Besides…you're the one who mentioned your butt first. Not me."

Maria grinned. "You're right. No biggie. I was just being curious."

"Oh. Well, if you're really curious about my pickup lines…I find that I get pretty good results with flashing my badge, holding out my hand and telling the lady she needs to come with me…that she's on my Ten Most Wanted list."

Maria snorted. "And they fall for that?"

"Every time," Bodie said.

"Bull," Maria said. "I don't believe a word of that."

Bodie chuckled. "You're good. And you're right. I don't have pickup lines…or a Ten Most Wanted list. At my age, I'd happily settle for one true love and a couple of kids."

"Awww, that's really sweet."

Bodie arched an eyebrow and then grinned.

"Ha. That's the true pickup line…and it *does* work. Mostly because it's true. My mom won't consider me fully raised until there's another woman in my life to take care of me."

Maria eyed the six-foot-plus man, the wide shoulders, the long, muscular legs and that stubborn-looking chin, and shook her head.

"You don't really come across as someone who needs to be taken care of."

"Neither do you," Bodie said. "But I want that life. Don't you?"

Maria leaned back against the seat and sighed softly.

"Yes, of course. I'm twenty-four. Not quite over-the-hill yet, but I think about having a family a lot. Probably because I saw how close Mom and Dad were. Well… the people I thought were my mom and dad."

Bodie heard a quiver in her voice and reached across the seat to give her hand a quick squeeze.

"No need to qualify titles. In every way that counted, those people were your parents. Don't ever apologize for that."

His fingers curled around the top of her hand. The warmth and strength of his touch made her heart skip a beat.

"You're right," she said. "Thank you."

He squeezed her hand once more, then turned her loose and glanced at his watch. They'd been on the road a little over an hour.

"We're coming up on Muskogee. Once we get into

town I'll stop to gas up before we head down south to the lake. It'll give you a chance to stretch your legs, freshen up…whatever you need to do."

Maria's stomach knotted. For a few minutes she'd forgotten the reason for the trip. Now she was getting nervous all over again.

"What if I don't recognize the man?" she asked.

"Then you don't recognize him."

"But how are we going to get past this huge roadblock in the case if I can't remember?"

"Have you thought about hypnosis?"

Maria blinked, then shivered. "No."

"It might be a path to take later, if things don't pan out the way we need."

"Yes, all right."

"Don't be afraid," Bodie said. "You aren't in this alone. You've got the Tulsa P.D. behind you."

She nodded, then looked away. She didn't want him to know that she'd teared up again. It was a sign of weakness, and she had learned at an early age that wit, wisdom and strength were qualities that Andrew valued—qualities he had fostered in them from their youth.

Within a few minutes she began seeing signs for the city of Muskogee. True to his word, Bodie exited, and when he came to a large convenience mart, he pulled in to gas up.

"If you're hungry, the deli in there is pretty good, and the bathrooms are clean."

"Okay, thanks," Maria said, and began walking toward the store as Bodie scanned his credit card, then started pumping gas.

Ed Underwood managed to stay far enough behind Bodie's car and to keep enough vehicles in between them that Bodie never noticed him.

When he saw them pulling in to the gas station, he glanced down to check his own gauge. The car was down a quarter. He would fill up later. Right now he didn't want to take the chance of gassing up somewhere else and losing them.

He took a turn into a business across the street and backed into a space near the curb, then watched the cop's car in his rearview mirror.

As soon as he saw the woman coming back, he backed away from the curb and got into position to pull out behind them again. He took a couple of pictures with the zoom lens on his camera; then, when they drove away from the gas station, he let a couple of cars pass by and fell in behind them.

"I got you a cold Pepsi," Maria said, as Bodie hung the hose back on the pump.

He turned, a smile of delight on his face as she put the cold bottle in his hand.

"Thanks," he said. "It's my favorite."

A spurt of pleasure shot through her as she got into the car. It was just a small thing, but she was pleased by his reaction.

Bodie slid behind the steering wheel, took a big drink of the cold pop, then put the bottle in one of the two console cup-holders. Maria put her own soda in the other, then dug in to her purse.

"What else you got in there?" Bodie asked.

She laughed out loud. "You have some nose on you, cowboy. Snacks. Take your pick." She held out a trio of goodies. Two different kinds of candy bars and a bag of taco-flavored corn chips.

"You choose first," he said.

Maria took the chips.

"I'll share."

"Deal," he said.

The candy bars went into the second cup-holder as she settled her bottle of pop between her legs and the bag of chips on the console between them.

Bodie put a couple of chips in his mouth as he pulled out of the parking lot.

"We're gonna take Highway 69 South and drive straight to the lake. It's a big one, and I'm not familiar with the location of Vincent's bait shop, but I've got a GPS. We'll find it."

"I have no doubt," Maria said, and crunched into a taco-flavored chip, then slowly licked the dusting of orange from her fingers.

When her tongue came out of her mouth and licked all the way up the first finger, Bodie started to sweat. He grabbed his Pepsi and took a big swig, then winced when it burned all the way down.

"Now. Where were we?" he asked.

"Discussing the finer points of your pickup lines," she said, and popped another chip into her mouth.

Eight

They'd reached Lake Eufaula more than twenty minutes ago and were still driving around in search of Tank Vincent's Bait and Beer.

"This lake is huge," Maria said, pointing first to one lush, green vista and then another. Montana had its own kind of beauty, but it didn't look like this. There were trees everywhere—and water. So much water.

"That it is," Bodie said. "I'll give you the tour-guide stats to go with the trip. It has 600 miles of shoreline, more than 102,000 surface acres, and it's the largest lake in the state. It's also the fifteenth largest lake in the United States."

"Wow," Maria said, then scooted to the edge of her seat, pointing to a large gray bird just taking flight from the shore. "Look at that thing! It's huge."

"Looks like some kind of crane," Bodie said.

"Oh! Oh, my gosh…see that log. There are three turtles sunning on the end nearest the water. Can you see them?"

Bodie grinned. Before he could answer, her focus had shifted again.

"Wait! Did you see that fish jump? Was that even a fish? It was awfully big."

Bodie grinned. "Looked like a fish to me."

"Dad would have so loved this place. He really liked to hunt and fish."

At the mention of her father, Maria's mood seemed to shift, as if she'd just remembered the reason they were here was to try and solve a murder. Bodie felt her emotional withdrawal as she leaned back in the seat and folded her hands in her lap.

There was nothing he could do to make things better except find the person who killed her mother. He was interested in what this man, Tank Vincent, had to say. As they approached a curve in the two-lane blacktop, he tapped the brakes.

"This place *is* beautiful," Maria said.

Bodie looked at her profile. "Yeah...very."

Something in his voice made her turn, but by the time she did, he was focused on driving.

"At the risk of sounding like a brat, are we there yet?"

He grinned. "According to the GPS, it should be just up ahead. I'm betting we'll find a small inlet, presumably with a boat dock and bait shop."

Her interest in natural beauty took a nosedive when she realized their trip was coming to an end. Her stomach started to roll, and her hands became sweaty.

"Really? Oh, Lord," she whispered.

Bodie heard the fear in her voice.

"It's gonna be fine. As far as we know, you have no reason to fear this man. I keep wondering if the P.D. even knew she had a pimp. There was no mention of one in the file, which was strange." He didn't mention Frank McCall's name. No need for her to know yet, if at all, that a dirty cop had been the lead detective on her mother's case.

Maria's face was pale. "I'm still scared."

Bodie touched her shoulder lightly. "I'm here. You'll be fine."

Her posture shifted, her head came up and her jaw clenched as if she was preparing for battle.

"Yes. You're right. I can't believe I'm reacting like this. I need to get a grip."

Bodie chuckled. "Ease up, lady. I'm thinking you're something of a control freak."

Maria shifted nervously. "That's what my sisters claim. Is it that obvious?"

"Psychology 101. When a child loses control of their world, as they grow up, it often manifests into a refusal to let anyone share a part of their adult lives, because that might mean having to relinquish total control. I think what happened to you would traumatize anybody, let alone a child."

She took a deep breath. She'd never thought of her behavior as having anything to do with her childhood. Of course, she hadn't known the truth of that childhood, either, until just last week. But it helped put some things in perspective. She'd watched her mother being murdered and then been thrust into a completely foreign environment with strangers, albeit loving ones, who finished raising her. Looking back, she had to wonder how she'd gotten through it without losing her mind. The only thing that made sense was the resilience of children to adapt to their environment—not because it was ideal, but because it was all they had.

"There it is," Bodie said, pointing.

Maria leaned forward to see a small log cabin up in the trees and a smaller building closer to the lakeshore. Obviously the bait shop. There was a boat dock, as well as a shabby-looking pier, ostensibly from which to fish.

"Not a very noticeable place for a business," she muttered.

"Sometimes people are where they are because they don't want to be found."

"Ah," Maria said, and then braced herself as they parked in front of the Bait and Beer.

Twenty years ago, Tank Vincent had been in the business of making men happy. He'd found women willing to participate, treated them fairly and pocketed the profits, thereby making himself happy, too. Every so often one of his girls would run into a little trouble with the police, but all he had to do was bail them out of jail and set up shop in a new location. Tulsa was a big city. Prostitution was reputed to be the oldest occupation in the world. He didn't know about that, but he knew that as long as there were men, it was never going to go out of style.

He had a tough reputation on the streets and a body to match: a body-builder physique and a pretty face that belied his cold demeanor. If a man messed with one of Tank's women, then he messed with the man and made him sorry in ways that defied explanation. Clients knew it going in. The men who wanted kinkier sex or were into bondage knew better than to use Tank's women. He took being a pimp seriously. The women took care of him. It was good business to return the favor.

Over the years, he'd had women quit the business, which was fine with him. There was always someone new ready to step in. The money was good. The work was easy. A blow job. A quickie. And sometimes an all-nighter, which was worth plenty to Tank and the girl he sent out. But he'd never had a woman die on him… before Sally.

Only Sally didn't just die. She was murdered. Someone had snuck into his world, taken out his best girl and gotten clean away.

It had destroyed him. Word got out on the street that Tank couldn't protect his women and lowered his street cred—but even worse, he lost faith in himself. He'd failed in the worst way.

He'd buried Sally Blake, taken the money he'd been socking away, packed up his belongings and driven as far as the gas in his car would take him, which happened to be Lake Eufaula. Down there he was just plain Sam Vincent, looking for a place to live. Within a week he'd bought the acre of land on which his home and business now sat.

Sally's murder had changed him.

Over time, he'd built the cabin, then the business, trying to find purpose in his life that would not be at anyone else's expense. Now he got up every morning knowing that no matter what he did in the course of his day, it was not going to involve another living being.

Today was no exception.

Today he'd sold twenty dollars' worth of bait to a local, some cold pop and snacks to some teenagers and a six-pack of beer to a guy who smelled like he hadn't bathed in a month. It was nearing eleven o'clock, and for him, that was a busy day. He was thinking about closing up and taking the boat out onto the lake to do a little fishing when he saw another car pulling up in front of the shop.

He frowned. He didn't like his plans being changed. When he saw the driver emerge, his frown deepened. He knew a cop when he saw one, and from the way this guy was dressed, he hadn't come to fish. Tank was verging on the notion of locking the door and turned the Open sign to Closed when he realized the cop wasn't alone. A tall, dark-haired woman got out on the passenger side. Probably another damn cop. They usually traveled in pairs.

Then he saw her face.

He gasped, certain he was just imagining what he saw. Then she circled the car and started walking toward the shop. The closer she got, the more certain he was that he was seeing a ghost. At that point, he nearly came undone. Either he was losing his mind, or the ghost of Sally Blake had finally come for justice.

Subconsciously, he'd been expecting this day for the past twenty years. Every soul deserved justice. She'd obviously come seeking hers. He put a hand to his chest, somewhat surprised to realize that his heart was still beating.

Then he heard footsteps on the porch. He stepped out from behind the counter, not certain how this was going to go. All his life, he'd expected to feel scared. He'd never wanted to die, but now that death had come for him, it seemed right. He'd lived how he'd wanted to, even when it had been at someone else's expense. He didn't have the guts to ask for an extension.

The bell jingled over the door.

The cop entered first, then held the door. All of a sudden, Sally was silhouetted in the doorway.

His vision blurred. He took a deep breath, closed his eyes and prayed it wouldn't hurt.

"Tank Vincent?"

The cop's voice was almost as shocking as the name he spoke.

Tank had buried that name with Sally. Down here, he was Sam, and for some reason, Sam Vincent was still breathing.

"I'm Sam Vincent," he muttered, as he opened his eyes. Sally was no longer in the doorway. Had he imagined her? Maybe this wasn't the day he was meant to die after all.

"Where is she?"

Bodie frowned. Was this guy drunk? The moment they'd walked into the shop, he'd shut his eyes. Now his question seemed to indicate he'd been expecting them, which made no sense.

"Where's who?" Bodie asked.

"Sally. Where's Sally? I saw her. I saw her plain as day."

Maria stepped out from the shadows.

"I'm not Sally. I'm her daughter," she said.

Vincent flinched, then inhaled sharply. "Sweet Jesus… Mary…Mary…my sweet little sugar baby."

He opened his arms, and before Maria could move, he enfolded her.

Bodie was stunned. He wasn't sure what he'd expected, but this certainly wasn't it.

Vincent was sobbing, alternating between cupping Maria's face with his massive hands, patting her shoulders and touching her hair, as if unable to believe she was there.

"You look just like her…just like her. You sound like her. You even walk like her. Oh, my God…you were a baby…just a baby, the last time I saw you. You liked Uncle Tank. Do you remember? Do you remember me?"

Maria shook her head and took a step backward.

"No, I'm sorry," she muttered. This was beyond overwhelming. She had braced herself for the fear. She had not expected love.

Sam's expression fell, but it didn't last long.

"That's understandable. You were such a little thing. Oh, man, how did you find me? Why didn't you come before?"

"I didn't know. I don't remember," Maria kept saying, but it wasn't getting through.

Bodie slid an arm across her shoulders and gave them a slight squeeze of assurance, then focused on Tank.

"Can we talk?"

Vincent was still trying to wrap his head around what was happening.

"Yeah, sure, I was about to lock up anyway. Follow me. My house is right behind the shop."

Then his gaze fell on Maria, and he started to cry all over again. "My little Mary…all grown up."

Ed Underwood had lost track of the cop and the woman a couple of times, and was cursing the meandering paths and trails encircling the lake. It was pure accident when he saw the car parked up in the trees beside a bait shop near the shore.

"What the hell? There's no way they came all the way out here just to buy bait," he muttered.

He pulled off the road and into some trees, then grabbed his camera, popped on the telephoto lens, and got out of the car and into position.

The moment the trio came out of the shop, he began snapping pictures, taking note of the way Scott stayed near the woman in a protective fashion. It appeared they'd come for a visit of some kind, because the older man with them kept smiling and touching the woman's arm, then shoulder, as they walked.

He got in a couple of close-up shots of the shop owner before they all moved toward a cabin a short distance away. He thought about trying to get closer, then decided to give Sheets a call first.

Franklin Sheets was on his way out of the courthouse. His client had been a no-show, and a warrant had been issued for his arrest. Franklin didn't care. He'd been paid up front. He had a lunch appointment with a man he was thinking of hiring as his campaign manager when he ran for district attorney. It was the next step in his desire to be governor. For as long as Franklin could remember, he'd aspired to be "someone." Even as a child, he'd embellished his family status and his father's job to his friends just to verify his own worth. Instead of outgrowing the urge, it had manifested into a hunt for power that bordered on maniacal. He knew it. He thrived on it. And nothing and no one was going to stand in his way.

The Oklahoma heat slapped him in the face as he exited the building and headed for the parking lot. When the sweat started pouring out of his hairline and down the back of his collar, he increased his pace, anxious to get to his Mercedes and turn on the A/C. Sweat was for blue-collar workers.

He slid behind the wheel, cursing slightly at how hot the leather was against the backs of his legs, and quickly started the car, then jacked up the air. His cell phone rang as he was reaching for the seat belt. When he saw who it was, he stopped and gave the call his full attention.

"Yeah. What do you have for me?" he asked abruptly.

Ed snorted beneath his breath. *Hello to you, too.* "I've got a couple of quick questions."

Franklin ignored Ed's words for a question of his own. "So…did you find her?"

"Yes. I've been tailing them for most of the morning."

Franklin frowned. *"Them?"*

"She's with a cop. His name is Bodie Scott. I knew him from back in the day when I was still on the force."

Franklin's heart skipped a beat, but he shrugged it off. It meant nothing. She'd met with the cop before. Maybe they were dating. Cops had personal lives.

"Yeah…so, where did she go? Why is she with him? Where does she live?"

Ed sighed. "I just started this morning, okay? They're at Lake Eufaula. I don't know why she's in Tulsa, but she listed Missoula, Montana, as her home at the hotel."

The knot in Franklin's belly began to ease. Montana. So she wasn't a local. Talk about a coincidence that he happened to see her.

"So they're fishing. What else?" he asked.

"They're not exactly fishing," Ed said. "Hang on a minute. I need to move locations."

Franklin cursed beneath his breath as Ed disappeared.

He decided to do some maneuvering of his own as he switched the call to Bluetooth and pulled out of the parking lot. He didn't want to be late for his lunch appointment, and this way he could talk while he drove.

Ed shifted the phone from one ear to the other and moved to another tree to make sure he was still secluded as the trio walked into the cabin. As soon as he heard the door slam, he moved a little closer, making sure to stay out of sight. "Okay, I'm back," he said.

"So they're not exactly fishing. What does that mean?" Franklin asked.

"It means…they drove all over the fucking place before finally stopping at some off-the-beaten-path bait shop. Turns out they were looking for the owner, not a fishing spot. When they arrived, he locked up and they all went up to his cabin."

"Really? Who is he?" Franklin asked.

"I'm not psychic. I don't know yet," Ed said. "I've got pictures. You'll get copies with my report."

"Which I want on my desk with the rest of the answers to my questions ASAP," Franklin said.

"You'll have them," Ed said, then winced at the click in his ear.

Sheets was an asshole.

Ed glanced toward the cabin. There was no way he was going to hear what was being said inside. Not for the first time, he wished he'd invested in that parabolic microphone he'd seen online. Ran on two nine-volt batteries with a 400-yard listening range. If he was in the mood to drop fifteen hundred bucks on a spy toy, it could be his. Unfortunately, if he did that, his third ex-wife's alimony check would bounce, which would not be cool. She was a piranha and sadly lacking in compassion.

He thought about trying to get closer when he realized the man they'd come to visit had a dog. A huge dog! The battle-scarred mutt suddenly rounded the cabin with his ears up and his nose in the air.

Shit. I'm upwind.

The dog barked four times in rapid succession. Ed read that as a "get the hell out" warning, did an abrupt about-face and headed for his car as fast as he could go, imagining that the dog was right on his heels.

He didn't look back until he was behind the wheel. The damn dog hadn't even gotten off the porch. Ed cursed. So the animal was all bark and no bite. Whatever. He started the car and backtracked to a public landing, parked amidst an assortment of trucks and SUVs, and settled down to wait. To be able to follow them back, he needed the cover of traffic or he would be spotted. The only thing that might foul up his plan was if Bodie Scott knew another way out of that godforsaken place besides the way he'd gone in.

"Sit down, sit down!" Sam said. "Can I get you something to drink? It's hot as hell out there. Got sweet tea. Made it this morning. Also got pop and beer. You name it."

"Iced tea for me," Bodie said.

"Make that two," Maria said.

Sam beamed. The cabin was one big room with a sleeping loft above. He poured three glasses of tea and handed them around, then settled down into what was obviously "his" chair—an old brown faux leather recliner that leaned to one side. Like Sam, it had seen better days.

Sam's gaze immediately moved to Maria, and from the look on his face, Bodie wondered if the man had once been in love with Sally Blake. His attention to Maria was nothing short of adoration.

"So what's up?" Sam asked.

Bodie glanced at Maria. Her hands were shaking as she took a quick sip of her tea. This wasn't going to get any easier.

"The reason we're here is…the Tulsa Police Department is reopening the investigation into Sally Blake's murder."

Sam's entire body seemed to shrink.

"Are you shitting me?" he asked softly.

"No."

Sam leaned back in the chair and covered his face. The silence in the room was at first surprising and then uncomfortable. Bodie was beginning to wonder if they'd been wrong all along—if this was the place where Tank Vincent confessed to a twenty-year-old crime.

Last night, while going through the file, Bodie had written down several questions he wanted to ask. He pulled out his notebook to make sure he didn't forget one.

"There's no mention of your name in the file. Where were you when Sally Blake was killed."

Sam drew a deep, shuddering breath, then dropped his hands in his lap. His face was wet with tears.

"Bullshit. I told that detective, Frank McCall, everything. I crashed my car that night. I was in the E.R. getting stitches. I should have been there for her, but I wasn't."

Bodie's gut knotted. The dirty cop *had* perpetrated a cover-up. But why? Who had paid him off?

Maria was starting to get it. Sam Vincent's reaction had a lot to do with guilt, something she hadn't expected from a pimp. Yes, his response to her had been positive, but she'd been a kid. Lots of people related to kids. But something in her gut said the man had cared about Sally Blake, not just her kid.

All of a sudden a thought popped into Maria's head. Considering the fact that her mother had been a hooker, she'd just assumed her father's identity was a nonissue. But had she been wrong? Did Sally Blake know who had fathered her child, and even more…could it be Tank?

She glanced at Bodie. His mouth was already parted, another question on his lips. She could wait. Maybe she would ask. Maybe not. Maybe this was something she didn't need to know, because in her heart, no one could replace Andrew Slade.

Bodie shifted in his seat. Like Maria, he hadn't expected this kind of reaction from Tank.

"Did they ever have any suspects?" Bodie asked.

Sam shook his head. "Not that I ever heard. It was

Sally's night off. She always kept Sundays for her and Mary." He smiled at Maria, then took a drink of iced tea. By the time he'd swallowed, he had control of his emotions once more.

"Do you think she could have made a date without your knowledge? You know...one now and then on the side without giving you your cut?" Bodie asked.

Sam frowned. "No, she wouldn't have done that. And even if she had, she would never have taken them home. That was her one unbreakable rule. No dates where she lived."

Maria's estimation of her mother shifted up another notch. Not only had she found a reason as to why Sally had chosen her line of work—an abandoned baby raised in the Oklahoma welfare system, unable to read or write—but she'd also refused to bring her work home where she lived with her child. What kind of a dichotomy was this—a hooker with morals? Was there such a thing?

Bodie frowned. "I don't think I read that anywhere in the file."

Sam shrugged. "Not surprised. Nobody gets excited about a dead hooker."

As hard as that was to hear, Bodie knew he was right. It also helped explain how McCall had gotten away with burying the facts.

"So were there any of your other girls interviewed? I didn't read anything except one statement from a woman named Becky Thurman, a neighbor who lived across the hall. Was she one of your girls?"

Sam's demeanor shifted with the tone of his voice. "Hell no. Becky is my sister. She was Mary's babysitter when Sally went out on dates."

"That's what my father wrote in my journal," Maria said.

"Your father? You got lucky. Not many kids get adopted out of the Social Services program in this state. They usually get moved from foster home to foster home until they age out of the system."

"I was never in the Social Services program," Maria said.

"Then how—"

Bodie didn't want to get into anything that would reveal the fact that Maria had witnessed the murder, no matter how friendly this witness seemed, so he interrupted quickly.

"So did Becky ever mention anything to you that she didn't tell the cops…like who might have been in Sally's room?"

"No," Sam said. "And believe me, if she'd known, she would have told. We loved Sally. Everyone loved Sally."

"Someone didn't," Bodie said. "Someone killed her."

Sam seemed to shrink. Bodie almost felt sorry for him, but what the hell? As a man, how did you reconcile yourself to the fact that you're selling women and pocketing the profits, and make it okay? *He* couldn't do it, that was for damned sure.

"Sam, I want you to think back. Did Sally ever have

a trick who gave her trouble…maybe wanted more from her than she was willing to give…someone who might have roughed her up or threatened her?"

"No, and if she had, I would have taken care of it," Tank said. "That was my rep on the street. No one messed with my girls and walked away. Everyone knew that."

"Did she have a lot of repeat customers?" Bodie asked. "Maybe someone who would have imagined that he and Sally had a 'real' relationship and flipped out when he realized it wasn't true? We both know that can happen."

"Not that I ever knew," Sam muttered, then pushed himself up from the chair. Even from across the room, he seemed to tower over them. "Don't you think I already thought of all this? If you knew how many nights I lay awake thinking over every fuckin' man who laid one of my girls, trying to pick out one who might have held a grudge… Her murder is why I quit the business."

That surprised Bodie.

"So you came to Lake Eufaula because you were running away?"

There wasn't an ounce of emotion in Sam's voice when he said, "Hell no. I came here to die."

Nine

The answer hit Bodie like a fist to the gut. He didn't have to ask why. In his own crazy way, Tank Vincent had loved Sally Blake, and his inability to protect her had taken the heart right out of him.

As a man, that was something Bodie understood.

"Is your sister still alive?" he asked.

Sam nodded. "Yes, but she's not Becky Thurman anymore. She got married again about fifteen years ago, but she's been divorced around six or seven years now. Her name is Clemmons now. Becky Clemmons."

Ah…the reason I couldn't find her name in the phone book, Maria thought as Sam gave Bodie his sister's address and phone number.

When he finished, he turned to Maria.

"I have something I need to give you," he said, then headed for the sleeping loft. His steps were slow and lumbering, his massive shoulders stooped as he dragged himself up the stairs.

"Why do I feel sorry for him?" Maria muttered.

Without comment, Bodie understood where she was coming from. Sam did elicit a certain amount of empathy. He glanced up, watching as the man lumbered back down the stairs with something in his hands. It wasn't until he started toward them that Bodie recognized it as a picture frame, and the man was carrying it next to his heart.

Sam stopped by Maria, then hesitated. Every night for the past twenty years, this photo had been the last thing he'd seen before he'd closed his eyes and the first thing he'd seen when he awoke. As much as he hated to part with it, his gut told him it was going to mean even more to Sally's child.

"Here," he said softly. "After you disappeared, it was the only thing of hers I had left. I want you to have it."

His hands were shaking as he held it out to her.

The moment her gaze fell on the face behind the glass, she gasped. It was like looking at her own reflection.

"Oh, my God."

Bodie didn't bother to hide his shock. The bloody crime scene photo had not done Sally Blake justice. Now Vincent's reaction to seeing Maria made sense. She could have been a clone of the smiling, dark-haired woman in the photo, instead of just her daughter.

But Maria's shock was for a reason far removed from what the others might have imagined. All these years—every time she'd looked at her own image— she'd never once remembered that she had a mother with the same face. Granted, she'd only been four and it had taken her twentysomething years to mature into this body, but the fact that she'd completely forgotten all of it was shocking. What in hell had she witnessed that had been so vile—so unimaginably horrible—that she could block out the memory of a woman who had been her double?

Maria held up the photo. "How old was she when this picture was taken?"

Sam frowned. "Not sure, but I'm thinking about twenty-one or twenty-two. It was about a year before you were born."

I'm twenty-four. She was close to the same age I am now.

The fact that Sam had mentioned her birth was the opening she'd been waiting for.

"Do you think Sally knew who the father of her baby was?"

Bodie eyed Maria's face, watching the way she maintained her control by focusing on a point just beyond Sam's shoulder, rather than looking at the raw emotion on his face. Even more telling was the way she phrased the question; she had removed herself from the equation.

Sam visibly recoiled. "You mean…do you think your mother knew who fathered you?"

The anger in his voice was like a punch in the gut. Maria started to respond in kind, but when she opened her mouth her voice was shaking.

"Yes, I guess that's what I mean."

"Hell yes, she knew."

"Was it you?" Maria asked.

Sam exhaled slowly, then staggered back to his recliner and sat down.

"No, but I can say with all honesty, I wish to hell it had been."

Maria's voice was shaking. "I'm sorry. I'm not trying to be disrespectful. I'm not trying to insult you or besmirch Sally's...my mother's...name. But you need to understand something. Last week, my father—the man who raised me—died. I knew nothing about any of this until the reading of his will."

She started to cry.

Bodie's first instinct was to hold her, which surprised him. The feeling was beyond the normal empathy he should have been feeling. Distracted by his own reactions, he did nothing as Maria continued to struggle her way through the explanation.

"I have no memory of my past. None. I had hoped by coming here that something would click. Someone's face, the place where we used to live, the sound of a voice. Something...anything...that would remind me of the first four years of my life." Her shoulders slumped as she looked down at the photo in her lap. "I'm overwhelmed by the fact that I've been looking at my mother's face every time I looked in the mirror and didn't know it."

Sam sighed. Her explanation had taken away his indignation.

"It's all right, sugar. Maybe if you're here a while it'll come back. You should go see Becky. She was with you almost as much as Sally. Maybe seeing her will ring a bell. I could call her. She'll be over the moon, I swear. You and your mother were family to us."

Maria glanced at Bodie. He shook his head slightly, which she took as a warning not to tell the rest of her story. She sighed. He was right. The fewer people who knew her secret, the safer she would be.

"I don't know," Maria said, glancing at Bodie.

He spoke up. "Considering the shock factor of Maria's appearance, it might be best if you did give her a call. See if she'll agree to talk to us." He eyed Maria. "You up for another round of this?"

"You know why I'm here. I'll do whatever it takes."

Sam frowned. "What do you mean?"

"I came back to find the man who murdered my mother," she said.

Sam's eyes widened, then a slow smile broke across his face.

"By God, you don't just *look* like Sally. You got yourself a fair amount of her grit, as well."

"Thank you…I think," Maria said. "And thank you for this." She held up the photo. "I can get it copied and send one back for you."

Sam shook his head. "She already copied herself when she gave birth to you. As for that photo, I don't really need it. I'll see her face in my mind for as long as I live."

Bodie took a card out of his wallet as he stood. "I think we're done here. If you think of anything… anything at all, call me. And I'll be waiting to hear if Becky's up for seeing us."

Sam's focus was on Maria as he slipped the card into his pocket. He wasn't often at a loss for words, but Sally's daughter took his breath away.

"Mary…uh, I mean Maria…I know you feel like I'm a stranger, but that's not the way I feel about you. You don't have to, but it would mean a lot if you stayed in touch. Nothing big, you understand…just a card now and then to let me know you're okay."

Before she thought, Maria found herself walking into his arms, and this time, she hugged him back.

"I will."

The delight on his face said it all.

"I'll give Becky a call right now," he promised, as he saw them to the door.

Bodie paused at the door. "If it's not convenient for her to see us this afternoon, call me back. I've got her number. I'll call and arrange it myself."

"Yeah. I'll do that," Sam said. "If you don't hear back from me, just assume she'll be expecting you this afternoon."

As he followed them out of the house, his dog, a Rhodesian Ridgeback, stood up from his resting place on the front steps.

"Whoa," Bodie said. "That's one big dog. Where was he when we walked up?"

"That's Pooch. He was probably in the woods chasing squirrels. When I'm in the house, he's on the steps. No one sets foot on the porch until I tell him it's okay."

"Damn good burglar alarm," Bodie muttered, eyeing

the huge beast as it ambled over to where he was standing and sniffed his boot.

"Let 'em alone, Pooch," Tank said.

Pooch gave Bodie's boot one more sniff and then flopped down against the side of the house.

Sam grinned. "I'll walk back to the car with you. If I don't go fishing, I'll have to open back up, and I'm not in the mood for business right now."

Within a few minutes they were in the car and heading down the drive. Maria stared down at the photo in her lap and found herself struggling with emotions she couldn't identify. She glanced over her shoulder. Sam Vincent had not moved a step since they'd driven away. As Bodie turned onto the road, she lost sight of him and settled back into her seat.

"Did anything ring a bell?" Bodie asked.

She shook her head.

"So what do you think?" he asked.

"About him? I think he was telling the truth about everything…and I think he was in love with…Sally."

"So do I."

"How do you feel about visiting his sister?"

"Not as nervous, now that I know the relationship between him and Sally was…what it was."

"Yeah, love has a way of smoothing out all kinds of wrinkles, doesn't it?" Bodie said.

"So it seems," she said softly. "So it seems."

"It's getting close to lunchtime," he said. "How do you feel about stopping somewhere along the way to eat?"

"Can we spare the time?" she asked. "I mean...do you have to get back to the police station at any certain time today?"

"My lieutenant knows I'm working on the cold case today, and my partner's out sick. We're good. Do you like fried catfish?"

"I like fish. I've never had catfish."

"Ah...then it's about time to rectify that gap in your culinary education. You can't be from Oklahoma and not have at least tasted fried catfish."

"But I'm not from—" Maria stopped in mid-sentence.

"It's in your blood," Bodie said softly. "The first four years of your life, you had the red earth of Oklahoma between your little toes, and one of these days you're going to remember it, too."

"I hope so, or this entire trip will have been a waste."

Bodie frowned. Two days ago he hadn't known Maria Slade existed. But now that he did, he knew that he was changing. He'd gone from a thirtysomething, didn't-want-to-talk-about-commitment bachelor to a man who had begun to want. No matter how this turned out, whatever came from having known her would never be a waste.

Becky Clemmons had been a 911 dispatcher for the city of Tulsa for eleven years. It was where she'd gone to work not long after her second marriage and where she'd found her niche in life. To her surprise, she was not only good at the job, but she also liked it.

Today was her day off, and she was trying to cram a week's worth of chores into twenty-four hours, which she had yet to make happen. However, she was making a big dent in the grocery list as she pushed her basket along the bread aisle in Wal-Mart. She grabbed a package of hamburger buns and dropped them in the basket just as her cell phone rang. When she saw who was calling, she smiled. She didn't hear from her brother nearly often enough.

"Hey, Sammy, what's up?" she asked.

Sam smiled. No one called him by his childhood name but his sister.

"Hi, Beck…how's it going?"

"About the same. How about you?"

"I'm better than I have been in years."

Becky's grin spread. She couldn't remember the last time she'd heard this much life in Sam's voice.

"Why? Did you finally catch that big flathead you've been after for the past ten years?"

"No. Better than that. Are you sitting down?"

"No. I'm in Wal-Mart doing the shopping. Quit being so dramatic and spit it out."

"Mary Blake came to see me today."

Becky's heart skipped a beat. "What?"

"You heard me. Sally's little girl. Oh, my God…Beck. Scared the shit out of me when I first saw her. She's the spittin' image of Sally…right down to the way she walks."

Becky couldn't focus. Her mind had gone straight back to the night of Sally Blake's murder: hearing the gunshots and then running footsteps, dashing across the hall to find that preacher kneeling over Sally's body... and Mary—four-year-old Mary—staring blindly at the arterial spray on the wall as the blood flowing from her mother's body pooled on the hardwood floor beneath her.

"Beck? *Becky?* Did you hear me?"

She shuddered.

"What...uh...yes, yes, I heard you. Mary came to see you."

Then it hit her. "How on earth did she find you?"

"Here's where the story gets wild. She has no memory of ever living in Oklahoma and only found out about her mother after her father—the man who raised her—died."

"Sweet Lord," Becky whispered.

"I tell you, Beck, she doesn't just look like Sally. She's got her momma's grit, too."

"What do you mean?"

"She said she came back to Oklahoma to solve her mother's murder. She and the cop she's with want to come by and talk to you. Is that okay? I gave them your address and phone number. I didn't think you'd mind."

"No, no, of course I don't mind. When are they coming?"

"Today, but they just left my place. It'll take them a while to get back into town."

Becky felt faint. "Today. Wow. Then I'd better get finished with my shopping and get home. I need to pick up the house and—"

"Oh, hell, Beck…they're not gonna care what your house looks like. I can't wait for you to see her. You gotta call me tonight. Tell me what you think."

"Yeah, sure…I'll do that," Becky said, and disconnected. She dropped the cell phone back into her purse and then fumbled for her grocery list, but when she glanced at it, the words blurred. Instead of finishing her task, she headed for the checkout stand. All she could think about was that she needed to get her head together and get home. If Mary Blake had no memory of what had happened, she wondered if she knew yet that she'd been the only witness to the crime she wanted solved.

It was midafternoon when Bodie and Maria got back into Tulsa. He called in to the precinct to make sure nothing urgent was pending, got the go-ahead from Lieutenant Carver to follow up with the Becky Clemmons interview and then stopped at a station to gas up.

"I'm going to find a bathroom," Maria said. "Want anything from inside?"

"Maybe something cold to drink. That catfish was good, but it made me thirsty."

"It wasn't the catfish. It was that bushel basket full of hush puppies you had with it. Pepsi okay?"

Bodie laughed out loud. "Why, thank you. That'll be fine, Miss Tell-it-like-it-is Slade."

Maria grinned. She was beginning to think she could like this man. Too bad their meeting had been under such ugly circumstances.

"Back in a few," she said.

Bodie watched her walk all the way inside the quick stop, marveling at the heavenly engineering that was responsible for that slow-motion sway in her stride. It wasn't until a cop car went screaming past, running hot with lights and sirens on full blast, that he yanked himself out of his slightly lustful reverie and remembered to put gas in the car.

A few minutes later Maria was standing at the counter waiting in line to pay when she glanced outside. There was a middle-aged man sitting in a car that was parked on the other side of the street. From where she was standing, it appeared that he was watching Bodie.

"Ma'am, can I help you?"

Maria jumped, then realized she was holding up the line.

"Oh. Yes. Sorry."

She paid for her purchases and was on her way out the door when she remembered the man. To her shock, he had a camera in his hand and seemed to be snapping pictures—and the camera was aimed directly at her.

Rattled, she started running across the parking lot, yelling at Bodie as she ran.

"Bodie! Bodie!"

Bodie caught the urgency in Maria's voice. He looked up, saw her running and bolted toward her.

"What is it?" he said, as he grabbed her by the arms.

"That man in that gray SUV...there! Across the street! He was taking pictures of me!"

Bodie turned just as the SUV shot away from the curb, leaving a trail of rubber on the street as the driver sped into traffic.

Bodie dashed into the street to get a tag number, but he was too late and the traffic was too thick. Cursing beneath his breath, he jogged back to the car, where Maria had taken shelter. He slid behind the wheel, slamming the door in frustration.

"Did you get the tag number?" she asked.

He frowned. Her voice was shaking.

"No. He put too many cars between us before I could get to the street."

"What do you think this is about?" she asked.

He shook his head. "I don't know. Did you get a good look at his face?"

"Not really. I noticed him first when I was inside the store. He seemed to be staring at you. Then when I came out, he had a camera...with one of those telephoto lenses. It was aimed at me. I panicked. It was stupid. I mean, a camera can't hurt me."

"No, but those photos might. Have you told anyone else besides the police that you were a witness to your mother's murder?"

"No."

"Dammit," Bodie said, then glanced at his watch. It

was close to four. "You still okay to go talk to Becky Clemmons?"

"Yes. I was rattled for a moment, but I'm not the fainting type. I'm ready when you are. Oh…there's your Pepsi."

She pointed to the two plastic bottles sitting in the console.

He picked it up and started to twist the cap when it began to fizz.

"Shit," Bodie muttered, then blushed. "Sorry."

Maria grinned. "I think I'm the one who should be apologizing. It got a little shook up while I was running."

Bodie opened the door and then held the bottle away from the car as he opened it, holding it there until the spewing had stopped. Then he shut the door and took a long drink.

"Here," Maria said, handing him a handful of tissues.

He wiped down the outside of the pop bottle, then sat it back in the console and eyed her purse.

"Did you happen to get anything sweet to go with these?"

Maria rolled her eyes, then pulled out a Snickers candy bar. "You are one serious bottomless pit. After all that lunch you ate, I can't believe you're still hungry."

"That doesn't count. Sweets go in a completely different part of the stomach."

Maria laughed. "Oh, really? Okay, fine. But you can't have it all. You have to share."

Again, Bodie had to admire her spirit. She'd quickly bounced back to her usual wise-ass persona.

"Of course. You take what you want, and I'll be grateful for whatever's left over."

Maria rolled her eyes. "Seriously…a bit too much Oliver Twist for a man your size." She eyed the candy bar, then broke it in half, stringing chocolate and caramel as she pulled the two pieces apart. "Here—and you're welcome, because I'm giving you the big half."

Bodie popped the whole thing into his mouth at once and started to chew.

"Thanks," he muttered, then licked his thumb before putting the car into gear and driving away.

Maria tried not to stare. She'd grown up around a mob of hungry cowboys, but she'd never been attracted to any of them in the way this man attracted her.

Thirty minutes later, Bodie turned off a residential street into a driveway and parked in front of a redbrick house. Before they had time to get out, the front door opened. A middle-aged woman wearing white Bermuda shorts and a loose yellow blouse came out onto the porch. Her short spiky hair was a dark smoky gray, and from the expression on her face, she was just as shocked by Maria's appearance as her brother had been.

Maria sighed. She wished she could return the favor. "Struck out again," she muttered.

"What?" Bodie asked.

"Total stranger," she said, then grabbed her purse. "I'm ready when you are."

Bodie took her hand. "Hang in there. It's been twenty

years. Don't expect too much too soon, and remember,
we're just getting started."

"Right," she said, and then they got out of the car
and started toward the house.

Ed Underwood almost missed the fact that Bodie
and the woman had reached a destination. There were
five cars between them when he saw their car pull into
a driveway. He stopped a block back and grabbed his
camera, snapping a quick couple of pictures of the
middle-aged woman who'd come out to greet them and
made a note of the address. He'd gotten enough for today
and wanted to go back to the office and run some info
through the computer. He was still rattled as he drove
away. Who knew that damn woman would have made
him so fast?

Ten

After Sam's call, Becky thought she had prepared herself, but she was wrong. The shock of seeing a living version of Sally Blake getting out of the car brought a lump to her throat, followed by an onset of fresh tears. Waiting was difficult. She wanted to run to meet her—to rejoice that her baby girl had come home. But that wasn't going to happen. She could tell from the look on Mary's face that she didn't remember her at all.

Becky's gaze shifted to the cop. Between the Stetson sitting firmly on his head and the dusty boots on his feet, he walked like a man comfortable in his own skin. In her younger days, she would have given him a run for his money. Blinking back tears, she reached for the porch post to steady herself as they started up the steps.

"Lord, Lord, it's a good thing Sammy called me or I'd be fainting dead away," Becky said as she stared at Maria. "You are the image of your mother, God rest her soul. Come in, come in."

Bodie had a hand under Maria's elbow as they started up the steps and felt her trembling. He took a quick glance at her profile. Despite what she was feeling, she gave nothing away.

He took off his hat as they entered the house. "Mrs. Clemmons. I'm Detective Scott from the Tulsa Homicide Division. This is Maria Slade. I believe you knew her as Mary Blake. Thank you for agreeing to talk to us."

"Yes, I knew Mary Blake," she said softly, and smiled at Maria as they settled in her living room. Once they were seated, her teary gaze immediately slid back to the woman she'd known as Mary. When she began to speak, her voice broke.

"Forgive me for staring, but you don't just look like Sally. You could *be* her. The resemblance is actually a little spooky…as if Sally was back from the dead."

"I'm sorry," Maria said. "I don't remember anything."

"No, no…no need to apologize," Becky said. "Believe me, I understand better than most why you wouldn't remember any of this."

Maria knew from reading her father's journal that Becky Thurman had not only been her babysitter and lived in the room across the hall, but she'd also been instrumental in helping get her away from the murder scene unobserved.

Maria smiled nervously, then folded her hands in her lap to keep them from shaking as Bodie took charge of the interview.

"Since you've already spoken to your brother, you know that the Tulsa police are reopening the case of Sally Blake's murder," Bodie said.

Becky nodded.

"I know it's been a long time, but what do you remember of that night?"

Becky swallowed past a lump in her throat as a fresh set of tears rolled down her cheeks.

"Everything…I remember everything." She shuddered, then made herself focus. "I'd pulled a double shift at the bar the night before and had gone to sleep early. I'd been asleep about two hours when I heard Sally scream. There were two gunshots, followed by someone running down the stairs. By the time I got out of bed and into the hall, the preacher who'd been in the room next to Sally's was running inside. I followed him in."

Maria felt numb. This was her life. She'd been a witness to this horror. Why in hell couldn't she remember?

"Was Sally able to speak?" Bodie asked.

"Barely."

"Didn't anybody ever ask her who shot her?"

"Yes! God yes! Over and over, but all she kept saying was, 'Hide Mary. He'll find her and kill her. Just like he killed me.'"

A wave of nausea swept over Maria. All of this was in the journal. She'd read it a dozen times, but hearing the emotion in Becky Clemmons' voice brought the horror to life.

Bodie glanced down at his notes. "Why do you think

she was so adamant about giving her child to a total stranger? Why wouldn't she want you to take care of Mary? You two were obviously friends."

Becky grimaced. "Actually, Andrew Slade…wasn't a *complete* stranger. We'd visited with him more than once during the week that he'd been in town preaching. I know Sally was real taken with him. She even went to hear him a time or two and took Mary with her. Said she wanted Mary to know there was a better life than the way they were living. She told me more than once that she wished she'd met a man like Andrew earlier in her life. So, besides the fact that Mary was a witness to a murder…you wonder why she didn't want Mary to live with any of us? The truth isn't pretty. My brother was a pimp. I worked in a bar. You tell me. What would you have done? Who would you have wanted to raise your daughter? She wanted her out of Tulsa—and fast."

"So you and Dad were the only two people who knew I witnessed the murder?" Maria asked.

Becky nodded.

"And you never said a thing?" Bodie asked. "Not even to the cops or your brother?"

Becky shook her head as she pulled a tissue from her pocket. "Sally said it would get Mary killed. I'd already lost my best friend. I wasn't going to put her daughter in danger."

Bodie nodded.

"What did the police say about the absence of the child while they were working the crime scene? It had to be obvious that a child lived there."

Becky rolled her eyes. "Are you serious? Yes, it was obvious. There was only one bed. Sally and Mary slept together. Mary's clothes were in the dresser beside Sally's. Some of her toys were on the living room floor close to Sally's body. One cop came over and took a look at her, but by that time she was in bed in my room, asleep. I told him that I babysat her at night when Sally worked. They didn't pursue the issue, which was exactly how the preacher and I wanted it. Their immediate assumption was that the murderer was one of her tricks. I told them she never brought business home, but they didn't believe me. They didn't believe me because no one cared. Someone killed a hooker. Big deal. It garnered a couple of lines in the newspaper and a mention one night on local television. Never mentioned Sally's name. Never mentioned that she'd left a child behind. There was no outcry about a killer running loose in the city, because the feeling was, a woman living the life that Sally lived deserved to die."

"Your brother was also adamant about the fact that Sally never brought clients to her place."

"Never," Becky stated firmly.

"Do you know if she'd had any previous trouble with a client? Was she being stalked or harassed in any way by someone she'd been with before?"

"Not to my knowledge, and if there had been, Sammy would have dealt with it. If anything bad had ever happened to her, I think she would have told me, or I would have seen the physical evidence for myself…you know, like if she'd gotten beat up or something."

"Do you know who my father was?" Maria asked.

Bodie eyed the expression on Maria's face but couldn't get a reading on what she was thinking.

"No, but *she* did," Becky stated firmly.

Bodie tensed, then leaned forward. "Really? How do you know?"

"She told me she had proof."

Bodie wondered if that proof could have been a motive for murder.

"Do you think the father knew? Was she trying to get money from him?" Bodie asked.

Becky shrugged. "I don't know. What I do know is that Sally wanted out of the business before Mary got old enough to realize how her mother was making a living."

"Did you ever see any one man come and go from her room with any regularity?"

"No, but like I said, she never did business at home."

"Did she ever refer to any particular man often enough that you thought maybe he was important?" Bodie asked.

"No." Becky's shoulders slumped. "I never thought of her death from this angle before. Do you think the man who killed Sally was Mary's father?"

"I'm not thinking anything," Bodie said. "I'm just investigating all possibilities, and that's one of them. Do you know if anything was stolen from the apartment? Nothing was mentioned in the report, but her death could have been something as simple as a robbery gone bad."

"She didn't have anything to steal," Becky said.

"But she had information someone might not have wanted to get out," Maria said.

Becky shrugged. "Anything's possible. I'm sorry I'm not more help. I would do anything to see her killer caught." Then she glanced back at Maria. "You really don't remember anything...not me...not Sammy...not a thing about your mother, do you?"

"No," Maria said. "In the past twenty years, not even a nightmare about it, which is why learning about all this was such a shock."

Becky turned back to Bodie. "I don't know if it would be any help, but I do have some of Sally's things in storage. There was no one to claim them after she died, and I couldn't bring myself to throw them away. I work tomorrow, but I'm off the day after. I could go get the boxes and bring them home, if you were interested."

"I'm interested!" Maria said, and then glanced at Bodie.

"It wouldn't hurt to take a look," he said. "Where do you work?"

"I've been a 911 dispatcher for the city of Tulsa for the last eleven years."

"Oh, wow," Maria muttered. "I would not want that job."

Becky grinned. "I've had that thought a few times myself, but for the most part, I actually enjoy it."

There was a brief moment of silence, and then Becky stood up.

"I have some cold sweet tea. And I made cookies. Would you care for some?"

Bodie glanced at Maria. He wasn't hungry, but from the look on her face, she still was. Maybe not for food, but she wasn't ready to leave.

"Yeah, sure…why not?" Bodie said. "How about you, Maria?"

She nodded.

Becky beamed. "I won't be a minute," she said, and scurried out of the room.

Maria combed her fingers through her hair, lingering on the back of her neck as she rubbed absently at a sore muscle.

"You okay?" Bodie asked.

"Yes."

He wanted to say more, but she cut him off without further comment when she refused to look at him. Then Becky was back, carrying a tray loaded with glasses of iced tea and a plate of cookies.

"Here you go," she said, as she served each of them a napkin and a drink, then passed the plate of cookies.

"Oh…snickerdoodles," Maria said, as she looked up at Becky. "They're my fav—"

Becky's eyes were shimmering with unshed tears. All of a sudden Maria realized that Becky already knew those were her favorites—that it was the reason she'd made them. It rattled her to think total strangers knew more about her than she knew about herself. She'd never had doubts about her ability to cope. Andrew had raised all his girls to believe they were capable of solving their own problems—that they didn't need a man to survive. And then he'd died and turned their world upside down. They had been living a lie—all of them. She no longer trusted herself to cope, because her memories were a lie. She stared at the cookie, then sank back into the depths of the easy chair without tasting it.

Becky cupped the side of Maria's face. "I also know your favorite color is blue, and that when you were little, you liked meat loaf with a browned mashed-potato crust. You're allergic to sulfa and when you're sick, you talk in your sleep."

Stop talking. Stop talking, Maria pleaded silently, then drew a deep, shuddering breath.

"It's all right, sugar," Becky said softly. "You're still in there. When it's time…everything you knew will come back."

She moved to where Bodie was sitting and held out the plate of cookies. "Detective?"

"Thank you," he said.

The first bite revealed the cookies were still warm. It was obvious that Becky Clemmons still cared, even if Maria didn't remember.

He didn't realize that Maria was slowly coming undone until she stood abruptly and asked him, "Are we finished here?"

Bodie jumped. Where the hell had that come from? "Uh…yeah, sure."

"I just remembered…I need to get back to the hotel," Maria mumbled.

"Would you like to take some cookies with you?" Becky asked.

"No, no…thank you, but no," Maria said. "Detective Scott?"

"After you," Bodie said, then followed her to the door.

Becky was right on his heels, obviously reluctant to lose contact.

"I'll call you just as soon as I get the boxes out of storage," she said. "I don't think there are more than three or four."

Bodie nodded. "Okay, and thank you, Mrs. Clemmons. If you think of anything else—anything at all—call me."

"I will," she said, then patted Maria's arm. "Sally would be so proud of you."

Maria frowned. "I don't think so. The one thing I can't remember is the only thing that will catch her killer."

"It will happen."

"I hope sooner rather than later," Maria said, and then hurried out the door.

"How do you feel?" Bodie asked a minute later, as they drove away.

Her stomach was in knots. "Rattled. Frustrated. Who the hell knows? Did you learn anything today that might help?"

He hedged his answer. "Maybe."

"The possibility that Sally might have been trying to blackmail someone…?"

"We don't know that," Bodie said.

"Becky said Sally wanted out of the business. Maybe she was using me to shake down the guy who fathered me. He could have been married…maybe somebody with enough prestige that he didn't want anyone to know he'd fathered a child with a hooker."

Bodie frowned. "That's harsh."

Maria shrugged. "The whole thing is a mess. I keep seesawing between empathy for what a tough life she had and disgust for the way she lived it. Did I tell you the old man I talked to at the mission said she couldn't read or write?"

"Really? No, you didn't."

"She was also abandoned as a baby on the steps of a church, or so the story goes, if you want to believe it."

Bodie frowned. "That's hardly something a person would lie about."

"I guess."

"Don't feel like you have to disapprove just because of her lifestyle. From all accounts, she was a good mother and loved you very much."

Maria turned away. For the first time since she'd learned the truth about herself, she was wishing she hadn't come—wishing she'd never learned about the whole sordid affair.

Bodie could tell that she was withdrawing emotionally, but there was nothing he could say or do to change what was.

"There's something I want to run by you," he said. When she didn't respond, he kept talking. "I know a doctor who's trained in hypnosis. If I can make an appointment for you, are you willing to give it a try?"

"Whatever it takes to get this mess behind me."

Now he could hear anger in her voice. That was a defense mechanism if he'd ever heard one.

"I'll give her a call when I get back to the precinct. Okay if I call you later with the information?"

"Yes."

They were almost back at the hotel, and Bodie found himself wishing their day together wasn't over.

"Are you going to be okay?"

She turned to face him, her eyes blazing with an emotion he couldn't read.

"Of course I'll be okay. I'm always okay," she said.

He frowned as he wheeled into the drive leading to the hotel. Defiant. Angry. Hurt. All her defenses were firmly in place.

"I'll call you tonight," he said.

"Thank you for taking me with you," she said politely.

He resisted the urge to curse, and then she was out of the car before he had time to answer. Still, he waited until she was inside the hotel and tried not to take offense at the fact that she never looked back.

Maria strode through the lobby with her head held high and her chin up—and without looking at a single face. She made it to the elevator, then up to the sixth floor. Her steps grew faster as she neared her room.

There was a pain in the middle of her chest that just kept growing, radiating outward into every fiber of her body. All she wanted to do was get into her room before she fell apart. Thrusting her hand into her purse, she began fumbling for her room key.

She began shifting things around, unzipping different compartments and going through her wallet, trying to find the key card. Then her hands began to shake. Her vision blurred, and still she kept digging and digging, until finally she lost it. She dropped to her knees in front of her door and emptied her purse onto the floor, then rocked back on her heels as harsh, painful sobs tore their way up her throat.

Bodie was waiting for an airport shuttle van to move before he could leave when a cell phone began to ring. It took him a few moments to realize it was Maria's phone and not his, which meant she'd left it in his car.

"Dang it," he muttered, and headed for a parking place.

He pocketed the phone as he got out and hurried into the hotel, then loped toward the bank of elevators. A couple of minutes later he got off on the sixth floor, checked to see which direction he needed to go to get to 604 and then took a right. Just as he turned a corner, his heart skipped a beat. Maria was sitting on the floor with the contents of her purse spilled all around her, and he could hear her crying all the way down the hall.

"What the hell?" he muttered, and started to run. He

reached her within seconds and pulled her to her feet, then into his arms.

"What's wrong? What happened?" He began to look her over, trying to see if she'd been accosted. "Did someone hurt you? Did you fall?"

She just kept sobbing.

He grabbed her by the shoulders. "Maria! Honey! Talk to me!"

"I can't find it. I looked and looked, and it's gone. Everything's gone."

"If you're talking about your phone, that's why I came back. You left it in my car. Don't cry...don't cry."

"Not my phone...the room key...my memory...my life...my father...my sisters...it's gone...everything is gone. It's all messed up."

Bodie sighed. He knew today had been stressful for her, but he'd had no idea how deeply she'd been affected. He glanced down at the contents of her purse strewn about their feet and immediately spied the key card.

"Here it is," he said, and quickly unlocked the door.

She swayed on her feet as she turned to get her things, but he stopped her and gave her a gentle push inside.

"I'll get everything."

She didn't argue.

Moments later, Bodie followed her in and set her purse on the table.

Maria was standing in the middle of the floor with a blank expression on her face.

Bodie hesitated. He wasn't sure about what to do

next. Instinct told him she needed comforting. It might not be proper police procedure, but she was definitely at the end of her rope.

He put a hand on her shoulder, then took a step forward. When she didn't pull back, he cupped the back of her head with his other hand and pulled her close. She sagged against his chest as his arms enfolded her.

"I—"

"Shh," he said softly.

She shuddered, then slowly, slowly, he felt the tension leaving her body.

They stood without moving…without talking.

The air conditioner kicked on. Outside, someone's car alarm was triggered, followed by a series of sharp blasts from the horn before it turned off as abruptly as it had begun. The sound of an argument in progress came and went out in the hall as a couple walked past the door. The phone in the next room began to ring, then stopped when the call went unanswered.

The vibration of her heartbeat was strong against his palm. Her hair was soft against his cheek. The urge to tilt her head and kiss her was overwhelming.

Then her cell phone began to ring again.

The sound yanked them back from the brink on which they'd been teetering.

Bodie sighed, pulled her phone out of his pocket and handed it over.

"Thank you," Maria mumbled, as she glanced down at the caller ID. "It's Bud," she said.

"I'll let myself out," Bodie said.

Before Maria could stop him, he was gone.

Still struggling with what she'd been feeling, she locked the door behind him, then answered her cell.

"Hello."

"I've been trying to call you," Bud said. "Everything okay?"

"Everything's fine," she said as she sat down on the side of the bed and lied through her teeth.

Eleven

Ed was still tailing Maria Slade and the cop, but in a different car and from a safe distance. When they finally got back to the hotel, he watched until she walked inside, then headed home. Sheets hadn't requested—or paid for—twenty-four-hour surveillance, and he was butt-numb from so much driving, not to mention tired and hungry.

As soon as he got home, he took the memory card out of his camera, downloaded it onto his computer, then printed out the shots he'd taken before adding them to the file he was compiling.

He leafed through his snail mail and listened to his messages while heating up some leftovers from Olive Garden, then ate them at the computer while he was researching ownership of the Bait and Beer shop at the lake.

Samuel Gene Vincent turned up as the owner. The cop in him wondered why Sheets wanted this information, then he shrugged it off. Information paid, and he was no longer in the cop business.

Using a reverse directory, he plugged in the address of the woman they'd visited and turned up the name Rebecca Clemmons.

On a whim, he typed in Clemmons' name on Facebook. Her photo popped up, mentioning she was a 911 dispatcher, divorced and not looking for a relationship.

"Too bad for me," he said and then laughed aloud at his own wit. The last thing he wanted was another wife.

He carried his dirty plate to the sink, dug a pint of Ben & Jerry's Cherry Garcia from the freezer, and snagged a spoon before heading back to the computer.

"Now, Samuel Gene Vincent…let's see what dirt I can dig up on you," he muttered, then scooped up a bite of ice cream and let it melt on his tongue as he began to type.

Being a cop had paid off more than once since he started this second profession. But this time his search was a bust. Vincent had never served time or been arrested, and he'd been at his present location for the past twenty years. He reached for the ice cream, then kicked back in the chair and finished it off before tossing the empty carton into the trash.

"Time to see what comes up on Maria Slade," he said, and started his search from another angle.

He typed in the name and got a hit on a professional horse trainer with a Missoula, Montana, address. It was the right state, but he hadn't expected a horse trainer's website; then he found a photo and knew he had the right woman.

"Hmm…okay…so what brought you to Oklahoma? Maybe a job?"

Lots of people raised horses in Oklahoma, Remington Park in Oklahoma City hosted quarter horse races, and rodeo was popular in parts of the state. Best-guess scenario: she was here in a professional capacity.

After a few more minutes of research, he logged on to the website of the local Missoula paper and searched Maria Slade's name again. Within seconds he was reading about the death and funeral of a man named Andrew Slade. One of the surviving daughters happened to be named Maria. Ed didn't know how it all fit together, but the cop in him loved a good mystery.

He printed out the info and added it to the file, then headed for the shower. Tomorrow was another day.

Franklin Sheets strode into Jamil's Steakhouse on 51st Street with a swagger and a smile. He thrived on the status he'd achieved as a criminal lawyer and used every public appearance as an opportunity to campaign. Even though he had yet to declare for the district attorney race, his intent was becoming common knowledge.

The woman on his arm was Amelia Paige, a fellow lawyer. She was as ambitious as Franklin, and it showed, from her perfectly tailored butter-yellow suit to the slicked-back chignon that was her trademark. Her eyes were as dark as her hair, making her expressions difficult to read. As a trial lawyer, she used all the tricks in the book to win her cases, and if her personal appearance helped hide what she was thinking, then so much the better. Words were power. She used them well.

There was nothing romantic between her and Franklin, but they often used each other as a convenient dinner companion. Tonight was no exception. The event Franklin had been invited to was the mayor's birthday party. All the city's movers and shakers would be there, and he considered it no small feat that he'd wangled an invitation.

As soon as the restaurant hostess arrived, Franklin cupped Amelia's elbow.

"We're here for the mayor's party."

The hostess nodded. "This way, please."

They followed her through a central dining area, past two smaller rooms packed from wall to wall with more hungry diners, to the room that had been reserved for the party.

Inside, the lights were up and the air was alive with energy. A waiter was circling with a tray of drinks. Franklin snagged one for himself and another for Amelia as they began to mingle, wending their way through the gathering toward their host and hostess.

"Happy birthday, Joe," Franklin said, as they reached the mayor. "Nice party."

Joseph LaBlanc slid an arm around his pretty wife's slender shoulders. Not only was she his third wife, but she was also seventeen years his junior. His peers were secretly jealous, but their women generally felt threatened by Julie's presence, as if their time on their husbands' arms was as limited as Julie's predecessor's had been.

"Thanks to my darling Julie," the mayor said, and gave his wife a hug.

"You're just in time," Julie said. "We're about to be seated."

"Happy birthday, Joe," Amelia added. "I've been looking forward to Jamil's famous appetizers all day."

"I know," Julie said. "I don't know which I like best… the tabbouleh or the cabbage rolls."

The restaurant's Lebanese focus was reflected not only in the food, but also the décor. Even though Jamil's was a five-star restaurant and named for its steaks, the array of ethnic appetizers that came included with every meal was what had given the place its reputation.

The guests took their seats. Franklin found himself seated across the table from Burch Westbrook, the chief of police, and next to Harry Korn, the editor of the *Tulsa Herald*. The dynamics of the seating arrangement were interesting. Korn was always looking for a scoop, and Westbrook was always angling for good PR. It remained to be seen how the evening would play out.

As predicted, the appetizers began coming, which slowed down the conversation drastically. The laughter started up at their end of the table when Amelia began bartering with Franklin for his food.

"I'll trade you my tabbouleh for your cabbage roll," she offered.

Franklin grinned. "You'll owe me big-time. I love their cabbage rolls."

But he traded anyway, and laughed when the chief's wife, Elinor, tried to pull off a similar trade, but without success.

"Married too many years to take the threats seriously," Burch said, and then softened his claim by giving his wife the last bite of his cabbage roll anyway.

The meal progressed to entrées as the waiters began carrying in plates. Franklin tackled his prime rib with gusto, while the scent of Amelia's bacon-wrapped filet teased his senses. He was in deep discussion with Harry Korn about the impact that epublishing was having on print news when a woman walked past the door leading into their dining area. Even though he only caught a glimpse, his heart skipped a beat. Was that Maria Slade? He could hardly concentrate on Harry's tirade for watching the doorway. When she walked back a few minutes later, he breathed easier. The only resemblance was height and dark hair.

Then he wondered to himself why it mattered. Maria Slade didn't know him from Adam, and he had no intention of changing that fact.

It wasn't until the tables had been cleared and the waiters were readying for the birthday cake to be brought in that Franklin realized Korn had come to the party with an agenda.

"Say, Burch, I heard your office is looking into another one of Frank McCall's old cases. I thought all those had been dealt with."

Franklin frowned. He knew that name but couldn't place the inference.

Burch Westbrook arched an eyebrow, then glanced around as if to say this was hardly the place. But Korn was a news hound, and he had the chief cornered.

"Is this going to impact the legal outcome of the case?" Korn asked.

Burch smirked. "No, not at all."

Korn frowned. "How can you say that with such conviction? I mean…it's a proven fact that McCall was dirty. He's serving time for it."

"Normally that might be the case," Burch said. "But this is actually a cold case that was just reopened, so there's no judgment in question."

Franklin hid a smile as Korn visibly wilted. The front-page story Korn was probably envisioning had been mentally moved to somewhere on page ten.

Still, Korn wasn't ready to give it up. "So this case was never solved…. Care to talk about it?"

"Now, Harry…I'm not going to discuss an ongoing investigation, and you know it."

"Okay, fine. But surely you can at least comment on which case has been reopened. It'll become common knowledge soon enough—unless you have something to hide?"

Franklin grinned. He had to admit, Korn was a master at getting what he wanted. Westbrook was notorious for his open and aboveboard approach to law enforcement, and was diligent in looking into anything dirty associated with the Tulsa P.D.

"It's not a secret," Westbrook said. "It's an old murder case. Dead hooker. No witnesses. No conviction. McCall just happened to be the lead officer on the case."

Westbrook frowned. "And you know I'm not going to discuss this any further."

Korn shrugged, but backed off.

Franklin started to sweat. This was why Sally Blake's daughter had come back. Obviously she was pressuring the P.D. to reopen her mother's murder case. But why? And why now?

Everyone started to clap. It took him a few moments to realize that they were carrying in the birthday cake.

Amelia elbowed him. He turned toward the front of the room and made himself smile as he joined in, but his joy in the evening had been dampened.

A token candle was lit. Joe blew it out. His wife stood up, then lifted her wineglass.

"Happy birthday, my darling husband," she said brightly. "And here's to many more of the same."

"Hear! Hear!" the guests shouted, and the evening continued, with cake and coffee being served.

Franklin went through the motions, but he'd already lost focus. All he could think about was calling Ed Underwood and finding out what he'd learned.

Maria was still reeling from her breakdown. She'd talked to Bud, who'd assured her that Savannah and Holly were fine, and then he'd pushed her for details she didn't have. His main question had been when would she be coming home. Having to tell him that she didn't know had been difficult, when all she really wanted to do was pack up and leave. But the more she learned about Sally Blake, the more of a connection she began to feel. The knowledge that her mother's last words had been on her behalf sat heavily on her heart. And her inability to remember their bond left her with, among other things, a huge dose of guilt.

She'd changed into sweats and a clean tee, then crawled into bed and leafed through her journal until she found the notations Andrew had left during the year she'd turned twelve.

Christmas: Five feet of snow outside. Holly fell coming up the steps this morning and made her nose bleed. When we heard her crying, we all ran out...you, Savannah, your mother and I. We were all concerned with Holly and didn't realize what was happening to you. We didn't know you hadn't come back in with everyone else until your mother missed you. I went back outside and found you standing in the blood with a blank expression on your face. I called your name several times, but you never responded. It frightened me, thinking you were going to regress to the child you'd been when you first came to live with us, but by the time we got your shoes cleaned, you had snapped out of it.

I watched you for days afterward, trying to see if there were any signs that you were beginning to remember, but, sadly, it was as if it had never happened.

Maria shut the journal and laid it aside, then leaned back against the headboard and closed her eyes.

"Help me, Lord," she whispered. "Help me. The answers are in me. Help me find them again."

She slid down beneath the covers and rolled over on her side. Today had been exhausting and, in an odd kind of way, so very sad. Sam Vincent was as lost in his own way as she was. It seemed as if he'd never been able to move on. It was obvious that his sister, Becky, had cared for her. But she felt no emotional connection to either of them, which made her feel guilty all over again.

The only good part about this entire day had been Bodie Scott. In any other circumstance, he would be the kind of man she would be interested in knowing. But she was just a case to him, and the sooner she got over the fantasy that anything else could be possible, the better off she would be. Defeated in ways she'd never known, Maria pulled the covers up beneath her chin and fell asleep.

It was almost 10:30 p.m. and Bodie was just finishing up a report at the precinct when Lieutenant Carver came out of his office and stopped at Bodie's desk.

"Is that the report on the pawnshop owner?"

Bodie nodded. The man had been gunned down only

minutes after he'd dropped Maria off at the hotel. He'd spent the rest of the evening taking witness statements and then notifying the next of kin, which he hated.

"I'm nearly through. As soon as I print it out I'll leave a copy on your desk."

Phil Carver nodded, but he still lingered.

Bodie hit Print, then looked up.

"Anything else, sir?"

"What happened with your cold case today? Anything lead you to believe Frank McCall sullied the case?"

"Yes, sir. Missing info. Her pimp, Tank Vincent, was interrogated and cleared, but there was no mention of him in the file. I took Maria Slade with me, hoping that something would click when she saw some of the people from her past, but it didn't happen."

Carver sat down on the corner of Bodie's desk. "Dammit. I was afraid of something like this. Where did you go?"

"Lake Eufaula to talk to Vincent. He runs a bait and beer shop, and has for the past twenty years."

"Was he the only interrogation today?"

"No. Turns out the woman mentioned who called the cops is the pimp's sister. She's a 911 dispatcher for the city of Tulsa now."

"Really?" Carver said. "And Miss Slade didn't recognize or remember either of them?"

"No, sir, but I have a plan to which she's agreed. I'm going to try and set up an appointment for her with Dr. Rachel Stewart, that hypnotherapist the D.A. used a couple of years ago as an expert witness."

Carver nodded. "Might work."

"And it might not, but we don't have anything to lose."

"You'll let me know the results, of course," Carver said, then added, "Someone leaked it to the press that we found another case with Frank McCall's fingerprints on it. The chief is furious. Called me a little while ago and said Harry Korn cornered him about it at the mayor's birthday party tonight. He read me the riot act. Told me to clear this case and clear it fast."

Bodie frowned. "That's odd. Didn't take long for it to become common knowledge. Somebody probably put two and two together when I requested Sally Blake's file."

"Don't I know it," Carver muttered. "At any rate, the sooner we can put this to bed, the better."

"I'll give Dr. Stewart a call first thing tomorrow morning and set up an appointment."

"Keep me informed," Carver said, and left the room.

A few minutes later Bodie dropped a copy of his report on the lieutenant's desk, then headed for the elevator. He was tired and hungry, and wanted nothing more than dinner and a good night's sleep.

On the way down, Maria Slade popped into his brain, and as soon as he got into his car, instead of going home, he found himself back on the streets and heading for the hotel where she was staying.

The phone was ringing. Maria rolled over and reached for the house phone, then realized it was her cell. Still groggy, she dug it out from beneath the journal and the covers, and answered without looking at the caller ID.

"Hello?"

"It's me," Bodie said. "Were you asleep?"

"Yes."

He grimaced. "Damn, I'm sorry. I'll—"

"Don't hang up now that you woke me," Maria snapped. "What's up?"

"Obviously now *you* are," Bodie said.

"Ha, ha," she muttered, then yawned and combed her fingers through her hair.

"Did you eat dinner?" he asked.

"No."

"I have pizza."

Maria's stomach growled as she glanced at the clock. "That sounds good, but I don't feel like getting dressed all over again."

"So open your door and let me in, and you won't have to."

Maria's gaze went straight to the door.

"You're outside my room? Right now?"

"Look and see," he said.

She threw back the covers and crossed the floor on the run, then put her eye up to the peephole. Sure enough, there he was, holding a pizza box. She opened the door.

"What kind?"

"Sausage and mushroom."

"You may enter," she drawled.

He stepped inside, not bothering to hide his pleased

expression. He set down the pizza box, then began pulling pop cans from his jacket pockets.

"I got Pepsi from the machine down the hall."

"You are one fine Boy Scout, aren't you?" Maria said.

He laughed. The tacit reference to "being prepared" was not lost on him.

"I have my moments," he said. "Where do you want to sit?"

She glanced around the room. There was one straight-back chair at the desk and one easy chair with an ottoman by the window.

"The bed?"

"Damn straight," Bodie said, and toed off his boots one at a time, took a handful of napkins from the inner pocket of his jacket, tossed them on the bed and then laid his jacket over the back of a chair.

Maria eyed his gun and shoulder holster.

"Oh," he said, and took the holster off and hung it by his jacket. "After you, ma'am," he said, and gestured toward the bed.

Maria yanked the covers back up, then crawled onto the bedspread and curled her legs up under her like a child.

Bodie grabbed the pizza box, laid it open between them, handed her a cold Pepsi, then sat down at the foot of the mattress with his pop between his legs.

"As my Daddy used to say, 'bless this food to the nourishment of our bodies.' Dig in."

Maria grinned. She didn't know which she appreciated most—his foolishness and company, or the pizza and pop. But she did as he asked and took the first slice of pizza.

The cheese was still hot and stringy, the meat warm and spicy. She plucked a mushroom off the end of her slice and popped it in her mouth, then took a big bite.

"Oh, my gosh…this is so good," she said, licking her thumb.

Bodie nodded and took a huge bite of his own slice.

For a few minutes the conversation lulled. It wasn't until he was about to begin his fourth slice that he paused.

"So it's okay that I'm here? I mean…you don't think it's weird, me showing up like this?"

Maria glanced up. "Yes, it's okay. No, I don't think it's weird."

It wasn't the declaration of adoration he would have liked to hear, but he would settle.

"Good."

"But just out of curiosity, why *did* you come?" Maria asked.

He wondered what she would do if he told her the whole truth, then decided a fraction of it would have to suffice.

"I like you. I was concerned about you. I don't like to eat alone. Feel free to choose any or all of those answers."

A twinge of something unnamed tugged at Maria's heart.

"I choose all," she said softly, then quickly looked away.

"Good answer," Bodie said, then took a deep breath and another bite of pizza to keep from following through on the notion of kissing her.

Twelve

Bodie swigged the last of his Pepsi, then eyed the lone piece of pizza growing cold in the box.

"You gonna eat that?" he asked.

"I'm stuffed. Knock yourself out," Maria said.

"No need letting it go to waste," he said, making sure he picked the remaining cheese off the paper to go with it.

"I need to wash my hands," she said, and rolled off the bed and strode across the room to the bathroom.

Bodie eyed her walk and knew that he would never be able to flaunt a pair of sweats like that. They cupped her curves while accenting her long legs and slow stride. He thought it quite gentlemanly of himself that he'd managed to ignore the fact that she was wearing that tee without a bra, then sighed with admiration as he took out half the pizza slice in one bite.

She didn't bother to close the door as she washed her face and hands at the sink, and didn't think, until she was coming back into the room, how easy he was to be around.

At that moment he looked up and grinned at her. A surge of emotion shot through her, startling her with an unexpected longing. It shook her enough that she went straight to the window instead of sitting back down on the bed with him. To her surprise, when she looked out, she could see lightning in the distance.

"Hey! I just saw lightning. Do you think it's going to storm?"

There was a tinge of panic in her voice as he reached for the remote.

"I don't know, but we'll soon find out," he said, and turned on the TV, then flipped it to a local channel. "See that map of the state up in the corner?"

Maria forgot to be wary as she hurried back to where he was sitting and sat down on the edge of the mattress beside him.

"Yes, I see it. What county are we in?"

Bodie pointed to Tulsa County. "That's us…right here. So if they change the color of the county from yellow to red, that means the county has gone from a storm warning to a tornado warning, okay?"

The concern was still in her voice when she said, "We don't have tornadoes in Montana much."

"Don't be scared," Bodie said. "The city will blow sirens if it gets really bad."

"Then what?" she asked.

"Then you grab some shoes and get to the lowest level, which means the ground floor. Use the stairs, not the elevator. Sometimes the power goes off, and you don't want to get stuck. They'll show you where to go once you're down in the lobby, but if you get confused, the best thing to do is get to an inner room, like a bathroom, and stay away from windows."

"Lord," Maria muttered.

"It'll be okay," Bodie said.

"You don't know that," she muttered.

He grinned, and without thinking, he slipped his arm around her shoulders and gave her a quick hug.

"You're right. I don't. But it sounded good, didn't it?"

He'd made her laugh.

"You're quite the charmer, aren't you, Bodie Scott?"

It was the sound of her laughter that hooked him. His gaze locked on her lips, and as hard as he tried, he couldn't bring himself to look away. He knew she was still talking, because her lips were moving, but he didn't hear a word. All he could think about was kissing her. Then, before he knew it, he was leaning forward. When she didn't move back, he captured those unheard words with a kiss.

Maria inhaled sharply, but she didn't flinch. When his lips centered softly on hers, she responded by leaning into the kiss.

Time stood still up to the moment when the kiss began to morph into wanting more.

She shuddered.

He groaned.

At that point they both broke contact and pulled back.

The look that passed between them was one of shock and then discomfort. To Maria's relief, Bodie took the initiative and smoothed over what could have been a very uncomfortable moment.

"Thanks for the dessert," he said softly, then flipped his finger beneath her chin. "I've got an early day tomorrow, and you've had a hard day. I think we both need to get some sleep."

She nodded.

"Are you gonna be okay?" he asked. "I mean…the weather and all?"

"I'll be fine," she said. "Thank you again for thinking of me, and thank you for the food and company." She put a hand on his arm. "It was very much appreciated."

"Even the dessert?"

She poked a finger against his chest. "Don't push your luck."

He grinned. "I think that's my exit line."

He slid off the bed, stepped back into his boots, put on his shoulder holster, then his jacket. When he turned around, Maria was holding his hat.

He settled the Stetson on his head and gathered up the pizza box just as a huge crack of thunder rattled the windows.

"Just thunder," he said.

Maria nodded. "I'm not scared of storms. Just unsure of tornadoes."

"I could stay."

She frowned. "I think we'd have more than tornadoes to deal with if that happened, don't you?"

He shrugged. "Pretty crazy, right? Two days' worth of acquaintance between us to this?"

Maria's heart began to pound. "What's 'this'?"

"You tell me," Bodie said.

"I don't know you." Her chin quivered slightly. "I don't even know myself."

"I get that. But I'm not the kind of man to hide what I'm thinking or how I feel."

Their gazes locked.

"How do you feel?" she asked.

"Like I want more. I want to know you beyond this thing that's connected us, and I'm afraid you're going to disappear from my life before I can make that happen."

"Wow," Maria whispered.

"Too much too soon?" he asked.

"I'll have to let you know," she said.

"Fair enough," Bodie said, then gathered up the trash and headed for the door. "Come lock it behind me."

Maria followed him to the door.

When he turned around, she shook her head, but softened her refusal with a grin.

"No seconds."

He laughed out loud. "Damn, woman. That's scary. You just read my mind."

"Drive safe," she said, as another clap of thunder rocked the room.

"I'll call you as soon as I get some info about the

hypnotist," he said, then pulled the door shut behind him. But when he didn't hear her lock it again, he yelled, "Lock it!"

She turned the dead bolt.

"That's what I'm talking about," Bodie said, and left.

Maria was smiling when she crawled back in bed. Later she fell back to sleep with the television playing, even though the storm had long since blown over.

Bodie's morning began with a call from his partner, Dave.

He was climbing out of the shower when the phone began to ring.

"What's up?" Bodie asked, as he wrapped the towel around his waist and sat down on the side of the bed.

"I'm on the way to Mini-Mall 31, just off 31st Street. Patrol car found two bodies this morning while making rounds."

"I'll be there in twenty," Bodie said.

"See you," Dave said, and hung up.

Bodie dressed quickly, grabbed his gun from the lockbox in his closet and headed for the door, stopping long enough to retrieve his hat and car keys from the hall table.

Early morning traffic was, as usual, bumper to bumper, so he drove hot all the way to the mall with lights and siren. As he pulled up, he saw that the crime scene crew and the M.E. were already on site.

"What have we got?" he asked, as Dave approached.

"Two males, both dead on the scene. One in a car, one on the ground beside it. Both shot. Both of them carrying. The guns are still on the bodies. Can't tell for sure until forensics runs some ballistics and the autopsy results come in, but at first glance, looks like the one guy walked up to the guy in the car and opened fire. The guy in the car has two bullet wounds. One in the belly. One in the heart. The one outside the car has one bullet wound—in the head. If I had to guess, I'd say the dude who walked up fired the first shot. He either didn't know the dude in the car was armed, or he expected the first shot to take him out. But it didn't. Looks like the two guys fired almost simultaneously then."

"Do we have IDs?" Bodie asked.

"Yeah. They're both gangbangers. As my daddy would have said, 'Two less-than-prime members of society just did the world a favor,' but then, Daddy had a cold way of looking at the world."

Bodie grinned, thinking Dave took after his daddy more than he knew, because that sounded like something Dave would have said, as well.

"I don't suppose we have any witnesses?" he asked.

Dave pointed to a pole-mounted security camera a few yards away.

"As luck would have it…if it works."

"I'll go find mall security," Bodie said.

And so the morning progressed. It was nearly noon before he had time to think, and when he did, his thoughts went straight to Maria. Her case wasn't the only one they were working, by any means, but he had to admit, she was the draw that made it unique.

Bodie made a quick call to Rachel Stewart, the hypnotherapist, hoping to make an appointment for Maria, but struck out. According to her receptionist, Dr. Stewart was in Denver testifying as an expert witness in a trial and would not be back in the state until sometime next week. There were others in the area, but none he knew as well. He decided to get Lieutenant Carver's feedback before he went any further.

Ed Underwood was back on the job. He'd already confirmed that Maria Slade was still in her room, so he'd chosen a spot in the hotel parking lot where he could see the front door if she left. It was just after nine in the morning when he got a phone call from Sheets. Surprised that he was already being pushed for answers, he felt a little like the fat-cat lawyer was calling just to check up on him, then wondered if he'd misjudged Sheets' interest. Because he was on the defensive, his answer was a little abrupt.

"Yeah?"

Franklin frowned. This wasn't the way he expected his phone calls to be answered, and he lit into Ed as if he was no more than a lowly law clerk.

"'Yeah?' What the hell kind of a way is that to answer a phone? 'Yeah' what? Were you just agreeing to what I wanted before you heard the request, or should I blame your mother for the way you were raised?"

Ed gritted his teeth. It was all he could do not to hang

up the phone. But he wouldn't apologize. Especially when Sheets was dissin' his old lady. Sheets hadn't hired him for his manners. He'd hired him for dirty work he didn't want to do himself, and when the son of a bitch remembered that, then the phone call could progress.

Franklin had expected an immediate apology. When he got nothing but silence as a response, he realized he'd made Underwood mad. He didn't care, but on the other hand, he needed him and chose to let it slide.

"What can you tell me about Maria Slade?"

"She's good-looking," Ed snapped.

Franklin sighed. He'd pushed too far.

"Let's start all over here," he said. "I know it's early days, but what can you tell me about Maria Slade?"

"She's from Missoula, Montana. I don't know how she hooked up with Bodie Scott, but they went to Lake Eufaula yesterday, to a bait and beer shop owned by a man named Samuel Gene Vincent. After that, they drove back to Tulsa to the home of a woman named Rebecca 'Becky' Clemmons, a 911 dispatcher here in Tulsa. I've got pictures. Do you want them now? Do you want me to continue surveillance?"

Franklin's heart was pounding. There was a Becky who'd been Sally's babysitter. As for the owner of the beer and bait shop, he'd known him by another name. Tank. Sally Blake's pimp. The downside of that was, Tank Vincent had also known *him*. If they were reopening the murder case, they would most likely begin running down as many of her johns as they could find, and Tank would be the one who might remember them.

During the first investigation, Frank McCall had been lead detective and he'd confiscated Tank Vincent's "little black book." Unfortunately, Franklin's name had been in there and McCall had recognized it—had known he was a lawyer hungry for the big time and figured he would pay money to make it go away. It had cost Sheets five thousand dollars he hadn't had at the time, but it had been worth it for his name not to be associated with a hooker—especially a dead one—in any way. McCall had made his name, Tank's and the little black book all go away, dead-ending the case and leaving Franklin's own future an open book just waiting to be written.

He didn't know where that little black book had ended up, but certainly couldn't afford to let his name come up in any kind of a murder case—especially not now. However, at this point, he wasn't sure what he wanted to do about it. What he did know was that he didn't want an ex-cop on the case any longer. If this went bad, he didn't need a man with a conscience pointing the cops toward the fact that Franklin Sheets was having Maria tailed.

"No, there's no further need," Franklin said. "I thought her presence was pertinent to a client I'm representing, but I was completely mistaken. Just send me what you have, along with your bill."

Ed frowned. He'd been a cop too long not to pick up the tension in Sheets' voice, but he was more than happy to end this surveillance. He knew Bodie Scott. Bodie wouldn't like it that he'd been tailed, especially if he and the Slade woman were working a case.

"Will do," Ed said, and disconnected.

Satisfied that this job was over, he started his car and drove away.

Franklin's stomach was in knots. He didn't know what the P.D. had, but as a lawyer, he knew it took more than the wish of a surviving family member to reopen a cold case. There had to be new evidence. Something was out there that he didn't yet know about, but he would find out. He had to, or the house of cards he'd built around himself could very easily come tumbling down.

Maria's breakfast tray was still on the table where she'd eaten. The coffee cup she'd carried back to bed was near the phone, the contents long since gone cold. She was sitting cross-legged on the bed with a pillow for a table, reading from the journal again. She kept hoping that something she'd read before would suddenly make sense now that she'd come back to the proverbial "scene of the crime." But so far, all it had done was make her sad for what she'd lost.

I saw you every day during the time I was at the Hampton Arms. Sometimes you were with your babysitter, Becky Thurman, and sometimes you were with your mother. Your clothes were always clean, and your hair was always shiny and neat. I think you were a very happy child. I know you were bubbly and outgoing, not like you are now. You grew up a very guarded person, which is understandable, but I have grieved for the person you might have become, as much as I grieve for your mother's death. In a sense, you both died that night. Your rebirth came about out of necessity and a child's resilience.

Maria slammed the journal shut and then tossed it aside. It felt as if she'd been up forever, but it was just after eight o'clock. Inactivity was making her restless. Back at the ranch, there would be a hundred things to do and never enough time to complete them. Here, she was in limbo, wanting to right a wrong, but unable to recall what it would take to do it.

She got up from the bed and strode to the windows. Last night's storm had passed, but the sky was dark and threatening rain again. Even if she'd been in the mood, this wasn't the day to go sightseeing. She hadn't heard from Detective Scott and remembered Becky Clemmons would be at work. Then she wondered what was happening back home, and thought of Bud and went for her phone. She only remembered the time difference after it started to ring at the other end. It was an hour earlier in Montana than it was here in Oklahoma. She hoped he was still in the house.

Bud answered on the first ring.

"Hello?"

"Hey, Bud, hope I didn't wake you."

He snorted lightly. "Woman...you know better than that. I'm on my third cup of coffee and wading through these blasted invoices. I miss Savannah. This is usually her job. Truth be told, I miss all of you something fierce. It's too damned quiet in this house."

"I miss being there, too," Maria said.

"So how's it going there?"

"Yesterday the detective and I talked to the man who used to be Sally's pimp. I also found out that the woman who used to babysit me was his sister."

"Did you recognize either of them?"

"No."

Bud heard the frustration in her voice. "Look, honey. You've suppressed that stuff for twenty years. It's not like it's going to just pop back into your head just because you're back in Oklahoma. I'm sure everything, including the people, all looks different."

"I know you're right, but the bottom line is, if I don't remember, the case goes cold again and someone still gets away with murder."

"I hear what you're saying, but you're not giving yourself a break. I have faith in you, girl. Of all Andrew's girls, you are the one who doesn't know how to quit."

Maria's eyes filled with tears. "Thank you for the pep talk."

"You're welcome. I love you, sugar. Take care, and call me whenever."

"I love you, too, Bud. Thanks for always being there."

"Just get through and come home," he said.

"I will."

She disconnected, then laid her phone on the bed and headed for the bathroom. She needed to get out of this funk, and the only thing she could think to do was get moving. There had to be a shopping mall in the area. She could walk and look, and eat lunch somewhere besides here in the hotel. She grabbed the phone book, and leafed through the yellow pages until she found a listing for Woodland Hills Mall on 71st and Memorial. She stripped off her sweats and headed for the shower, even as it started to rain—again.

The rain was coming down in earnest by the time Maria reached the mall. She found a parking spot very close to one of the entrances, and thought about sitting in the car and waiting for the rain to subside, then decided she would rather be inside killing time than sitting in the car feeling sorry for herself again. God knew she'd been wet plenty of times before. It wasn't going to hurt her now.

She locked the door behind her as she got out, then bolted across the drive. The exhilaration of trying to outrun the rain had her laughing as she reached the covered walkway leading into the mall. She swiped water from her face, shook back her hair and slid the strap of her shoulder bag a little higher up on her shoulder, then strode into the mall. The immediate scents of a nearby food court, coupled with the piped-in music and the rumble of voices, were already lifting her spirits.

Straight in front of her was an escalator leading to the second floor and the source of all those delicious smells. Deciding to leave eating for later, she started walking slowly, eyeing window displays and people, watching when the opportunity occurred. A man was standing near a stairwell with a clipboard in his hand, trying to make eye contact and talk someone into participating in his survey. When he saw her coming, he smiled and started toward her, then almost stumbled as he stopped and changed his mind.

Maria glanced at her reflection as she passed by a store and then frowned. No wonder he backed off. As Bud would have said, she looked like she was ready to whip someone's ass. If she was so uptight, it stood to reason that she wasn't remembering anything. Then she reminded herself that she'd come here to kill time, not to start a war, and made herself relax.

As she continued down the promenade, she began smelling spices, then realized she was approaching a candle shop and remembered seeing decorative candles in Becky Clemmons' home. She was going to have to go back there when Becky got her mother's things out of storage, and while it wasn't quite the occasion for a hostess gift, Becky was going out of her way to help. A token of appreciation might be nice.

She went inside, and soon got lost in the myriad number of shapes and sizes, not to mention the array of scents from which to choose. Finally she settled on a fat white one in a silver stand. The scent was white cotton—a clean, crisp scent that reminded Maria of clothes drying outdoors on a line. She exited the store with a lighter heart and a slower stride, the small gift bag dangling on her arm.

A few stores farther along, she noticed a trio of young

black men coming toward her. They were laughing and bumping against each other as they walked. Within moments she realized she knew one of them—Tyrell, the teen from the John 3:16 Mission. And it didn't take long for her to see Tyrell recognized her, too. What did surprise her was that when they came abreast, he stopped.

"Hey, lady."

Maria smiled. "Hey, Tyrell, did you already forget my name?"

He grinned. "Maria. I ain't forgettin' nothin'."

"How's Preacher Henry?"

Tyrell's friends were eyeing him curiously, a little taken aback that he was bothering with this woman.

Tyrell gave them a look, which sent them moving along.

"He's good," he said.

"You tell him I said hello, will you?"

Tyrell nodded his head. "Yeah, I'll do that."

"Your friends are going to go off without you," Maria said.

He grinned. "Nah…they're ridin' with me. They ain't goin' nowhere unless they're wantin' to walk."

She laughed.

Tyrell shifted from foot to foot, as if a little embarrassed, then jumped right into what he needed to say.

"Hey, lady…what you did for the mission…that was real good of you."

"Maria. My name is Maria."

"Yeah, okay. Maria. What you did was big. Real big. Preacher Henry ain't been that happy in a long time."

"My daddy was a preacher, too. I'm glad it helped."

"Yeah. Well. I just wanted to say thanks."

"Then you're welcome. You take care, okay?" Maria said.

"You, too, lady."

"Not lady...*Maria*."

He laughed, and then he was gone.

Maria's heart was even lighter as she began to retrace her steps back down the promenade toward the escalator. It was almost two o'clock, and she was hungry, so she headed up to the food court.

A short while later she was digging into a plate of egg rolls and broccoli-chicken stir-fry from the Chinese eatery. A young woman with two small children was sitting at a nearby table. The kids were digging through Happy Meal boxes from McDonald's, while the mother was tackling an order of chili cheese fries. The children were talking and eating and playing with their toys. Their mother's smile as she listened was both complacent and proud. Maria couldn't help but wonder if there had been times like this between her and her own mother, and wondered what their lives would have been like now if her mother hadn't been murdered.

Before she could think herself into another funk, her cell phone rang. She quickly swallowed, checked the caller ID and smiled as she answered.

"Hello."

"It's me," Bodie said, as he leaned back in his chair and pushed a desk drawer shut with his boot.

"Hi, me."

He grinned. "What are you doing?"

"Eating stir-fry and egg rolls at the food court at Woodland Hills."

"Yum. So...you've been shopping."

"Not so much. Just looking for a way to kill time. I'm not good at sitting around and waiting. Do you have anything new to tell me?"

"Not pertaining to the case," Bodie said. "But I wondered if you would like to have dinner with me tonight. It'll be close to eight before I can get away. If that's too late just—"

"How rude. First invite me out to eat and then start making excuses for why I shouldn't accept."

He grinned again. This attitude was exactly why he wanted to see her again.

"So are you saying you'll go?"

"That's six hours from now. I'm pretty sure I'll be hungry again by then, and I suppose I can squeeze in a little time for you."

He laughed out loud, then frowned when Dave pointed at him from across the room and grinned. He lowered his voice and swiveled his chair away from Dave's line of sight.

"I'll pick you up at your room around eight o'clock."

"Why don't I just watch for you from the lobby?

When you pull up in the breezeway, I'll come out, and you won't have to park the car."

"Yeah, sure…whatever," Bodie said.

"Where are we going to eat?" she asked.

"It's a surprise."

"Do I have to dress up? Tell me now, because I'm at the mall and I didn't bring any dressy clothes with me."

"It's a nice place, but not crystal-and-china nice. Just really good food."

"Okay. I can handle that. See you later, then."

"Yeah. Later," he said, and was still smiling when he hung up. When he turned around, Dave was leaning against his desk.

"Who's the woman?"

Bodie frowned. "None of your damned business."

Dave arched an eyebrow. "Dang. You usually share info. What's up with this one?"

"She's not for sharing," Bodie said.

From the moment Becky Clemmons got to work and sat down in her chair, she was on the job. There was no time to think about Mary's unexpected return or Sally's belongings, which she'd promised to get out of storage. As always, the weather had an impact on the calls that came in, and when it started raining, the number of wrecks and fender benders went up. By the time her shift was over, she was tired, but the adrenaline was still racing. The storage company wasn't far from her house, and she had a good two hours before it would get dark. Even though it was still raining, she couldn't get the task out of her mind. The sooner she got the boxes, the quicker she would see Mary again.

And hopefully whatever was in those boxes would be the trigger Maria needed to remember what she'd seen.

Thirteen

The rain had abated by the time Bodie left for the hotel to pick Maria up. As soon as he pulled beneath the breezeway, she came out, smiling at the doorman who held the door. She was wearing a pair of dark pants and a pink knit top beneath a light gray jacket, but he smiled when he saw her shoes. She was still wearing boots. A woman after his own heart.

Bodie tried not to mind that the doorman was watching her. He couldn't blame the guy. Maria Slade was worth way more than a second look. He jumped out and opened the car door for her as she approached.

"Hi," she said, flashing a smile at him this time.

"You look beautiful," he said softly.

"Thank you," she said quickly, and ducked her head as she slid into the seat and he closed the door behind her.

Last night Bodie had made it patently clear how he felt about her. She wished they'd met under different circumstances. Part of her wanted to get to know him better, but she kept reminding herself that this wasn't why she'd come. She felt guilty about being attracted to the detective who was leading the investigation, as if those emotions would lessen the honesty of her quest.

Bodie slid behind the wheel. "Hope you're hungry."

"I won't waste your money, if that's what you're worried about," she drawled.

He laughed. As he drove away, it occurred to him that he'd probably laughed more with her in the last two days than he had in months with anyone else. It also occurred to him that this was moving way too fast. He was still a cop, and she was the only witness in a murder case—if only she could remember what she'd seen. His lieutenant would frown on the fact that he'd asked her out, but he figured if sometime during the night they talked about the case, dinner could loosely be classified as part of the investigation.

Becky got home with the boxes just before dark. She pulled her car into the garage, then closed the door behind her. Too tired to unload them now, she opted to leave them in the trunk and went inside to change clothes and make herself some dinner.

Later, as she was cleaning up the kitchen, her curiosity got the better of her. She went after the boxes and carried them one by one into the living room and stacked them against the fireplace. She wanted to go through them right now but felt as if she should wait for Maria.

Instead, she turned on the television and tried to concentrate, but her thoughts kept going back to the boxes. What if the clue to bringing Mary's memory back was inside one of them? What if there was something in there that would be instrumental in bringing a killer to justice?

Finally her curiosity won out. She turned off the television. Maybe she would open just one. She didn't remember a thing about what was in any of them, and as she tore into the first one, it hit her that this felt a little bit like digging into Sally Blake's grave.

Franklin Sheets' eyes narrowed as he slipped the throw-away phone he'd bought earlier out of the desk drawer. If he followed through on this call, he would be setting a wheel in motion that had the possibility of crushing him. On the other hand, there was too much at stake for him to just sit back and hope his name never came up in the investigation of Sally Blake's murder. He thought of the man he was going to call. A man he knew only by the name of Harley.

The number began to ring. Franklin shifted nervously in his chair, then glanced toward his office door, making sure it was firmly shut.

"Hello?"

The voice was raspy and abrupt. Franklin tried to match the layer of testosterone and failed miserably.

"I want to speak to Harley."

"I'm Harley. How did you get this number?"

"Melvin Powers."

There was a long moment of silence, and then the sound of someone hawking and spitting. Franklin's belly rolled, but he gritted his teeth and waited.

"So what do you want?" Harley asked.

"I have a problem I need to go away."

"Permanently?"

"Yes."

"Twenty-five thousand. Ten up front. The balance after the job is done."

Franklin's gut rolled. He was unable to believe he was really doing this.

"That's agreeable," he said.

"I need a name and location," Harley snapped.

"A man named Samuel Gene Vincent. Might go by the name of Tank. Owns a beer and bait shop down at Lake Eufaula. I don't have exact directions."

"I'll find him," Harley said. "Transfer the first ten thousand dollars into this account." He recited a string of numbers. "The balance goes into the same account only after you hear from me. Screw me over and it'll be the last thing you do."

"I'm good for it," Franklin said. "Is there anything else you need?" he asked.

"Your patience," Harley drawled.

Franklin could hear the man laughing as the line went dead in his ear. He swallowed nervously as he slipped the phone into his pocket. From all accounts, Harley was a bad-ass of the first order—a man without a conscience. But Franklin also knew that if he was going to scour his past clean, that was the kind of man he needed to do the job.

"Hot or mild sauce?" Bodie asked.

"Some of both?" Maria countered, as the waitress slid a heaping plate of barbequed pork ribs in front of her, accompanied by tangy cole slaw and a mountain of hand-cut home fries.

"You got it," Bodie said, and set the two bottles of extra sauce in front of them in the middle of the table. He slapped a handful of extra napkins right beside them, then looked up. "You think you can wade through that bad boy?"

She arched an eyebrow and reached for the sauce. "I already told you, I won't waste your money. You just worry about your own plate, and leave me and mine alone."

He grinned. "My dad is gonna love you," he said, and then stopped and sighed. That was a huge assumption that hadn't needed to be voiced. "Well, hell, sorry. That just slipped out. I'll be putting some food in my mouth now, instead of my foot, okay?"

"It's okay," Maria said, pointing a French fry at him. "*My* dad would have liked *you*." Then she popped the fry in her mouth and chewed.

They ate and bantered, traded sauces and sides, while the time slipped away. By the time the meal was over, they were both satiated, and so at ease with each other that they no longer thought about the fact that three days ago they hadn't even known each other existed.

As they left the restaurant, they realized right away that the wind had risen and, once again, the sky was threatening rain.

Maria eyed the clouds. "Doesn't the sun *ever* shine in Oklahoma?"

Bodie grinned. "I think maybe you ate too many ribs in there, sugar. It's nighttime. The sun never shines after dark."

Maria laughed. "You know what I mean."

"It's spring. Right now we're grateful for the rain, 'cause the likelihood is we'll get a two-month dry spell come July and August."

"Oh. Well. Forget I complained. I just hope it's not another stormy night."

Bodie slid an arm around her shoulders as they walked across the parking lot toward the car.

"I know...but it's par for the course around here this time of year."

By the time they were pulling out of the parking lot, the rain was coming down. Bodie turned on the windshield wipers, then the car radio. "If there are any storm warnings, they'll broadcast them on this station."

As he drove, she nervously eyed the night sky and the intermittent cloud to ground lightning, then decided to change the subject from storms to the turmoil in her own life.

"You said during dinner that the hypnotherapist you were going to call is away, right?"

"Yes. There are others, but I can't vouch for them personally, like I could her. I'll run it by Lieutenant Carver in the morning, but if you have the time to spare, I'd rather wait for her."

"I'm making time to see this through to the end, no matter how long it takes," she said.

"Have you heard from Becky Clemmons?" Bodie asked.

"No. Have you?"

Maria frowned. "She was going to call you, remember?"

"Have you thought about spending some time with her? Maybe spending a little time with someone who knew you and your mother that well would help."

When she didn't comment as he braked for a red light, he glanced at her profile. Other than the fact that he thought her beautiful, which was becoming more and more of a fact to him, the streetlights coming through the windows cast the shadows of raindrops on her face, making it appear as if she were crying. It looked so real, he took a second look to make sure it was just an illusion.

"Is there anyone else mentioned in that journal that you're planning to see?" he asked.

"No. Remember, Dad only knew Sally and me less than a week before…before it happened. And he spent a good portion of each evening and every night at the church that was hosting the revival."

Bodie accelerated through the intersection as the light changed. "So was your dad always a traveling preacher?"

"Yes, but he quit after Holly came to live with us. At least that's what my sisters and I finally figured out after all those secrets were revealed. He married Mom... Hannah, after Holly joined the family, then quit traveling and preaching, but I barely remember our life before Hannah. The family ranch was in Montana, and that's where we all grew up. It's actually kind of weird, learning about all this from the journals since he died...like we never really knew him. Our whole perception of who we were is skewed."

"I don't think you're going to remember all that much without hypnosis, though, do you?"

"I don't know...maybe," Maria said. "Are you getting flak about the case? I mean...you reopened it, but you still don't actually have any new leads to follow."

"I'm optimistic," Bodie said, then grinned. "I'm always optimistic."

"I've noticed," Maria said. "Can we say...steamroller?"

He had a feeling she was talking about more than the case—like maybe his declaration of interest in her last night—and decided to say so.

"There you go, putting me back outside your boundaries. How are we going to make any progress if you continue to keep me at arm's length?"

"And here I thought the progress we were hoping for had to do with my mother's murder."

"Well, yeah...that, too."

She shook her head, then pointed. "There's the hotel."

Bodie sighed. Unless he could work some magic, this meant the end of their evening. He pulled up by the front entrance, then put the car in Park.

"Call me in the morning and let me know what your lieutenant thinks about another hypnotherapist," Maria said.

"So this means you're not inviting me up?"

"You're such a good detective. You figured that out without me having to say a thing."

"A man can hope."

"I'm not saying it's impossible. I think it's good to set goals for yourself," Maria said.

Bodie slipped a hand behind her neck and gently pulled her close.

"I'll settle for this," he said softly, and leaned forward until their lips met.

The kiss was brief, but there was no mistaking the urgency behind it.

"Sleep well," Bodie said, as he turned her loose.

"You, too, and thank you for the company and that wonderful meal."

"You're welcome, honey. Don't worry about the storm, okay? If it gets really bad, I promise I'll call and wake you up so you can get to shelter."

"My knight in shining armor," Maria said, then got out of the car and headed for the hotel door. She paused just before she went inside, turned and waved.

Bodie waved back, then waited for her to go in. It wasn't until she finally disappeared from his sight that he put the car in gear and drove away.

* * *

Harley had no problem finding Vincent's bait shop. His plan was to check the place out during working hours and see what he was up against. He wheeled into the parking area, then strolled inside as if it was something he did on a regular basis. He paused in the doorway long enough to locate the cooler where the beer was housed, then moved toward it. A six-pack of Coors was calling to him. He picked it up, along with a large sack of chips, and headed for the cash register.

Sam eyed his customer as he moved toward the cooler. He'd never seen him before, which didn't mean anything, but considering the location of his shop, not many strangers found him. When the man headed toward the counter with his purchases, Tank got himself a better look.

His head was shaved like a skinhead, and his clothing reflected a biker lifestyle. He sported several tattoos, was wearing a black leather vest and had cut the sleeves off his T-shirt. His boots were studded with silver studs, and his jeans were faded from countless washings. When he walked, he jangled from the amount of chain he was wearing. But despite all the gear, Sam couldn't help thinking it was all for show.

"How you doin'?" Sam asked, as the man set the beer and chips on the counter.

"Good. Good. Looks like it's gonna rain tonight."

Sam nodded as he rang up the purchases. "Anything else you need?"

"Nope. That'll be it," Harley said, and pulled out a

handful of bills and peeled off enough to pay for his stuff, then pocketed the change. "See ya'," he said, and flipped Sam the peace sign as he left.

At that point Sam glanced at the clock. It was after six. Time to close up. He emptied the till into a bank bag, and then locked the front door, turned the Open sign to Closed and locked the back door on his way to his house.

Harley popped the top on one of the beers as he got to his car. He watched as Vincent began locking up for the night, then smiled to himself as he drove away. He'd seen all he needed to see. Granted, the man was big, but he was old and out of shape. He wouldn't be an issue.

Harley intended to wait 'til later, when the man went to sleep. No need making things harder than they had to be. He backtracked to a restaurant a few miles away, went in and ordered a chicken-fried steak that was half the size of his plate, with mashed potatoes and gravy, and a side order of corn.

He took his time eating, waiting for time to pass. Taking out one lone man in a location so far away from prying eyes was going to be a piece of cake. And as the thought crossed his mind, he flagged down his waitress and ordered some dessert.

By the time Sam had cooked and eaten his supper, it was nearly dark. He carried his table scraps out the back door of his cabin and scraped them into Pooch's bowl. A low rumble of thunder reminded him that the weatherman had promised thunderstorms for the area. He glanced up at the darkening sky, then circled the cabin so he could see toward the bait shop, making sure he'd left the night-lights turned on. A soft yellow glow from the neon Coors light in the window cast shadows on the ground beside the building. As always, everything was locked up and tied down.

After scratching Pooch's ears, he went back inside and finished cleaning up the dishes, then headed for the living room to watch a little TV. But it was hard to concentrate. He hadn't been able to get over Mary Blake coming to see him. Granted, she wouldn't have been here without the cop and the fact that they were reopening her mother's murder case, but that was fine with him. He was still blown away by how much she looked like Sally, and had high hopes that Sally's killer would finally be brought to justice. By the time he was ready for bed, Pooch was scratching at the door, wanting to come in, and Tank went over to oblige him.

The giant Rhodesian Ridgeback sauntered in slowly with his tongue lolling off to the side, dripping water from a swim in the lake.

"Looks like you already had your bath," Sam said. "Do me the favor of staying off the furniture while I take mine now...you hear?"

The dog paid him no mind, and Sam didn't wait to make sure the dog stayed on the floor. They both knew the routine.

Time passed slowly as Sam took his shower, then puttered around the cabin, until finally he headed up the stairs to the loft where he slept. Out of habit, his gaze slid toward the table where Sally's photo used to sit, and then he remembered that he'd given it to Mary. Smiling to himself, he turned back the covers and crawled into bed.

The thunderstorm moved closer. Intermittent flashes of lightning were followed by angry rumbles of thunder. When the rain began pelting the roof over Sam's bed, he finally drifted off to sleep.

Downstairs, Pooch had curled up at the bottom of the stairs leading to the sleeping loft, lulled—like his master—by the sound of wind and rain.

Harley turned off his lights and engine, and coasted toward the bait shop. It was still raining, but the worst of the storm had moved past. His tires made little popping noises as they rolled along the graveled road, but the sounds were muffled by the rain and wind coming off the lake.

The neon light from the Coors beer sign was shining in the bait shop window, casting a pale glow out onto the ground. The cabin behind the shop was in darkness. He didn't even have to deal with a halogen yard light.

Perfect.

He parked the car beneath the trees nearest the shop, then grabbed his gun and a flashlight and got out, wishing he'd thought to grab a jacket before he left Tulsa. The rain was cold, and while the leather shed water, his shirt and jeans didn't, and he was soon soaked to the skin.

As he reached the cabin, he paused beneath a window and listened, making sure the old man wasn't sitting inside watching television in the dark. The roof was minus a rain gutter, and as he leaned forward and peered into a window he got a steady flow of rainwater down the back of his neck, which pissed him off a bit more.

The house was completely in darkness, not even a night-light inside to tell him how the place was laid out. His best guess was that it was one big room, maybe two at most.

His boots made soft little squishing noises in the grass as he circled the cabin. When he got to the back door, he aimed his flashlight toward the door long enough to see that it had a dead bolt. Frowning, he made his way back around to the front of the cabin and then started up the steps.

Sam was sound asleep on his side with his hand hanging off the side of the bed. Suddenly Pooch's cold wet nose was in his palm.

He woke immediately, then sat up, his head cocked to the side, listening.

Pooch woofed softly, then turned and ran swiftly down the stairs and across the room as Sam slipped out of bed and into a pair of pants. He grabbed a twelve-gauge shotgun from the rack above his bed, and then opened the drawer in the table near his bed and pulled out a handful of shells.

He knew the house as well in the dark of night as he did in broad daylight, and now he peered over the loft down into the room below. From where he was standing, he had a straight line of sight to the front door.

It took him a few moments to locate Pooch, and when he saw him with his ears up, silently trailing along the wall from the back of the room toward the front, marking the path of whatever was outside the cabin, he knew he had a visitor.

It occurred to him that it might be a cougar. They were seen in the area from time to time, although since it was raining, he doubted it would have picked up Pooch's scent, which would be the only reason a big cat would come around human habitation.

Then all of a sudden Sam heard the front steps groan and knew his late-night visitor had to be human. It would take considerable weight to make those steps creak, and whoever was out there had just come up onto the porch.

Confident that his approach had been muffled by the rain and wind, Harley swept his flashlight across the locks. Another damn dead bolt. Whatever. He'd kicked in plenty of doors before, and there was no time like the present.

He lifted his knee toward his chest, then lunged forward, putting all of his two hundred and twenty pounds into the kick.

The door splintered, and he was inside the cabin and reaching for the light switch when something huge hit him chest high and took him down to the ground.

The old man had a dog!

He saw a flash of white teeth, heard a deep, angry growl and threw his arm up to deflect the bite aiming for his throat. The bite went bone-deep into his forearm, and he was screaming as he swung his handgun up against the dog's furry belly and fired twice as fast as he could.

The dog yelped and went down, howling and writhing, as if confused by the pain. He rolled the animal off himself and swiftly crawled behind an easy chair.

Whatever surprise he'd been planning was over. He was dog-bit and bleeding, and the room was still dark.

All of a sudden the inside of the cabin was flooded with light. He peered out from behind the chair, his gun at the ready. That was when he saw the stairs at the back of the room leading to a sleeping loft. He looked up, just as a huge silhouette loomed over the railing.

"Tank!" Harley yelled, hoping that would distract the man enough for him to get off a good shot.

Instead, Sam emptied the twelve-gauge shotgun he was holding into the easy chair—and right into Harley's chest.

Harley screamed, not unlike the dog still writhing on the floor, as fire spread throughout his body.

Sam came flying down the stairs, reloading as he ran. He recognized the intruder immediately and realized that the earlier visit had been to case the joint. Assuming the man had come to rob him, he shoved the shotgun in his face.

"What's your name?" Sam yelled.

"Tank…come on, man, help me. I'm hurt real bad."

Sam froze. It suddenly hit him that this man he didn't know had twice called him Tank, a name he hadn't used in twenty years. Not just that, down here he was Sam Vincent. No one knew him as Tank.

"Who are you?" Sam yelled, and then poked the barrel of the shotgun in the man's belly.

Harley moaned from the pain, and then he started to seize. Before he could answer the question, his eyes rolled back in his head, and then he was gone.

Fourteen

Sam wasn't the only one having a problem with crime. Back in Tulsa, a man named Marino had gotten sick at his night job and clocked out early from the warehouse where he loaded trailers for tractor-trailer rigs. Battling a fever and sick to his stomach, it was all he could do to get home. Expecting sympathy and some much needed rest, he walked into his bedroom and found his wife in their bed with another man.

Shock escalated to fury, and before he took time to think it over, Marino killed the man, then his own wife, in a fit of rage. In a state of shock and still reeling from the sickness that had sent him home, he took some medicine and passed out on his living room sofa. When he woke the next morning, he made himself some coffee, then sat down on a kitchen stool and called the police.

A couple of hours later, a lab tech from the crime-scene crew was taking photos, while two others were bagging evidence, even though Marino had already confessed and been taken into custody. They continued to gather evidence as if the killer was an unknown. It wouldn't be the first time a perp connected with a lawyer and decided to change his plea. Bodie was already guessing that a wily lawyer was going to put the man's illness and state of mind into play when it came time for trial. However, evidence told its own story, even when killers changed theirs.

Dave was still on the porch talking to a uniformed officer and Bodie was heading for the car when his cell phone rang. He glanced at the caller ID, saw Out Of Area and started to let it go to voice mail, then changed his mind.

"This is Detective Bodie Scott."

"Detective…Sam Vincent."

Bodie stopped. Tank? "Uh…yeah, hi, Sam. How's it going?"

"I've seen better days," Sam said.

Bodie frowned. "What's wrong?"

"Last night I had a visitor break into my house around two a.m. Killed my dog and tried to kill me."

Bodie thought of that huge Rhodesian Ridgeback coming at him in the dark and winced.

"Sorry to hear it. What happened? Robbery gone bad?"

"That's what I thought at first, but just before he died, the guy called me Tank."

Now Bodie was paying attention. "He's dead?"

"Yeah, a twelve-gauge will do that to you if you're in the wrong place. So…I've been thinking. I left Tulsa twenty years ago, and when I did, I left Tank Vincent behind. Even though my sister lives there, I haven't been back. Everyone down here knows me as Sam. No one ever calls me anything but Sam. Then you show up with Mary Blake all grown up telling me that you're reopening the case. You interrogate me, and the next night some thug breaks into my house, calls me by my pimp name and tries to kill me, and now I'm starting to get antsy."

"Son of a bitch," Bodie muttered.

"Took the words right out of my mouth," Sam replied.

"Are you okay?" Bodie asked.

"Hell no. I had to bury my dog and get a new door. I haven't decided whether I'm gonna get my easy chair recovered or just toss it. Gonna be hell trying to pick all the shot out of the stuffing."

"Are you good with the local law?"

"Yeah. They know me. Besides, it was pretty obvious after they saw the door kicked in that he hadn't planned on knocking."

"Did you know the shooter?"

"No, but he came in the bait shop a few hours earlier, I guess to look me over. Thinking about it, if he'd been planning to rob me, he would have done it then and been long gone, instead of waiting 'til dark and hitting my house."

"Have the police identified him?"

"I don't know. You can call the county sheriff about all that."

"Yeah, I will, and thanks for letting me know."

"Look. I'm not trying to tell you how to run your business," Sam said. "But I'd be paying attention to Mary right now, if I was you. If this was connected to the investigation, she could be their next target."

A chill went up Bodie's back as the line went dead in his ear. He signaled to Dave that they needed to leave, and then got into the car. Dave came running and jumped in next to him.

"What's up?"

"I need to talk to Lieutenant Carver about that cold case we reopened. I think someone's leaked information that's already gotten one man killed. I don't want Maria Slade next on the list."

Franklin Sheets had a habit of turning on the television set in his bedroom as soon as he woke up. It was his way of catching up with what went on in Tulsa after he went to bed and what news was breaking that morning. It played in the background as he began his morning routine. He'd already showered and was standing in front of the mirror swiping shaving cream on his face when he heard the television anchor mention the word *shooting*, then Lake Eufaula.

He grabbed a hand towel and ran out of the bathroom, grabbed the remote and upped the volume.

"*...attack took place in the early morning hours at the home of Samuel Vincent, owner of the Bait and Beer on the far southwest shores of Lake Eufaula. After the intruder invaded his home, shot and killed his dog and took aim at him, the home owner shot back in self-*

defense. The perpetrator was pronounced dead on the scene. Identification is being withheld until notification of next of kin. The authorities are surmising this was a robbery gone bad. In other news…"

Franklin's stomach rolled. Harley was dead. He was out ten thousand dollars, and Tank Vincent was still alive. What had started out as nothing more than house-keeping was turning into an issue. His cell phone rang on the stand next to his bed, but he ignored it. He needed to think. Then he glanced at the clock.

He needed to think fast, because he was due in court in a couple of hours.

Becky Clemmons was pouring her second cup of coffee when her telephone rang. When she saw it was Sammy, she smiled. This was a treat. Hearing from him twice in one week was unusual.

"Good morning, brother," she said.

"Yeah, thought I'd better call you before you heard about it on the news."

Becky frowned. "Heard what?"

"Someone broke into my house early this morning around two a.m. Kicked in my front door, killed Pooch and tried to take me out."

"Oh, my God…Sammy…are you okay?"

"I'm not hurt, if that's what you're asking."

Becky's thoughts were tumbling. "What do they think…that he was trying to rob you?"

"I don't know what *they* think, but I know what *I* think."

"What?"

"It has to do with reopening Sally's murder investigation."

"Why would you—"

"The man who broke into my house called me Tank. Tank is from twenty years ago. Tank never came to Lake Eufaula. Sam lives at the lake."

Becky started to shake. Was this horror starting all over again?

"What do you think we should do? Do you think I'm in danger? Oh, my God…Mary…what if they find out about her?"

Sam shrugged. "Hell, Beck…they obviously know she's in town, because she was with the cop who came to interrogate me."

Becky's voice dropped to a whisper. "No, you don't understand. The reason they've reopened the case is because a witness has come forward."

A chill suddenly ran up Sam's spine. "What do you mean? Who is it? Why didn't they come forward back then? And how the hell do you know this? Why did they tell you and not me?"

Becky sank into a chair and closed her eyes.

"It was Mary. Mary was in the apartment the night Sally was killed."

Sam's heart skipped a beat. "No. She was with you. You said all along that she was with you."

"I lied. With her last breath, Sally begged us to hide her. She begged the preacher to take Mary. She kept saying that if he knew she saw him, he'd kill her, too."

"Sweet Jesus," Sam muttered. "She didn't say a word when she was here. Why are they interviewing people if she already knows who it was?"

"Because she has no memory of her past, which means she doesn't remember that night, either. She only learned of all this after the preacher died. She came back to do the right thing, and I think coming to see us was part of the plan to bring back her memory, only I don't think it's working."

"Son of a bitch!"

"I told the cop I had some boxes of stuff from Sally's apartment. She and that cop are supposed to come back and go through all of it in the hopes that something will trigger some memories for Mary...for Maria. I brought the boxes home last night, so..."

"Have you called them?"

"I was just about to when you called."

"I already told that detective what happened here last night, and I warned him Mary could be in danger. You could be, too. Pay attention to what's going on, and don't let any strangers in your house."

"Like you did?"

"I didn't *let* him in. But I made sure he didn't leave. I'm still dealing with the mess down here. As soon as I get squared away, I'm coming to your house."

"You don't even know where I live," Becky said.

"I have an address. Tulsa can't have changed that much. I'll find it. In the meantime, be careful."

"You, too, Sammy. I love you."

Sam sighed. "Love you, too, Beck. See you soon."

* * *

For the first time since she'd checked in, Maria went down to the hotel restaurant for breakfast. She was mad at herself for caving in to emotions and determined to gain some control. Eating alone in her room was too much like hiding. Andrew had not raised his girls to hide, and she wasn't about to start now.

She saw a trio of young women exit the elevator and start across the hotel lobby. They were laughing and talking and trading bites of a huge cinnamon roll as they headed for the exit. There was a disparity in their ages, but not in their appearance. It was obvious they were from the same family. All three had thick, curly red hair. Just watching them made her lonesome for her own sisters, and she decided to give them a call. She didn't know for sure where they were, or how their journeys back to their pasts were playing out, but she had a sudden urge to reconnect, and she pulled out her phone as soon as she was seated.

She knew Savannah was in Florida. With the time difference, it was already after 11:00 a.m. there. Savannah wasn't an early riser by choice, but she should be up by now. Maria punched in the number, then waited to hear her sister's voice. When the call went to voice mail, she left a message.

Holly was in Missouri, which was in the same time zone as Tulsa, but once again, her call went straight to voice mail.

Frustrated, she was about to call Bud just so she could

hear a familiar and friendly voice when her food was served. She laid the phone aside.

Belgian waffles with fresh strawberries and whipped cream were a luxury they didn't often have at the ranch. Theirs was usually a stick-to-your-ribs menu, like ham and eggs, or eggs and biscuits with sausage gravy. She dug into the food and found herself enjoying the treat.

The waitress had just refilled her coffee cup when her cell phone rang. Thinking it would be one of her sisters, she answered without checking the caller ID.

"Hello?"

"Hi, Maria...this is Becky Clemmons. I wanted to let you know that I got the boxes of your mother's things out of storage last night. They're here at my house, and I'm home all day, in case you want to come over."

Maria's disappointment that it wasn't one of her sisters quickly shifted to interest at the thought of going through those boxes.

"Did you call Detective Scott?" Maria asked.

"Just now, but I couldn't get him, so I left a message on his cell phone."

Maria frowned, then glanced at her watch. It was after 10:00 a.m. Obviously he was otherwise engaged. But she didn't want to wait. She was a big girl. She could find Becky's house by herself.

"If you don't mind, I'd like to come over now, rather than waiting for him. I'm not very good at navigating Tulsa, though, and it may take me a little bit to find your house."

Becky started to say something about what had

happened to Sammy, then decided it could wait until Maria's arrival.

"What hotel are you at?" she asked instead.

"The downtown Doubletree on 7th Street."

"Oh, okay. I can give you directions that will get you here faster than following a city map."

"Just a minute," Maria said, and picked up her purse, shoving the journal aside as she dug for a pen and paper. "Okay, I'm ready."

Becky spoke carefully, giving Maria time to write as she dictated a route to her house.

"Okay, I think I've got it," Maria said, and read it back.

"That's it. You have my number on your cell. Call me if you get lost."

"Will do," Maria said.

Now that she had a purpose to the day, she was anxious to get started. She started to call Bodie, then changed her mind. If he was too busy to answer Becky's call, it stood to reason he was too busy to answer hers, as well.

She charged her meal to her room, got her valet parking ticket out of her purse and headed across the lobby. A short while later, she was in the car and headed west, following Becky's directions.

Lieutenant Carver was finishing up on some paperwork when Bodie knocked on his door.

"Come in," the lieutenant said as he flipped the file

shut and set it aside, then waved his detective toward a chair. "Heard you caught a weird one this morning."

"Yes, sir," Bodie said, thumbing the button to put his phone on silent mode. "Hell of a deal for all concerned. Sick husband checks out of work. Goes home, catches cheating wife in bed with another man. Kills both of them, then takes some medicine and sacks out on the sofa. Doesn't bother running. Doesn't pretend someone else did it. Just made himself some coffee the next morning before he called the police."

Carver shook his head. "Takes all kinds. So, what did you want to see me about?"

Bodie slid forward on the edge of his seat.

"I think someone leaked information about that cold case we reopened."

Carver frowned. "Are you accusing—"

"Sir. I'm stating a concern, not trying to point a finger."

Carver's frown deepened. "So explain yourself. What makes you think we have a leak?"

"Remember a couple of days ago Maria Slade and I drove to Lake Eufaula and interviewed Tank Vincent, the man who used to be Sally Blake's pimp?"

"Yes. What about it?"

"I got a call from him this morning. Sometime around two a.m., someone kicked in his door, killed his dog and was aiming for him when he emptied a twelve-gauge shotgun into the intruder's belly."

"A robbery gone wrong. What does that have to do with us?"

"Down there, no one calls him Tank. According to him, he's known only as Sam. They have no knowledge of his life before he moved there."

"I'm failing to see the point here," Carver said.

"Point is…according to Sam Vincent, the intruder called him Tank before he died. Sam finds it too coincidental that we show up looking for Tank Vincent, and then the next night someone else comes looking to *kill* Tank Vincent."

Carver cursed beneath his breath, then sighed. "I tend to agree with Sam."

"Yes, sir. So do I. Which brings me to the next bit of concern. I can think of only one reason why Sam Vincent became a target. Sally Blake's killer is still around, learned the case was reopened and intends to get rid of anyone from before who was connected to the case in any way."

Carver frowned. "That's pretty far-fetched, considering you have no facts to back it up. As for your witness…do we know anything new?"

"No, nothing yet, but Maria Slade was with me the other day when I talked to Vincent. She was also with me when I went to Becky Clemmons' house—and she's Tank's sister, if you can believe that. If someone leaked word that Maria's our witness, she's going to be at risk right along with Vincent and Mrs. Clemmons."

Carver's eyes narrowed as the silence grew. Finally he nodded.

"You make sure no more people die and I'll see what I can find out about who leaked info and to whom."

"Yes, sir," Bodie said.

As soon as he left the office, he checked his voice mail and saw that Becky Clemmons had called while he was in with his boss. Her message was clear and brief.

"Detective, this is Becky Clemmons. Just wanted to let you know I have Sally's things that were in storage. I'll be home all day if you want to come by."

Bodie frowned, then dialed Maria's number, but his call went to voice mail. All he could do was leave a message for her to call him immediately, and then he returned Becky's call.

Maria found Becky's house without one wrong turn. As she pulled into the driveway and got out, Becky opened the front door and came out on the porch to meet her.

"You made good time," Becky said.

Maria smiled. "You gave me amazingly good directions."

Becky grinned. "Probably all those years as a 911 dispatcher telling people what to do in times of crisis. Come in, come in. After last night's rain, it's like a sauna outside today."

"The weather is certainly different from Montana this time of year," Maria said, and followed Becky into the house.

The promised boxes were in the middle of the living room floor, and Becky had pushed back a coffee table and a settee to make room for the contents.

"We're going to make a mess," Maria said.

"I don't care. I cleaned them off when I brought them in. They'd gotten pretty dusty in the storage facility. Truth is…I peeked in one of them last night and can hardly wait to see what's in the rest. It's been so long, I don't remember."

"Then that makes two of us," Maria said.

Becky patted her on the arm. "Don't push it, honey. There was a reason why you needed to forget this. And now there's a reason why you need to remember. I'm trusting that your strength as a survivor is going to get you through this, like it did before."

"Wow," Maria said softly. "I never looked at it like that."

Becky shrugged. "It's true that some wisdom does come with age." Then she giggled. "Then again, there are some people who just get old and hopeless. You can't change stupid."

Maria laughed. It was the first time she'd felt at ease with this woman, and she told herself to just let go and quit trying to control everything.

"So, do you want to get started?" Becky asked. "Can I get you something to drink?"

"Yes, I'm ready, but I don't need anything to drink right now," Maria said.

"Sit anywhere you like," Becky said.

Maria dumped her purse on the sofa, then sat down on the floor and tucked her hair behind her ear before she reached for the first box.

Becky gasped softly as she saw the small gesture, then quickly looked away for fear Maria would see her tears. That one little action—tucking her hair behind her right ear—was something Sally had always done without thinking.

Unaware of what she'd done, Maria pulled the nearest box closer, then reached in and pulled out the first paper-wrapped object.

"This is sort of like Christmas," she said.

Becky touched the top of Maria's head. "And all the gifts are from your mother," she said, then took a seat in a nearby chair.

Maria's hands were shaking as she began peeling back the paper. Dust motes rose into the air, then seemed to hover in the beams of light coming through the living room windows, creating an aura of shimmering gold around her.

One by one, she carefully unwrapped the simple treasures that had once been a part of Sally Blake's world. By the time the first box was empty, Becky was on the floor with Maria, sometimes laughing, sometimes crying, from the memories they evoked.

And while Maria was fascinated by the unveiling, part of her was beginning to panic. Nothing looked familiar. Nothing rang even the smallest bell of memory.

When she pulled the second box close, she paused, her hands on the lid. There was a tremble in her voice that she couldn't deny, and a growing knot in her stomach, when she asked, "Becky...what if this doesn't help?"

Becky cupped Maria's cheek. "You'll still have your mother's treasures, won't you?"

Maria's vision blurred. "I'm so determined to remember the bad stuff that I forgot I could still remember the good. Thank you for that. I never thought of it that way."

"I think it's time for that drink. Would you rather have iced tea or a cold pop? I have Dr Pepper and Pepsi."

"Pepsi. Bodie and I like Pepsi," Maria said.

Becky smiled to herself as she went to the kitchen. Maria didn't even realize how she'd paired herself with the detective.

She brought back the drinks and set Maria's to the side on a small end table beside the sofa, then resumed her seat on the floor just as Maria began on the second box. Within moments of taking out the first package, Maria's eyes widened.

"This one is kind of heavy...and round." She peeled away the last bits of paper. "Oh, wow! A Christmas snow globe. I have a collection of snow globes back home in Montana."

"That was yours," Becky said, watching Maria's eyes widen in surprise. "It used to play music."

An odd shiver slithered through Maria's memory. Lord. Her fascination with snow globes had been linked to her past, and she hadn't known it.

She turned the globe over, saw that the little key was still there and wound it up. She had doubts that it would work after all these years, but after she gave it a couple of shakes, the little Christmas tree in the middle of the scene began turning, and a tinny-sounding lilt began playing in accompaniment to the white, swirling snow.

Becky frowned. "I can't place that melody. It sounds familiar but—"

Something was pushing at the back of Maria's mind—the sound of laughter, the brush of a kiss against her cheek, with a "sleep tight, don't let the bed bugs bite"—but it was gone so quickly that she could have imagined it.

"It's 'Twinkle, Twinkle, Little Star,'" Maria whispered, then set the globe on the floor near her knee. She was reaching back into the box when Becky's phone rang.

"Rats. I left it on the hall table," Becky muttered, and hurried to answer.

"Hello?"

"Mrs. Clemmons, it's Detective Scott. I got your message. By any chance, have you heard from Maria Slade?"

"She's sitting on my living room floor as we speak, going through her mother's things."

Bodie breathed a quick sigh of relief.

"Have you talked to your brother?"

"Yes."

"Does Maria know what happened?"

"I haven't said anything about it yet. I thought this was enough to deal with for the time being."

"Good. I'll talk to her when I get there. Tell her I'm on my way."

"Will do," Becky said, then hung up.

She glanced across the room, and for a moment it was as if twenty years had never passed and she was seeing Mary sitting on her floor playing, just as she'd done so many times before. Then she blinked and the notion was gone.

"That was Detective Scott," Becky said, as she sat back down. "He said to tell you he's on his way."

Maria didn't respond. She was staring at a pair of salt and pepper shakers that she'd just unwrapped. A little white hen with a red comb, and a rooster with a big red comb and a tail painted in garish colors. Without thinking, she shook the hen, watching blankly as a few tiny grains of salt fell out onto the wrappings. And the longer she looked, the faster her heart began to beat.

"I've seen these before." She picked them up and turned them so Becky could see. "I've seen these before! Oh, my God…they had names. They did, didn't they?"

Becky started to answer, then stopped. It wouldn't help at all if she told. Instead, she held her breath and prayed.

Maria closed her eyes. The words were right there—waiting…waiting—just out of reach.

"The little hen and the big rooster…they had names. They had names. But what—" She gasped as her eyes flew open. "Matt and Kitty. Their names were Matt and Kitty."

"Yes, because you and your mother watched reruns of *Gunsmoke* all the time. It was her favorite show. I always thought it was because she identified with Kitty…them being in the same profession."

Maria's eyes filled with tears. "It's going to happen, isn't it? Like you said, it's going to take time, but this is a start. I'm going to remember."

Fifteen

By the time Bodie reached Becky Clemmons' house, Maria had emptied the second box and was on to the third. Her eyes were sparkling from the excitement of the hunt, and from the high of knowing that when it came to her memory, all was not lost.

Becky saw him drive up and went to the door before he could knock. She let him in the house, then put a finger to her lips and pointed.

The sight stopped him in his tracks. Maria was cross-legged on the floor, with a pile of wrapping behind her and the contents of two boxes spread out in front of her. Her head was down, her focus fixed on the paper-wrapped object in her lap. As if sensing his presence, she looked up, then broke into a smile.

Bodie's gut knotted. *Have mercy. How did this happen? I am falling in love with a woman I hardly know.*

"How's it going?" he asked, as he walked over toward the empty chair beside her.

"Careful," she said, pointing to her little unwrapped treasures. "See those?" She pointed to a hen-and-rooster salt-and-pepper set. "Their names are Matt and Kitty. I remembered that. It's because my mother and I watched reruns of *Gunsmoke*. Isn't that funny?"

Bodie sat with a thump, then looked up at Becky in surprise.

"She remembered on her own?"

Becky beamed. "Yes, and that snow globe, as well."

"It plays 'Twinkle, Twinkle Little Star,'" Maria said. "Mommy wound it every night when we were going to sleep."

Becky's eyes were filling with tears again, as they had off and on all morning. Maria didn't realize she'd unconsciously shifted how she referenced her mother. She'd gone from thinking of her as Sally to my mother to Mommy in the space of a couple of hours.

Bodie was elated. For the first time since Maria Slade had walked into the station, he was beginning to believe they might actually have a chance of solving this case.

"Oh, look! Is this a diary? No...I think it's a photo album," Maria said.

"Can't be a diary," Becky said. "Your mother couldn't read or write, remember?"

Maria opened the book, and the crudely printed and misspelled words literally leaped off the pages. "Oh, my God. Becky, look!"

Becky gasped.

    marys babe bok

"I never saw her write anything but her name," Becky said. "And even that was difficult for her." She handed the book back to Maria.

Bodie was watching Maria's face as she began leafing through the pages, and when she suddenly clutched the book against her chest and began to cry, he sat down on the floor beside her.

Maria took a deep, shuddering breath and then laid the open book back in her lap. When Bodie saw the pages, the love of a mother for her child came alive. Sally Blake might not have been able to write, but she'd kept a journal of her baby's life in the only way she knew how. In pictures.

"May I?" he asked.

Maria handed him the book, then got up and stumbled out of the room. Becky followed. Bodie could hear her guiding Maria down the hall to her bathroom as he opened the book at the first page.

A tiny footprint and handprint had been stamped on the page, along with an old Polaroid snapshot of a tiny baby in a hospital nursery.

The next page had a tiny wisp of black hair taped to the page.

Each ensuing page had a different photo. One of Mary having a bath.

One of her standing beside a sofa, able to pull herself up but before she was walking.

Then a photo of Mary standing alone in the middle of a floor wearing nothing but a bib and a diaper.

Someone had taken a photo of Sally and Mary standing in front of the gorilla cage in a zoo. Bodie wondered if Mary's absentee father had been on that trip, and if he was the one who'd snapped the photo.

Page after page, there were mementos of a little girl's life, marked in the only way Sally knew how. It was no wonder Maria had dissolved into tears. Love radiated from every page.

Then Maria came back into the room.

"Sorry," she muttered, as she sat back down on the floor. "It just took me by surprise."

Bodie stroked the side of her cheek, then handed the book back to her.

She thumbed through the rest of the pages until she came to the last photo and once again was taken aback. It was a picture of her playing on the floor and surrounded by a dozen or more tiny, brightly colored horses.

"Oh, oh, oh…my ponies…my ponies."

Her hands were shaking as she laid the book aside and began digging frantically through the contents of the last box. All of a sudden she pulled out a large shoe box and rocked back on her heels.

"What is it?" Becky asked.

Maria opened the lid, and then dumped them out onto the floor and began setting them up as she must have done as a child.

Her ponies.

"The herd. It's my herd of My Little Ponies. I remember playing with these. They were my favorite toys."

"And now you train real ones," Bodie said.

Maria shivered. Again the ghost of her past was rearing its head into the present.

"I always thought I loved horses because Dad and

Bud raised them. I didn't know… I didn't remember… about this…about having them before."

She picked up the book, absently flipping through the blank pages to the end.

"I guess that's all," she said, but as she came to the back flyleaf, she saw a few more words. Suddenly she gasped.

"Oh, my God, look. It says 'marys dade,' only there's no picture. Just the words. I guess the photo got lost."

"Let me see," Bodie asked.

Maria handed it over.

From where he'd been sitting, he'd seen a crease on the inside flyleaf, as if it had been pulled loose, then glued back down. He ran his finger along the edges, then frowned as he ran the flat of his hand across the page itself.

"There's something under here," he said as he pulled out a pocketknife. He carefully cut a slit along the bottom and side of the cover, then removed a single folded sheet of paper.

Bodie scanned the page, and when he realized what it was, he looked up.

"This is a lab report on a DNA sample. It doesn't have a name on it, but listen to what it does say.

"'Sample is 99.9 percent consistent with being the biological father of Mary Blake.' Wow. Sally Blake might not have been able to read, but she wasn't stupid. Somehow she got a DNA sample from your biological father and sent it off to some lab so she'd have proof."

Maria snatched the page out of his hands and quickly

scanned it, but he was right. There was no designated name for the donor. Only a series of numbers identifying the sample.

"Is there a way to find out who the donor was?" she asked.

"It's been twenty years. I doubt this lab is still in operation, but I'll check. I can, however, run these results through the computer. If the man had ever had an occasion to have a DNA sample run through CODIS, we might get a hit. Either way, it's still a long shot. Can I take this?"

"Yes, yes," Maria said, and handed it to him, then took Becky's hand. "I cannot thank you enough for saving all this. Not only have you given me the only link I'll ever have with my mother, but thanks to you, we're closer to finding out who killed her than anyone's ever been."

Becky was elated. But while she was happy the past was being revealed, even in small increments, there was something Maria also needed to know about the present. She stood up, then glanced at Bodie.

"It's after twelve. I'm going to make some sandwiches. Will you stay and eat with me? Nothing fancy, but I'd love the company."

Bodie glanced at Maria. She nodded.

"That would be great," he said. "But as soon as we've finished, I want to get back to the office with this."

Becky raised an eyebrow, then stared pointedly.

"I'm sure you two have plenty you need to discuss. Take your time. I'll call you when lunch is ready."

Maria began rewrapping her treasures to be shipped back to Montana, then stopped. Since some of them were breakable, she wanted to use bubble wrap instead of the old newspapers they'd been in to ensure their safe arrival.

Bodie stopped her with a touch, then took her by the hand and pulled her down beside him on the sofa.

"We need to talk."

The tone of his voice put a knot in Maria's stomach.

"What happened?"

"Last night, up at the lake, someone broke into Sam Vincent's house and tried to kill him."

Maria gasped. "Oh, my God. Is he all right? Did they catch the guy who—"

"Sam's fine. The man kicked in his door. Shot and killed his dog, and tried to take Sam out. *Sam* killed *him*, instead."

"That's awful…just awful. Was it a robbery gone bad?"

"Not according to Sam." He proceeded to tell her about Sam's belief that it had to do with the reopening of her mother's murder case. When Bodie mentioned that the killer had called Sam "Tank" and the implication of that, she paled.

"So you're saying…?" she began.

"That it probably wasn't a robbery, that the man was there to kill someone connected to Sally's past. What we don't know is why someone wants Sam dead now, when it didn't matter before, unless they've somehow linked you to the case, and then to him."

"But how? I didn't tell anyone but you."

Bodie frowned. "There might be a leak in the department. My boss is on it. We're not sure how it's all going to play out, but you and Becky need to be careful. Don't open your door to anyone unless you know them, and if you haven't ordered room service, don't open the door to anyone from the hotel, even if they're dressed in a hotel uniform."

"A man's dead—maybe because of me," Maria whispered, and covered her face.

"Don't feel sorry for him," Bodie said. "He took his chances when he messed with Sam Vincent. What you need to take heart in is the fact that maybe secrets are starting to unfold, which is what needs to happen to solve the mystery."

"Yes, okay. I get what you mean, but it's also frightening. I've never been involved in something criminal. I haven't even had a speeding ticket."

Bodie cupped the side of her cheek. "But that's just it, Maria. You *have* been involved…in a murder. And you're finally beginning to remember how."

Maria felt the weight of the world on her shoulders as she leaned into his touch. This was hard—so hard.

Suddenly Becky called them from the hall.

"Lunch is ready!"

"Be right there," Bodie said.

He got up, then offered Maria his hand. Their fingers laced as he pulled her up, but instead of stopping, she wrapped her arms around his waist and hid her face against his chest.

He pulled her close, his voice low and urgent when he spoke.

"I'm sorry for the reason you had to come back to Tulsa, and that you're having to go through all this, but I'm not sorry you came. I can't imagine living my life and never having known you."

He tilted her chin until their gazes locked.

Maria slid her hand behind his neck and pulled.

He groaned beneath his breath as their lips met, and then his hands were on her back and sliding down to her hips and holding her close—as close against him as she could be without him being inside her.

Becky came into the room, grinned, and did a two-step backward and out before they ever knew she'd been there.

The meal was nearly over when Bodie's phone rang. It didn't take long for him to make an apologetic exit.

"Duty calls," he said, then thanked Becky for lunch and eyed Maria. "Walk me to the door?"

She followed him out, then stopped just inside the front door. She knew he was going to kiss her even before it happened and would have been disappointed if he hadn't. It didn't matter that she hadn't known him long. She just knew she liked him, which was something she hadn't felt in years.

"Are you going back to the hotel soon?" he asked.

"Not for a while. I feel like I should stay as long as

Becky will put up with me. Being here with her, among all these things from my past, has given me hope that my memory will return in full. I don't want to miss an opportunity."

He pulled her into his arms.

"Lady…you're so getting under my skin."

Maria put her arms around his neck and tilted her face up for the kiss.

"I like you, too," she said softly, and then he swooped.

One kiss led to another, then another until he finally broke off with a groan.

"Lord, have mercy. I want. I want *you*," he whispered, then swept another quick, hard kiss across her mouth before leaving her standing in the doorway, wanting him back.

But he was gone.

Maria shivered as she went back into the kitchen to help clean up the dishes.

Becky eyed the pensive expression on Maria's face as she came back and smiled to herself. Her baby was falling for the cop. She just hoped no one got hurt out of the deal. When Maria grabbed a dishcloth and began cleaning off the table, Becky had a moment of déjà vu. She paused with her hands in the dishwater and just stared.

"You have to know, right now I feel like twenty years have disappeared, and Sally and I are cleaning up from lunch, like we have a hundred times before."

Maria looked up. "Tell me stories," she said, as she came back to the sink.

And so the afternoon passed.

When it came time for Maria to leave, Becky handed her a key.

"What's this?" Maria asked.

"A key to my house. I have a hair appointment in the morning, and you might want to start packing before I get back."

Maria frowned. "Oh, I don't feel right taking your key."

"Why?"

"Because you don't really know me. I might—"

Becky sighed. "Honey, I know enough. Take the key. I should be back around eleven. How about I bring some KFC home with me?"

"You don't have to feel obligated to keep feeding me, either. I could take you out somewhere later."

"We'll see," Becky said. "I don't suppose you'd consider moving out of the hotel and staying here until the case is closed? It would save you a lot of money, and you know I have room."

Now Maria was really touched. "I don't know. That's a huge imposition," she said. "Let's take this one day at a time and see how it goes."

Becky shrugged. "Okay. It's your call, but just know that from my standpoint, you're free to come and go as you please."

"Thank you," Maria said, then went into the living room to sort through what needed to be shipped, separating the things into piles of breakables and unbreakables, and getting them out of the middle of Becky's floor.

She left late that afternoon with a head full of stories and a peace in her heart that she hadn't felt since the day her drama had begun.

Franklin was desperate. He'd called in a favor to find out why the Sally Blake case had been reopened, and the news couldn't have been worse. Maria Slade had supposedly witnessed her mother's murder. There was added info about coming back with a journal and amnesia that he hadn't quite understood. It wasn't until he learned of an upcoming appointment with a hypnotherapist to help Maria remember what she'd suppressed that his blood ran cold.

He couldn't let that happen, but his go-to man had gone and gotten himself killed. He was getting desperate. Did he take the chance of trusting someone else? What if that went wrong, too? What if the perp was caught and, to save himself, confessed to who had hired him? The more Franklin thought about it, the more certain he was that he was going to have to do the job himself.

Then reason surfaced. He'd gotten away with murder once. He wasn't stupid enough to think he could go back in with guns blazing and get so lucky again. Maria wasn't her mother. She wasn't living in a seedy part of Tulsa and living a life that, to the general public, didn't count. She was obviously a reputable woman, and her death would raise a stink. No one would buy it was an accident. Not after she'd come forward as a witness to a murder. But this time there was no dirty cop to hide evidence, and this couldn't be helped. He had to control the situation, and for that to happen, the witness—the link between himself and Sally Blake—had to disappear.

He grabbed his Rolodex, desperate for a solution to his problem. As he was flipping through, a name caught his eye. He paused. This would mean shelling out more money, but he had that—though he'd planned on using it as a buffer during the election. However, if this woman really had seen what happened, there wouldn't be an election to worry about. As he reached for the phone, it occurred to him how convenient it was that he'd spent his life representing the criminal element. This would be a way for them to give back. Then he frowned. The only problem with that theory was that the criminal element didn't have a conscience, and he was going to have to do some fast talking to make this work.

Beads of sweat lined Tom Jack Bailey's upper lip as the blond-haired beauty astraddle him worked her hundred-dollar blow job.

She was good. But what she was doing felt better. The climax was only seconds away, and Tom Jack was already losing his mind, when his cell phone began to ring.

He cursed beneath his breath. What the hell had possessed him to download Merle Haggard's "Okie from Muskogee" as his ring tone? It immediately reminded him of where he'd come from and the father who'd beaten him on a regular basis, before he'd gotten big enough to fight back.

The cell kept ringing and ringing. He grabbed it and flung it across the room, where it hit the wall before falling to the floor. And kept on ringing.

"Don't stop," he growled, and closed his eyes, struggling to hold on to the feeling.

But the image evoked by the ring tone was too strong. The last time he'd seen his father, it had been pitch dark near the banks of the Canadian River, and he'd been covering his body with shovelfuls of red Oklahoma dirt.

He lost his erection and his temper, both at the same time, and slapped the blonde.

"Get the hell out!" he roared.

She scrambled for her clothes, dressing as she moved, and was out the door carrying her shoes before she'd buttoned her blouse.

Furious and frustrated, he stomped across the motel room and grabbed the phone, which had finally gone to voice mail. Some son of a bitch had left a message. It better be good. Then he heard the voice, remembered the man and, out of curiosity, returned the call.

Franklin was frustrated and pacing, trying to figure out who to call next when his phone rang. Since he was using another throw-away phone and the only person he'd called was Tom Jack, his hopes rose.

"Franklin Sheets."

"So it really was you."

Relieved, Franklin sank into a chair behind his desk. "Yes, it's me. I need a favor."

Tom Jack grinned. Maybe this was going to be worth the loss of the blow job after all.

"What kind of favor?"

"I have a problem I need cleaned up."

"Why call me?"

Franklin's voice shifted angrily. "Don't play games, Bailey. We both know what you do, and you're a free man right now because of what *I* do. Are you willing or not?"

Tom Jack frowned. He didn't like threats, and that had sounded a lot like one.

"I'm free because the fucking law made a fucking mistake and you caught them at it. I paid good money for your representation."

"And I'm willing to pay good money for yours," Franklin countered.

Tom Jack smiled. "Well now, if we're going to talk business, I need details."

Franklin proceeded to give them.

When he hung up later, the deal was done. But he'd learned something from the first hit man he'd hired. No money was changing hands until the job was done.

The next day came with more rain. Maria was sound asleep, dreaming about Montana and trying to pull a cow out of a snowdrift, when her cell phone rang. She had it to her ear before she opened her eyes.

"Hello?" she mumbled.

"Ahhh, dang it. I woke you, didn't I?"

The low whiskey-rough rumble in his voice was a surprisingly charming way to be wakened.

"It's okay," she said, and stretched, groaning softly as her muscles reacted.

The soft groan in Bodie's ear sent a shock wave of longing straight through him. He sighed.

"You sound sexy as hell when you wake up. Wish I was there to *see* it, too."

Maria smiled. The day hadn't even started, and already he was flirting. She loved it.

"Dad used to say 'if wishes were horses, beggars would ride.'"

He frowned. "So are you saying that will never happen…or that poor people can't own horses?"

She laughed out loud.

Again the sound ripped through Bodie like a knife. He was on the verge of hanging up and heading for her hotel when Dave came into the office and waved to indicate they had to go.

He nodded an okay, then wound up the call.

"I just called to say be careful today. I'm only a phone call away if you need me, and also…will you go out to dinner with me tonight?"

Maria rolled over on her belly and closed her eyes. "Yes. Call me later with details—and you be careful, too."

"Yes, ma'am," Bodie said, and hung up with a grin, dropped his cell phone in his pocket and grabbed his service revolver out of his desk drawer as he hurried to catch up with Dave.

* * *

Maria ate breakfast on the go, dodging rain showers as she went from store to store, buying bubble wrap and packing tape, then large boxes in which to ship the things back to the Triple S. She could just imagine Bud's expression when UPS delivered them to the doorstep. She would have to give him a call and a heads-up before their arrival.

As she shopped, Tom Jack drove his black, low-slung classic Camaro in her wake. And when she left her last stop and started toward Becky Clemmons' house, he slid the Camaro into the stream of traffic only a couple of cars behind her.

When she turned north off of Memorial and then into the neighborhood where Becky's house was located, he turned with her, taking care to stay at least a full block behind. Then he watched as, windshield wipers working overtime, she pulled up into the double-wide driveway to Becky's house.

Maria noticed immediately that the other woman's car wasn't under the carport, which meant she was still getting her hair done. Maria grabbed her purchases and headed for the front door as the rain pelted down. Thankful for the covered porch, she dropped her things long enough to locate Becky's key, then let herself in the house and locked the door.

She felt like an interloper being in this house alone, but Becky had been adamant that Maria was family, and that she could come and go as she pleased.

After a quick trip to the bathroom, she settled in to her task.

Outside, satisfied that the rain would provide him cover, Tom Jack pulled up closer, then got out and ran toward her car, everything he needed tucked under his arm.

Within a few seconds, he had disappeared beneath her car.

The rain continued to pour.

Thunder rumbled, followed by the occasional shaft of lightning.

A minute or so later, he rolled out from under the vehicle, leaped the curb, jumped in the Camaro and sped away. Then, just to make sure he'd been unobserved, he drove around the block and parked at the far end, waiting to see if someone came out or the police showed up. When fifteen minutes had passed and nothing had changed except the increasing rainfall, he put the car in gear and drove away.

Sixteen

The boxes were packed, the labels printed. All Maria had to do was get them to a UPS shipping office.

"By the time you drive clear across town, I think it will be too late," Becky said. "Why don't you just leave them here and come back tomorrow? It will surely have quit raining, and it will be easier to load and unload them then."

Maria swept her hair behind her ear, then moved her head from side to side, easing the crick in her neck. The packing had been more exhausting than she'd imagined, mostly because she'd gone over each object a second time, as if discovering it all over again.

"You sure? It will mean one more night with a mess in your living room," she said.

Becky grinned. "So? It's not like I've got a social life anymore. I'm going to bed soon, and I'll be up and at work before the sun comes up. It can't possibly be in my way."

"Okay. You talked me into it," Maria said, then

glanced out the window. "Looks like the rain is about to let up. It's still sprinkling, but nothing like it was before."

"You sure you won't stay for dinner?" Becky asked.

"Bodie's taking me out to eat."

Becky grinned. "That detective has certainly caught your attention, hasn't he?"

Maria shrugged. "Can you blame me? Where I grew up, every other man I know is a cowboy or has something to do with ranching. Bodie may be a homicide detective, but he stands out for me with that hat and boots."

Becky laughed. "And he's pretty, besides."

"I admit he's far from ugly. But it's his heart that gets to me."

"Okay, have a good time with your cowboy cop, and if there's anything you need, don't hesitate to ask. And remember what I said. When you get sick of that hotel room, pack up your stuff and come stay here."

Tears burned the back of Maria's throat.

"Thank you. I see why my mother thought so much of you," she said, and gave the older woman a swift kiss on the cheek. "I'll call you tomorrow."

"Have fun this evening," Becky said.

Maria smiled and waved as she headed out the door, only to be met with blowing drizzle. She jumped off the steps, hitting the remote control as she ran so that the door would be unlocked when she got there.

Then the world exploded.

* * *

It was just after five when Bodie and Dave arrived back at headquarters. They were on their way into the precinct to write up their report when Bodie's phone rang. When he saw it was from Becky, he stopped in the stairwell, waved Dave on and answered.

"Detective Scott."

All he could hear were sirens, and Becky screaming words that made no sense at him over and over.

"What? What? Becky! Slow down! I can't understand you! What happened? Why am I hearing sirens?"

When Dave heard Bodie's side of the conversation, he stopped on the stairs and turned around, watching intently.

At the other end of the line, Becky Clemmons took a breath, then made herself focus when all she wanted to do was scream.

"I said…Maria's hurt…bad! The paramedics are with her now. She was just leaving my house on her way to the car when it blew up. Oh, God, oh, God… Bodie, it was a bomb. Someone tried to kill her!"

Bodie's legs went out from under him. He grabbed onto the stair railing to keep from falling.

"Oh, Jesus…no," he whispered, and then adrenaline spiked as he shifted into cop mode. "Where are they taking her?"

"Saint Francis."

"I'll meet you there."

He disconnected, then looked up the stairwell at Dave.

"Tell Carver someone just tried to kill Maria Slade."

Dave already knew that Bodie had a thing for the woman. He'd teased him more than once about fraternizing with someone connected to a case, but he hadn't seen this coming.

"Oh, no…man, I'm sorry. How? What happened?"

"Car bomb. I'm on my way to Saint Francis now."

"Yeah, go, go…I'll do the report and tell the L.T. Call me when you know something more."

But Bodie was already down the stairs and out the door. And all the way to the hospital, all he could think about was that they hadn't had enough time. He wanted more. He *needed* more. Like a lifetime. The only thing he could do was pray that she survived.

Maria came to in the ambulance. The pain in her body and head was so intense that she woke up with a scream.

The EMT working on her quickly began talking, trying to get through to her enough to calm her down.

"Maria. Maria! It's okay. You're in an ambulance. There was an explosion, and you were injured."

"Hurts…" she mumbled, then started pushing at his hands and what felt like wire holding her down.

The EMT grabbed her hands to keep her from pulling out her IVs.

"Yes, ma'am, we're on the way to Saint Francis Hospital. Lie still. You need to lie still."

Enough of what he was saying soaked in, but before she could talk, she passed out again.

The next time she came to, she was in a room. People were moving all around her, and she could hear a man issuing orders but couldn't focus enough on what he was saying to figure out where she was. The last thing she heard was "We're losing her," and then everything went black.

Becky was sitting in a chair in the E.R. when Bodie rushed in. He took one look at the tears on her face and his stomach dropped. *God. Please don't let her be dead.*

"Becky!"

She looked up, the horror of what she'd seen still etched on her face.

"This is déjà vu hell. I watched Sally die in a pool of her own blood. Then…seeing Maria on her back like that… Blood…so much blood kept coming, and then the rain would dilute it and wash it away. Oh, my God." She covered her face with her hands.

Bodie sat down beside her. "Is she dead?" Even as he was saying the words, he wanted to scream.

Becky gasped, then looked up. "No! No! I'm sorry, I didn't mean for you to think that. I don't know how she is. They wouldn't let me see her."

He jammed his Stetson tighter onto his head. "I'll be back."

He strode toward the E.R. with his badge in his hand.

The first person who challenged his presence got a close-up view in their face.

"Where's the car bomb victim? Where's Maria Slade?"

The nurse pointed. "They're working on her in there, but you need to—"

He pushed past her and then hurried across the hall, moving as fast as he could without running, then slipped into the room unnoticed.

They'd cut off her clothes. Two nurses were picking tiny bits of glass from one side of her body, while another was slipping an oxygen cannula onto her nose. He stepped aside as a portable X-ray machine was wheeled into the room. It was a living nightmare. He began silently praying, making deals with God while his anger at whoever had done this grew into full-blown rage.

By the time they were finished, almost an hour had passed. She had six staples in her scalp, two stitches in one leg and four in an arm. They were waiting for X-ray readings on her ribs and monitoring the inevitable concussion.

A doctor started out of the room, and Bodie stopped him. He flashed the badge again, then asked, before he could be ordered out, "Is she going to live?"

"Yes, barring any unexpected complications. There's no internal bleeding. We're waiting on X-rays to determine if she has any broken ribs, which I'm expecting, due to the amount of bruising."

The room was spinning, but Bodie held on to the fact

that she was alive. Right now, he would ask for nothing else.

"Where are you taking her?" he asked.

"I'm putting her in ICU for the night, just to be safe," the doctor added. "If she wakes up and there are no surprises, she could be moved to a regular room in the morning."

Bodie started counting off his rules.

"There will be a guard posted at the door to ICU. She is not to have any visitors except for the names I'll leave with the nurse. She is the only witness in a murder investigation, and we have reason to believe this was an attempt to permanently silence her."

The doctor's eyes widened.

"Uh…yes, of course. I'll inform ICU."

"Can I talk to her?" Bodie asked.

"She's not conscious, and we're moving her shortly."

"I'll be standing guard until you do."

The doctor nodded. "Make sure you coordinate the guard situation with the RN in ICU."

"I want the names of the nurses and doctors who'll be on duty tonight."

The doctor frowned. "What for? Our staff is above reproach."

"Do you know their financial status? Are any of them nearing bankruptcy? Does someone have a gambling habit that's got him in a deep hole?"

"Well, I'm sure I don't know, but—"

"We're talking murder. And for some people, the

need for money can rot every principle known to man. I've already got one death to investigate. I don't want two."

The doctor's nostrils flared. It was the only sign he gave of his displeasure, but he nodded.

"You'll have your information, but you don't interfere with my nurses or the other patients, either. Understood?"

"You understand this...I'll do whatever it takes to keep Maria Slade alive."

Sam Vincent had just hauled the buckshot-riddled and blood-soaked easy chair out the front door onto the porch. First chance he got, he was hauling it to the city dump. He'd never used that chair anyway and didn't have much company. No need stressing out about getting it replaced.

He looked around as he started inside, then remembered Pooch was dead, which saddened him deeply. Pooch had been family, and he didn't have enough family left to afford to lose any more.

The new door squeaked as he went back inside, which sent him straight to the cabinet to get some WD-40 for the hinges. The bloodstain on the hardwood floor was another thing he would have to deal with. He wasn't sure if it would come out. If not, well...he didn't have a problem looking at it for the next twenty or so years. A good reminder not to drop his guard ever again.

He was squirting down the last squeaky hinge when

his phone began to ring. One more squirt of WD-40 and then he dug it out of his pocket.

"Hello?"

"Sammy…"

Becky was crying. The sound sent a shiver of fear straight through him.

"What's wrong, sugar? Tell me, Beck. What happened?"

"Mary…she's in the hospital. Someone put a bomb in her car, and it went off just as she stepped off my front porch."

Sam stepped backward, feeling for a chair, but couldn't find one, then slid to the floor, his legs shaking so bad they wouldn't hold his weight.

"Is she dead?"

"No."

"Are you hurt?"

"No."

"Thank God. How bad is she?"

"Stitches and cuts from flying glass. Concussion. Might have some broken ribs. She's in ICU in Saint Francis."

"They got a guard on her?"

"Yes. Detective Scott…I think he's in love with her…. He nearly lost it. He's raised hell all over this hospital. Got doctors pissed and nurses afraid to go into her room."

"I'm on my way."

"What are you going to do?"

"I couldn't keep Sally alive. This is my second chance to make things right."

"What do you mean?"

"I'm coming to the hospital, and I'm not letting Mary out of my sight until that damned killer is either locked up or six feet under."

The line went dead in Becky's ear.

Despite the fact that no one was allowed in ICU outside of visiting hours, Bodie was in a chair beside Maria's bed. He watched everyone who tended her with a hard, steely gaze, impervious to intermittent attempts to make him leave. A hospital security guard had arrived early on and been met with Bodie's badge and an angry look, a clear signal that Homicide Detective trumped Security Guard and he was making too much noise.

The guard left.

Bodie didn't.

Time passed.

Suddenly a nurse was tapping him on the shoulder.

"Detective…Robert Tate is on the phone. I've informed him of Miss Slade's condition, but when he found out you were here, he asked to talk to you."

"Robert Tate? Who's Robert Tate?"

"The man listed on Miss Slade's wallet card as the person to notify in case of an emergency."

He got up from the chair, glanced down at Maria, then at the machines they'd hooked up to her. Satisfied that nothing had changed, he followed the woman back to the nurses' station and picked up the phone.

"This is Detective Scott."

"Detective…I'm Bud Tate. What the hell happened?"

Ah. Bud was a name he knew. "Someone put a bomb in her car. We think when she hit the remote to unlock her door, it triggered the bomb. Thank God she wasn't in the car when it detonated. The doctor said her injuries will heal. I'm here to make sure she doesn't incur any more."

Bud felt sick to his stomach. He couldn't quit pacing and couldn't think what to do next.

"I can be there sometime tomorrow—not sure what time."

"Mr. Tate, she hasn't awakened yet. I won't leave her side until she does, and at no time will she be unguarded. You and I don't know each other, but if I have my way, one of these days we will. Of course you can come if you want, but don't think she won't be taken care of. I assure you, I will see to that."

Despite his panic, Bud managed a grin.

"The hell you say."

Bodie sighed. "Yeah. If you'll give me your number, I'll call you the minute she wakes up, then you can talk to her anytime after she's moved out of ICU."

Bud swiped a hand over his face, torn between the desire to board the first available flight to Tulsa and the overwhelming duties he was dealing with on the ranch on his own.

"Has she remembered anything? Last time I spoke to her, she was really down, afraid she would never remember."

"Bits and pieces, but nothing vital yet."

"Tell her I called."

"Yes, sir."

"Maybe you oughta start calling me Bud."

Bodie managed a grin. "Yeah, maybe so. What's your number?"

Bud gave him the numbers for the house phone and his cell phone.

"Stay in touch and take care of her. She's like my sister."

"Will do," Bodie said, then hung up and walked straight back to Maria's side.

He had strict instructions not to talk, because it would disturb the other patients, and he would honor that. But it didn't stop him from leaning over her bed and whispering in her ear.

"It's me, baby. Bud called. Becky's saying prayers. Everyone loves you…including me."

Then he brushed a kiss across her forehead and returned to his seat against the wall, so he could see everyone coming and going.

Franklin Sheets had driven twenty miles outside of Tulsa to a farm pond on the Bailey homestead. Tom Jack was the last living member of his family and resided in what was left of the old farmhouse with no regard for upkeep. Franklin knew the other man's demand for him to bring payment all the way out here was his way of controlling a man he didn't like. He also knew that what Bailey didn't know was that his target wasn't dead.

Franklin got out at the specified location, so mad he couldn't swallow his own spit. He was screaming and waving his arms like a madman.

"You fuck-up! What part of 'I want her gone' did you not understand?"

"What the hell are you talking about?" Tom Jack asked.

"She's alive. And according to the doctors, going to recover. The guard around her is tighter than a virgin's ass."

Tom Jack shook his head, trying to bluster his way through this debacle.

"Look. I planted a bomb that would put a hole in the side of a building. No way she lived through that."

"She wasn't in the car when it went off," Franklin snapped.

"But—"

"Apparently it went off prematurely. You fucked up!"

Tom Jack paled. "I don't see—"

Franklin pulled a handgun from his jacket pocket and fired point-blank.

The shocked expression on Tom Jack Bailey's face faded, like the light around him. He fell backward into the farm pond with a loud splash and slowly sank.

"For once, you were right. You *don't* see. Not any-more."

Franklin threw the gun into the deepest part of the pond and then brushed his hands off on his pants as he walked away.

Seventeen

It was just after 3:00 a.m. when Maria came to.

Pain, coupled with panic and confusion, rolled through her body in waves. She could hear muted voices and repetitive beeping. The room she was in was dim and scary. When she drew breath, the scent of antiseptic stung her nose. Her gaze fell on the thin beam of light beneath the door.

For no reason, she felt panic, then fear. She closed her eyes, willing the image away, but instead it grew. Something was out there. Something evil.

Mommy!

She flinched. That voice... It didn't belong here. Panic grew. A dark, swirling mist was right in front of her, and then it began to morph into a hall. There was a noise, then someone screamed.

Mommy Mommy Mommy!

She clutched her covers as her eyes flew open. The voice wasn't real. Unwilling to follow that hallway any farther, she made herself concentrate on where she was now.

It felt like a hospital, but she couldn't remember what had happened or why she would be here. Then she saw a Stetson hanging on the back of a chair. Her heart quickened as her gaze moved down.

Bodie. He was asleep in a chair, his head on her bed and his hand on her arm. Whatever had happened, he hadn't left her. She started to cry as she reached for him, her fingers tangling in his hair.

Bodie woke, then sat abruptly. Someone had pulled his hair. His gaze went straight to the bed; then he gasped. Maria! She was awake. He jumped up, talking in an urgent whisper.

"Maria...sweetheart...thank God, thank God."

She tried to speak, then winced as she licked at her lips.

"Don't talk," he whispered, then grabbed a damp washcloth and dabbed it along her dry lips. "You're in ICU. You're going to be okay, but you need to stay still."

Maria tugged on his hand.

He leaned closer.

"What...?" she asked, her voice trailing off.

He frowned. He wasn't sure how much to tell her, but he could see the stress and need to know in her eyes. He leaned closer. When her fingers curled around his, it felt as if she'd wrapped them around his heart. Then he bent down, whispering.

"I need to go let them know you're awake, so I'll make this quick. You were coming out of Becky's house when your car blew up. Someone put a bomb in it. We're dealing with it. All you need to do is get well."

Maria's fingers tightened on his. Her eyes widened, then closed. When tears rolled down her cheeks, Bodie wanted to cry with her.

"Maria...baby...don't cry. It's going to be okay. Are you in pain? I can go get the nurse."

Her grip tightened as she shuddered on a soft, quiet sob.

"Okay, I won't leave you." His voice broke. "I don't want to ever leave you again. Maria...sweetheart...I almost lost the chance to say this, so you're going to have to hear it whether you're ready or not." He paused, put his own finger to his lips and kissed it, then brushed it gently against *her* lips. "I'm falling in love with you."

The words affected Maria like water on a fire, cooling the heat of panic and filling her with a strength she hadn't known was missing. For a moment the uncertainty of the past seemed unimportant.

Her hands were shaking as she put a finger to her own mouth, then lifted her hand toward him.

He caught her hand, pressing the kiss against his lips.

"Thank you, baby. Hang in there for me. I'll be right back."

Bodie headed for the nurses' desk, where the RN on duty looked up as he approached.

"She woke up," he said softly.

The nurse came out of the chair and immediately went to Maria's bed. She began running a thorough check of Maria's vitals as Bodie stood out of the way.

"I need to notify her doctor," the woman said, and went back to the desk as Bodie resumed his seat.

Again Maria reached for his hand. The moment they touched, she took a slow breath and fell back asleep. But this time it didn't matter. This time Bodie knew she was going to get well.

When the shift changed at 7:00 a.m., Bodie stepped out into the waiting area to use his phone. To his surprise, not only was Becky there, but so was Sam.

The moment Sam saw him, he was on his feet. His expression seemed calm, until Bodie looked into his eyes. They were deadly.

"How is she?"

Bodie shoved a weary hand through his hair. "She woke up. At this point, the doctor is expecting a full recovery."

"Thank you, Jesus," Becky said, and dissolved into tears.

But Sam's expression never changed. "I'm here. I'm not leaving her. I won't walk away from this like I did before."

"Don't worry. When they move her out of ICU, I'll have a police guard outside her door round the clock."

"And I'll be right there with him. In fact, if no one's in the room with her, I'll be in a chair beside her bed. No one gets to her again while I'm alive."

Bodie hesitated. Allowing a civilian to participate in a police operation wasn't kosher, but in this case he had a feeling Sam was going to do his own thing, regardless.

"We'll work it out on a day-to-day basis," Bodie said.

"Can we see her?" Becky asked.

"As soon as the shift change is complete, the next visitation is allowed. She's allowed two visitors at a time, so you guys go. I'll wait until you're done before I go back in."

"They're letting you stay?" Becky asked.

"I didn't give them a choice," Bodie admitted. "I need to make a call to her family back in Montana…let them know about her progress."

"I'll be in there 'til you get back," Sam said.

Bodie eyed him. "Be right back," he said, then walked a short distance away to call Bud Tate, forgetting about the time difference.

Bud's call to Savannah and Holly about Maria's attack had been difficult. After getting them on a conference call, he told them what had happened. Their shock had turned into disbelief and then fear. The attempt on her life had driven home to them in the most brutal of ways that what they were doing was dangerous. After tears and plenty of warnings from Bud, they'd promised him faithfully that they would be careful.

After the call, sleep had been impossible. He'd finally drifted off around 3:00 a.m. When the phone rang only a couple of hours later, he woke up with a jerk. His first thought was that Maria had taken a turn for the worse.

He sat up, his voice shaking as he picked up the phone.

"Hello?"

"Bud, this is Detective Scott. Just wanted you to know that Maria woke up. The doctor is satisfied with her progress. I'm expecting them to move her to a private room sometime today, or early tomorrow at the latest."

"Oh, Jesus," Bud whispered, then swiped a shaky hand across his face. "Thank you, God."

"Yes, I agree. I don't have anything further to tell you about the bombing itself, because I haven't been to the station. As soon as I find out more, I'll call."

"You stayed with her last night?"

"Right beside her bed."

"I thought she was in ICU?"

"She is. Because of the danger, I forced them to make an exception."

"Thank you, sir. Thank you for watching out for our girl," Bud said.

"Make it Bodie, okay? Remember, I'm staking a claim on your family, if she'll let me."

Bud's relief was so great that he grinned. "Yeah, right. Bodie it is."

"Later," Bodie said, and hung up.

Despite the hour, Bud turned right around and called Maria's sisters. Savannah first, because she was in

Florida, where it was a little after seven o'clock, then Holly in Missouri, which was in the same time zone as Oklahoma. After reassuring them that Maria was going to get well, he lay back down, and for the first time since he'd gone to work for Andrew Slade, he overslept.

It was another day before they moved Maria from ICU to a private room. Bodie had a guard waiting at the door. And as they were wheeling Maria down the corridor, he realized that the guard already had company. Sam was sitting in a chair on the other side of the doorway, glaring at everyone who passed by, even though she wasn't even in the room yet.

Maria was awake, but still groggy from pain meds. She knew Bodie was walking beside the gurney. When she couldn't see him, she could still hear him—his stride was long, his steps solid.

As they stopped to turn the gurney into her new room, she saw the uniformed policeman on one side of the door, and then she saw Sam on the other.

She reached for his hand.

He patted her arm awkwardly, his eyes blurry with tears.

She was touched by his determination to watch over her. And Bodie… He had overwhelmed her in so many ways she couldn't count. He wasn't just becoming her knight in shining armor. He had claimed a place for himself within her world, whether she was ready or not.

"Bodie?"

"I'm here," he said, as they pushed her into her new room.

Bodie waited in the hall as they transferred her to the bed. As soon as the orderly came back out pushing the empty gurney, Bodie was back in the room and pulling up a chair beside her bed. He paused to sweep a lock of hair from her forehead.

She moaned.

"Are you hurting, honey?"

She exhaled slowly, then nodded.

"Hang in there. They said a nurse was bringing you something for the pain."

A muscle in her leg began to spasm. She clutched his hand even tighter as she tried to ride out the pain, and was exhausted and shaking when a nurse finally came in carrying a syringe.

The nurse nodded at Bodie, then moved to the other side of the bed, where the IV was hanging, reached for Maria's arm to check her identification bracelet, then eyed the drip before turning to Maria.

"Maria, my name is Carol. I'll be taking care of you until the shift change at midnight. Are you in pain?"

Maria nodded, then gritted her teeth as another muscle spasm racked her body.

I know, honey, I know," the nurse said sympathetically as she saw Maria wince. "That move from ICU was rough, but as soon as this kicks in, you'll be able to get some rest."

Maria eyed the meds she was being given. "Is this going to make me pass out?"

"Yes, ma'am, and I suggest you enjoy the ride," Carol said, and then winked as she emptied the syringe into the IV port, before leaving the room.

Outside, Sam had taken note of the nurse, as well as her name tag. He was watching her walk away when an elderly black man and a teenage boy half his size turned a corner and started up the hall. To his surprise, they stopped in front of the policeman guarding Maria's room.

The guard stood up as the older man spoke.

"Excuse me, but is this Maria Slade's room?"

Sam stood up.

"No visitors," the policeman said.

All of Sam's protective instincts kicked in. They'd barely gotten her moved and someone was already seeking her out.

Then the old man nodded his head, as if he'd expected the answer, and smiled.

"Do you think there is any way you might tell her Preacher Henry and Tyrell are here. I think she'd liked to know."

"Wait here," the guard said, and ducked his head into the room. "Detective Scott? A moment, please."

Sam eyed the newcomer's clerical collar with distrust, aware such things could easily be faked.

"You claiming to know her?" he snapped.

Henry smiled. "Yes, we do, don't we, Tyrell?"

Tyrell just glared.

When Bodie came to the door and saw the strangers, his first instinct was distrust.

"What's going on?"

Tyrell glared again.

Preacher Henry just smiled.

"We heard on the television about what happened to Miss Slade. I wanted to come say a prayer for her."

"You can pray in church," Bodie said.

"Yes, sir," Henry said, trying to hide his disappointment. "But maybe you would tell her we came. Tell her Preacher Henry and Tyrell from the John 3:16 Mission was here."

All of a sudden the connection clicked.

"Wait," Bodie said. "She *does* know you, doesn't she? She ate at your mission, right? You were talking to her about where she used to live."

Henry beamed. "Yes, sir, that's right! And she ate beans and corn bread with us, then washed dishes with Tyrell here, didn't she, son?"

Tyrell wouldn't give anything past a nod, but Bodie noticed the boy was at least eyeing him with curiosity rather than the baleful glare that was undoubtedly his normal reaction to "the Man."

"She also gave us a whole new kitchen," Henry said.

Bodie suspected that Maria would want to see them, but he wasn't sure she was up to it.

"Look. She's had a rough morning and is just falling back to sleep, but you can come in long enough to let her know you came, okay?"

"Thank you, thank you, and God bless," Henry said.

"Come on, Tyrell. Come say hello to your dishwashing partner."

They went straight to Maria's bed.

Bodie watched the shock come and go on the preacher's face, but the boy's expression was harder to read.

Then the preacher laid his hand on Maria's forehead.

"Hey there, young lady. What did you go and do to yourself, huh?"

Maria's eyes fluttered, then opened. The moment she saw the duo beside her bed, she managed a smile.

"Preacher Henry…Tyrell…I can't believe you came to see me."

"Why wouldn't we, girl? Looks to me like you need prayin' over. You got any problem with that?"

"No, sir," she said softly.

"That's good…that's good. So let me do my thing, and then we'll let you get some sleep."

He laid his hand on her arm, closed his eyes and prayed a simple "Says it all" prayer.

"May the grace and healing of our sweet Lord fill your body and soul. Amen."

Moved by the gesture, she touched his hand. "Thank you, Preacher Henry."

"You're welcome, young lady. Be well. I'll be praying for you."

Her gaze slid to Tyrell. "Good to see you again. Been back to the mall since I saw you last?"

"Yeah, I guess." Then he moved a little closer to her bed.

His eyes grew bigger as he stared at her injuries, then the machines and IV. "Someone really tryin' to kill you?"

Henry frowned. "Tyrell!"

He backed off a step. "You know I'm askin' for a reason, okay?"

Bodie frowned. "Like what kind of reason?"

"Where I live, I hear things," Tyrell said.

Maria's eyes widened as Bodie grabbed the boy by the arm.

"Outside. With me," Bodie said, and walked him out of the room.

"Sam. Inside with Maria."

Sam didn't have to be asked twice.

Bodie walked Tyrell to an alcove across the hall. "What do you hear?"

Tyrell looked defensive. "Stuff. Like someone wants her iced."

Bodie's heart skipped a beat. "Who's the some-one?"

Tyrell shrugged again. "Don't know who put out the hit, but I heard somethin' about who might have taken the job."

God in heaven... Was the first break in this nightmare going to come from a kid who hadn't even been born when this all began?

"I need a name," Bodie snapped.

Tyrell glanced over his shoulder, making sure there

was no one else around, then shoved his hands in his pockets.

"Maybe I heard someone say Tom Jack Bailey."

Bodie was writing down the info as fast as Tyrell talked.

"Do you know him? Do you know where he lives?"

"Uh-uh," Tyrell muttered. "All I hear is he's from somewhere up around Claremore, but that ain't sure."

Bodie took a card out of his pocket and put it in Tyrell's hand.

"Thank you. Very much. If you hear anything else, give me a call."

"Yeah, whatever," Tyrell muttered, but he dropped the card into a pocket, then looked around to spot the old preacher, who was standing by the door with Sam.

"You done, boy?" Henry asked.

Tyrell nodded.

Bodie stopped at the door. "Thank you for coming… both of you."

"We won't be bothering you again," Henry said. "But we'll still pray for her…for all of you."

Bodie was punching in the number of the precinct as they walked away. He counted the rings impatiently, then relaxed when Carver answered.

"Lieutenant…Bodie Scott. I just got a tip on our bomber."

Phil Carver reached for a pen. "I'm listening."

"According to my informant, there was a hit out on Maria Slade, and a man named Tom Jack Bailey took the job. Might be from up around Claremore, but that's not a firm location."

"Good news for a change," Carver said. "I'll start the ball rolling here, and I'll call the Rogers County sheriff. I'll have him send some men out to pick the guy up for questioning. If he's our bomber, we might finally find the man behind the money."

"Yes, sir," Bodie said, then headed back to Maria.

She wakened to a tapping sound, but it was the moonlight coming through the threadbare curtain hanging beside the bed that kept her from going back to sleep. It was making scary shadows on the wall.

When she swung her feet down to the floor, she gasped. The floor was cold.

"Mommy. Mommy. Where are you?"

Then she saw a light—a light under the door that led out to the hall. It was reassuring, but the noises in the hall were not. She was afraid to get out of bed. Something bad was out there—in the light.

Someone was yelling. It was Mommy! Mommy was yelling. She had to help.

It took all of her courage to open the door, and when she got into the hall and heard a man's voice, too, she stopped. He was yelling at Mommy, but it didn't sound like Uncle Tank.

Mommy screamed.

She stepped out of the shadows just in time to see her mother slap him.

"Get out! Get out now you, creep, and don't come back. You don't want us. Fine. We don't need you."

"Count on it! You'll never see me again, but just to make sure I never see you…"

"No! Oh, my God! No, Frankie, no! Please don't!"

The stranger had a gun and he was pointing it at Mommy!

Boom! Boom!

The dishes rattled in the cabinet as Mommy fell backward on the floor. Something red was on the wall. Something red was on her clothes. Something red was spilling on the floor underneath her.

The bad man kicked Mommy, then got down on his knees beside her. Mommy was grabbing at his shirt, leaving red spots all over it.

The man was laughing. Why was he laughing? Mommy was hurt.

"Too bad our little Mary isn't here or I'd put her down, too. Tie her up in a sack and throw her into the Arkansas like a litter of unwanted pups."

She clasped her hands to her mouth, afraid to move. Afraid to breathe. He wanted to put her in a sack and throw her in the river! He couldn't do that. She didn't know how to swim.

All of a sudden the stranger jumped up, kicked Mommy one more time and ran out the door. He was gone! They would be okay now—only Mommy wasn't getting up.

"Mommy! Mommy! I had a bad dream."

But Mommy didn't move.

Something warm was running down her leg. She was horrified when she realized she'd wet her panties! Her eyes widened as she looked at Mommy, certain Mommy would be mad. She was a big girl. Big girls didn't wet their panties anymore.

Then Mommy was looking at her, reaching toward her, and she was crying. Blood was coming out of Mommy's mouth. Mommy needed her to come, but her feet refused to move.

No, Mommy, no.

Maria screamed.

Her eyes flew open, her gaze frantic as she looked around the room. Like the dream, except for a night-light, it was in darkness.

Within seconds, Bodie was at her bedside. Out in the hall, both Sam and the guard were on their feet, then inside the room before she could draw another breath.

The guard's gun was drawn.

Sam's fists were doubled.

Bodie held out a hand. "I've got it. Bad dream. Just a bad dream."

They quietly withdrew as Bodie lowered the bed rail and then slipped onto the mattress beside her. She was sitting up and shaking, her hands covering her face.

"Easy, honey," he said softly, as he unwound the IV tubing from around her elbow. "Don't want to pull this thing out."

Maria moaned and leaned into his chest as his arms

surrounded her in a safe embrace. She was trembling so hard her teeth were chattering.

"Are you in pain?" he asked. "Want me to get the nurse?"

She shook her head, then dug her fingers into his forearms as she pulled away. The horror on her face was intense.

Bodie cupped her cheek. "Talk to me, sweetheart."

She closed her eyes briefly as the dream began a fast-forward loop inside her head, and all she could hear was one name over and over. Frankie. Frankie. The name of the man who'd shot her mother was Frankie.

She opened her eyes.

"Frankie. The man who shot my mother was named Frankie."

Bodie gasped. "You remembered?"

"I think I've been having flashes off and on ever since the blast, but I kept fighting it. Maybe it's the pain meds. Maybe they dulled my defenses enough that I finally let go. In my dream, I was in bed when a sound woke me up. Mommy wasn't in bed with me. The moonlight made scary shadows on the wall, and I went to find her. I could hear voices. She was mad. She was screaming for someone to get out. A man was yelling back. I hid, then realized Mommy needed help. I saw her slap him."

"Did you know the man? Had you ever seen him before?"

"I don't remember…. I don't think so. But right after she slapped him, he pulled a gun. She begged."

Tears spilled from Maria's eyes and down her cheeks.

"Oh, God…she begged, she begged. 'No, Frankie, no,' but he shot her anyway. Twice. It was loud. So loud." Maria put her hands over her ears, but the sounds wouldn't go away.

Bodie's heart was racing. This was the break they'd been waiting for.

"You did good, baby. You did good. This will help us find the man who killed your mother."

He needed to call the lieutenant, but Maria grabbed his hand, pulling him back. He could tell that she had to get it out. It had to be said to make it real.

"He kicked her…and kicked her. She was looking up at him while the blood bubbled out of her mouth and out of her wounds, and he still kept kicking her."

"Jesus," Bodie muttered.

"Then he got down on his knees beside her and said, 'Too bad our little Mary isn't here.' He said he'd 'tie her up in a sack and throw her into the Arkansas like a litter of unwanted pups.' Then he got up, kicked her again and ran away."

She was shivering now and gulping back sobs. "He said 'our.' He must have been my father, although I wouldn't have understood that at the time. And I didn't move, because I was scared he'd see me. I didn't want him to throw me in the river. I couldn't let that happen… because I didn't know how to swim."

Bodie pulled her head down to his shoulder and shut his eyes. No wonder she'd suppressed her memories.

"I kept calling Mommy's name, but my feet felt heavy. She looked at me. I could see her lips moving, but I couldn't hear what she was saying. Then I wet my panties, even though I was a big girl."

By now Bodie was crying with her as her body shook. Twenty years of terror were finally turning her loose, coming up her throat in hard, ragged sobs.

There was nothing he could say or do but hold her and let her cry herself out. His job was to catch the evil son of a bitch who'd done this, and make sure he and his fellow cops did everything right, because the day the State of Oklahoma put this man to death, he would be in the gallery, watching him take his last breath.

Eighteen

A little while later a nurse arrived and injected another syringe of painkiller into Maria's IV port. Within minutes she had fallen back asleep. Bodie waited until he was sure she was completely out, then he was out the door.

Both her guards—official and self-appointed—stood up.

Bodie pointed at Sam. "Inside with her."

After three days, Sam had the routine down pat and pivoted quickly, then disappeared into the shadows.

Then Bodie pointed at the cop.

"Do not—under any circumstances—let anyone in there until I get back."

"Not even the doctors?"

"Not even," Bodie said. "I won't be long."

The cop moved in front of the door and folded his arms across his chest as Bodie headed for the waiting room. He was counting on it being empty at this time of night, because he needed a place where he could talk without fear of being overheard. In spite of the hour, he had to talk to his lieutenant. It wouldn't be the first time one of the detectives had called the man at home, and it undoubtedly wouldn't be the last.

He was scanning his cell phone as he walked, searching for Carver's home number, then hitting Dial. It began to ring as he walked all the way to the back of the empty waiting room, where he dropped wearily into a chair.

Carver answered on the fourth ring, in a husky, grumpy voice.

"This better be good."

"Sorry to call you so late, boss, but it's Bodie. Maria Slade woke up screaming. Had some kind of emotional breakthrough. She remembered the name of the man who shot her mother. Said she saw the whole thing, including the man. We only have a first name, but we've caught bigger fish with less."

Carver threw back the covers and sat up on the side of the bed.

"Dammit, she couldn't make it easy for us, could she?"

"No, sir. Not after twenty years. She said her mother was screaming at the man, and when he pulled a gun, her mother began screaming and saying, 'No, Frankie, no.' More info may come as time passes. As soon as she's able to go home, we'll see about getting a sketch artist. Maybe then we can come up with a face to go with the name."

"When do you think she'll be released?"

"Doctors aren't committing themselves. Still not sure."

"Will she be able to be on her own after she's released?"

"It doesn't matter, because she won't have to make that decision."

Carver shoved a hand through his hair and then leaned back against the headboard, thinking to himself as he did that late calls like this were only one of the reasons why he was no longer married.

"She's pretty damned lucky to be alive," he said. "Oh. Finally got a report from the bomb squad. It was some kind of homemade job rigged to go off when she hit the remote. I don't think the bomber took distance into consideration when he rigged it, or maybe he was just a screw-up. Luckily, she was far enough away to escape the worst of what could have happened. If it had been made of the new high-tech explosives, it wouldn't have mattered where she was. She would be gone, along with a couple of houses around her."

Bodie's eyes narrowed. "Which tells me that whoever's behind this seems to be using some less than stellar local talent instead of calling in pros."

"I thought the same thing," Carver said.

"Did you hear back from the Rogers County sheriff about Tom Jack Bailey yet?" Bodie asked.

"Yes. They've made one sweep by there already, but no one was home. They'll go by the place again in the next day or so. Now, unless you have something else, I'm going back to bed. I have a meeting with the chief in a very few hours to brief him on this case. He's pretty uptight about it being one of Frank McCall's old ones. The sooner we close it, the better. Your info should make him happier."

"Yes, sir. Uh…are you all right with me focusing on just this case for now?"

Carver frowned. "As in…guarding a material witness, I presume? But don't we have a guard outside the room, as well?"

"Yes, sir."

"Are you on the verge of getting too involved?" Carver's voice had deepened, a sure sign he was getting perturbed.

"No, sir. Not at all. I'm way past the verge."

Carver cursed. "Dammit, Bodie. This is unprofessional conduct, at best."

Bodie was all set to plead his case. "It doesn't contaminate the case in any way. She's not a suspect. She's simply a family member who's seeking justice for a loved one."

"Don't feed me a line of bullshit. I am not the fucking media."

"Fine. No bullshit. When this is over, you're invited to the wedding."

"Holy shit! Maybe I really do need to replace you as lead investigator."

"No, sir. Please don't do that. I like my job. I would hate to quit it, which is the choice I'd make before I'd walk away and leave someone else in charge of her care."

"Double shit. How much vacation time do you have built up?"

"I don't know…maybe a month."

"Then use some of it. As of now, you are officially on vacation. If this ever goes to trial, we do not want to have to explain away Frank McCall's involvement *and* yours. Do you savvy?"

"Yes, sir. I'll send in the paperwork tomorrow."

"Fine. Enjoy your vacation," Carver snapped.

Bodie grinned. "Thank you, sir."

Carver hung up.

Bodie dropped his cell phone back in his pocket, then made a detour at the bathroom. After he stopped to wash up, he took off his hat, stared at himself in the mirror as he combed his fingers through his hair, then swept them across his whisker-rough chin. Dave had been bringing him clean clothes, and he'd been showering in the bathroom in Maria's room, but he couldn't remember the last time he'd slept in a bed.

He looked like hell and felt worse, but it was a good kind of tired. Maria was alive, and she'd had the breakthrough they needed. Now all he had to do was keep her breathing and let the Tulsa P.D. do the job.

When he got back to her room, the cop was still standing in front of her door.

"At ease, man," Bodie said. "Take a seat. When's your replacement due?"

"O-seven hundred, Detective."

"Have you had anything to eat or drink?"

"No, sir. I'm fine."

"Go take a bathroom break and get yourself some snacks from the vending machine. I'm here until you get back."

The cop strode away, then returned in record time, carrying a can of Coke and a cellophane-wrapped sweet roll. He nodded at Bodie, then resumed his position.

Bodie went back into the room.

Sam stood up. The expression on his face was questioning, but he didn't ask.

Bodie had to admire a man with restraint.

"Maria remembered what happened."

Sam's face seemed to melt. His lips parted, and even from where Bodie was standing, he heard the old man exhale as he turned and laid a hand on the covers over Maria's leg.

"Bless her little heart," he muttered. When he turned around, his cheeks were wet with tears. "Who killed my Sally?"

Bodie hesitated. Ordinarily, this kind of information would not be shared until the perp was in custody, but in this case, Sam Vincent was probably the only person who might be able to help.

"Did you ever know the names of Sally's tricks?"

Sam's attitude shifted again, this time to defensive. "At one time, I knew the name of every man she turned. Had it all down in a little black book, which I gave to that detective, McCall. It should be with the rest of the evidence. Why?"

Shit. The McCall connection the chief was afraid of

had just reared its ugly head again. One more thing he had to pass on to the lieutenant.

"What about the name 'Frankie'? Ring any bells?"

"Is that what Maria said? That someone named Frankie killed Sally?"

"She said she heard her mother scream, 'No, Frankie, no.' Then he shot her—twice. It was a brutal attack, but I'm not going into details. I think part of the reason Maria buried it so deep was because she also heard him threaten her own life."

"Son of a bitch. Do we know why he did it?"

"No, but he called her 'our' Mary. And threatened to put her in a sack and throw her in the river." Bodie's hands curled into fists; his voice was shaking as he went on. "She said she was afraid to cry out, because she didn't know how to swim."

A look passed between the two men.

"I will kill him," Sam said softly.

"Let the law deal with him," Bodie said.

"Then you better find him before I do. I'd gladly spend what life I have left behind bars to be able to watch him die."

A chill ran up Bodie's back. Except for a few details, that was the same emotional reaction he'd had when he found out someone had tried to kill Maria. If he'd needed proof that Sam had really loved Sally, he guessed it had just been offered.

"If you really want to help," Bodie said, "then sit down and make me a list of all the men you can remember who went by the name of Frank or Frankie."

Sam nodded, gave Maria one last glance, and then headed out the door.

Bodie leaned over the bed and kissed the side of Maria's cheek.

She flinched, then moaned as she shifted restlessly.

Bodie pulled the chair back up beside her bed. "Sleep, baby, sleep. I'm here. I won't let anything happen to you again."

Sunrise was breathtakingly beautiful. A burst of hot pink and soft yellow on a horizon that went on forever, and yet Franklin did not appreciate the heavenly display, because he hadn't been to bed.

He stepped back from the window and went into the bathroom, then stopped and stared at himself. Once upon a time he'd been considered handsome, with the world at his feet, and he'd taken advantage of it and all it brought.

It wasn't like his conscience was bothering him, because Franklin didn't have one. His theory was, you only lived once, and when you died, that was it. No afterlife. No God. No Devil. No one to answer to.

It had made his life choices too damn easy. But he'd never been backed into a corner before. The more he tried to cover his tracks, the worse his prolems became.

He'd paced the floor of his manor house throughout the night, reliving the life and the mistakes that had gotten him to this place, and, in the interim, emptying a bottle of good scotch.

He should be drunk.

Normally, he would have been.

He wondered if modern science knew that sheer terror could completely offset the effects of alcohol. At least it had helped him to a decision.

The bottom line was, nothing had changed. Maria Slade's return had been the impetus for the Tulsa P.D. to reopen the investigation into Sally Blake's murder. According to his source, she'd witnessed it and then suppressed it.

The people he'd hired to clean up behind him had been ineffective. Now he either sat down and waited for the cops to come knocking on his door, or he cleaned up himself, just like he'd done twenty years earlier. It was sometime after that last swallow of scotch that he'd come to a final decision.

He knew she was in the hospital, under guard. He also knew she would soon be released. That was when he would make his move. No sneaking in at night. No bombs. Face-to-fucking-face—and a bullet between the eyes…to her and whoever else got in his way.

End of problem.

End of story.

Maria was lying in her bed, a couple of pillows beneath her head. From the angle at which she was lying, she could see Bodie shaving. For her, it was the highlight of her day.

He was in her bathroom, minus his shirt and with his face covered in shaving cream, wielding a disposable razor as adeptly as she was sure he handled a gun on the firing range. What was making her smile was that he was softly humming beneath his breath. She wondered if he was even aware of it. As she watched, she flashed on what it would be like to live out her life with this man, watching him perform this morning ritual for the rest of their lives.

She shivered with sudden longing. It wasn't the first time looking at him had made her hot. He'd already made his plans for their future clear. The funny thing was, sometime over the past few days she'd begun to share his vision.

As she watched the play of muscles in his arms and across his back, she wondered what it would be like to be with him, feeling the power of his body, the rush of blood and the push of urgency as he drove himself into her, over and over. Just the thought made her shudder with longing. It was a miracle to her that he could still flirt and look at her the way he did. After everything she'd put him through, not to mention the way she looked now, he should be disgusted by all he'd seen.

But for whatever reason, he'd stayed steadfast, and she had come to appreciate him in ways she could never have imagined. He'd seen her through things that only a married couple would expect.

At one point, one of the pain meds they gave her made her sick. She'd spent hours throwing up, and God love him, Bodie was by her side the whole time, holding up her head and grabbing for the pan.

The first time she'd been able to get out of bed and

walk to the bathroom on her own, he'd been the rock on which she'd leaned.

The day the nurse announced she could go stand in the shower in her little bathroom instead of having another bed bath, it was Bodie who'd helped her back into a nightgown.

She hadn't seen the horror in his eyes when he'd first seen her naked body, but she could imagine it. The cuts and bruises, the tiny stitches and the staples in her head, which they'd finally removed, had all been vivid reminders of what she'd lived through. By the time he helped her back into bed, he had his emotions firmly back in control and his need to make someone pay even stronger.

For Bodie, what they were going through together only cemented his belief that they were meant to be. If they could get through this without freaking each other out, nothing would ever get in their way.

But for Maria, it was the knowledge that every time she woke up screaming, all she had to do was reach out and he was there.

By the time the day came for her release, she was ready for the next phase of this crazy sexless affair. Just a look between them was all the proof they needed that making love was on their minds 24/7.

Two days earlier, the plan for Maria's release had gone quietly into action. All her belongings had secretly been moved from the hotel to Bodie's home, but the room was still listed in her name.

The chief was all over whatever plans they'd made. After finding out that Tank Vincent's little black book had never turned up in evidence, it was apparent that Frank McCall had concealed it for his own profit. Probably blackmail.

A sketch artist had come to the hospital and spent an entire afternoon with Maria before coming up with a sketch that Bodie immediately knew would be impossible to use. Even after computer aging technology, the face had been too generic, which was why they were now at this crossroad.

A bait and switch.

Tulsa P.D. officer Nora Watts was in Maria's hospital room, checking herself out in the mirror while the others watched. She was wearing jeans and a blue blouse. She had on boots like the ones Maria favored, and was tucking a lock of her own blond hair beneath the dark brown wig, reminiscent of the style of Maria's own hair.

"How do I look?" she asked, posing for approval with all her makeup and bandages.

"Better than Dave," Bodie quipped.

His partner glared. He was wearing a Bodie-style Stetson, jeans and a sports coat, along with boots like the ones Bodie wore. From a distance, they would easily pass as Bodie and Maria, which was the plan.

"I don't know how you stand these freakin' boots," Dave muttered.

Bodie chuckled.

"I'm ready," Nora said, then turned and winked at Maria. "You get well, honey. I've got your back."

Maria made herself smile, but she was scared. Leaving the relative safety of the hospital was unnerving. But the plan was that the police escort waiting outside would take Nora/Maria back to the hotel under guard in the hopes that, if the killer was watching, waiting for another chance at her, he would make the mistake of picking on the policewoman instead.

"Be careful," Maria said.

Nora looked back over her shoulder as she seated herself in the wheelchair.

"Don't worry about me. I have PMS and a gun."

Dave groaned. "Dang it, Nora...TMI. Too much information."

Their lighthearted manner eased the tension, and within moments the fake-out began.

Dave jammed the Stetson down low on his head, grabbed the back of the wheelchair and pushed Nora out into the hall. A pair of armed and uniformed officers followed, leaving Maria and Bodie alone in the room.

Sam was outside in his motor home, waiting for his part in the drama to unfold. Everyone and everything was in place. As soon as they got Nora on the road, they would slip out of the hospital unobserved.

The media had been given word that the bombing survivor was being released. A couple of news vans were already out in the parking lot, hoping to get film of her leaving the hospital.

Four police cruisers were waiting at the entrance, along with a big SUV with tinted windows. When an orderly appeared in the doorway wheeling a dark-haired woman toward the SUV, everyone's attention shifted.

Nora had donned a pair of dark glasses, too, and when she went to get up from the wheelchair and into the SUV, it appeared as if Bodie Scott, well known for his boots and Stetson, was there to help her in.

Within moments, the small convoy drove out of the parking lot: two black and whites in front, the SUV in the middle, and two more black and whites behind. Both news vans followed as the procession began wending its way through the streets of Tulsa, back to the Doubletree Hotel.

Franklin heard the news that the bombing victim was being released. He'd driven into a parking lot across the street, waiting and watching long enough to confirm the fact. His ire rose as he saw her being wheeled out of the hospital, then loaded into the SUV. When they drove away, he slipped into the busy city traffic and followed, making sure to stay at least a block or two behind. As they turned off the street and into the hotel driveway, he stopped on the street long enough to see Maria exit with the cowboy cop on her arm and walk into the hotel.

Satisfied that he knew where she was, he drove away. There were plans to be made, but if all went as expected, by tomorrow, his troubles would be over.

* * *

"Easy does it, honey," Bodie—the real Bodie—said, as he helped her up the steps, then into the motor home.

Sam was hovering. "I got you a pillow and a blanket, if you want to lie down while we're driving."

During the past few days, Maria had grown accustomed to the presence of these men. One from her past. One from the present. Both joined in a common goal: to keep her safe. But she felt shaky. Standing up for just that short time had made her feel light-headed.

"I think I will lie down."

Bodie helped her back to the tiny bedroom, then took off her shoes as she sat down on the side of the bed. He watched her ease herself down, but he knew her well enough now to know she was jumpy. However, it was an understandable reaction to leaving the safety of the hospital. Someone wanted her dead.

"It's going to be all right. I promise you," he said softly.

She pulled the fake cap of bandages off her head, then reached for his hand.

"I'm scared, Bodie."

"Lie down, baby," he said, then pulled the blanket up over her legs before he leaned down and kissed her square on the lips.

"Trust me?"

She'd spent a lot of time watching this man in action over the past few days. One thing she'd learned was that he was a man of his word.

"Yes."

"Ready to go home?"

They'd already crossed that bridge a couple of days ago, when he'd informed her that he was taking her to his house, that she was no longer safe on her own.

"Yes."

Sam poked his head in the door.

"What can I do? You need anything else?"

Maria smiled. "You're taking care of it, Sam, just by helping me get home."

Sam nodded sternly, but he wanted to grin.

"Bodie…you ready to go?"

"Yeah. Just give me a minute to get to my car. You know the address. Head for my house. I'll be behind you to make sure we aren't followed."

"Got it," Sam said, and lumbered back through the motor home to the front seat.

Bodie looked down at Maria. There were so many things he wanted to say, but there would be time for that later.

"I'll be right behind you," he promised.

"I know. I'm okay," she said.

Bodie winked, then quickly made his exit.

Sam shut and locked the door as he watched the lanky cop lope across the parking lot. As soon as Bodie got in his car, he called back to Maria, "We're leaving now. Don't worry, sugar baby. Uncle Sammy will take good care of you."

Maria sighed, then closed her eyes. Sugar baby. He'd

always called her by that pet name. The fact that she remembered now was such a gift.

The old motor home began to move, slightly rocking the bed on which Maria was lying, but she didn't care. It felt a little bit like being rocked to sleep, which seemed like a good idea. So she pulled up the covers and closed her eyes.

By the time darkness fell on Bodie Scott's house, Sam's motor home was parked at the back of the property and hooked up to an outside electric pole. Bodie had invited Sam to sleep inside, but Sam had turned him down.

"I've slept in this old bus plenty of times before. It suits me. Besides, it'll give us an edge. I'll have eyes on the outside of your house while you're inside with Mary. If I see something fishy, I'll call your cell."

As far as Bodie knew, Maria was still asleep in her bed in the back of the house. He was in the kitchen, cleaning up from their dinner. The television was playing in the living room. He could hear bits and pieces of whatever was on but was more tuned in to the night sounds of his house.

He was pretty sure their plan to sneak Maria from the hospital without being seen had been successful, but he wasn't at the point of being willing to bet her life.

His parents had been planning on coming up this weekend and taking him out to dinner, but he'd put them off with a promise to reschedule later, claiming work-related duties that couldn't be avoided.

He would have loved to have them meet Maria—
and for Maria to meet them. But not now. He took no
chances when it came to involving his family in his
work, and until this case was over, Maria was off-limits
to everyone but him.

He was putting the last pan in the dishwasher when
he heard a noise behind him and turned around.

Maria was standing in the doorway, pale but upright,
which was a truly amazing sight.

"Baby! Did you call? I'm so sorry. I was running the
water and didn't hear you. What do you need?"

"I didn't call. I don't need anything. I just felt like
moving around a little, and I wanted to see you."

"So here I am," he said, and pulled her gently into his
embrace. "God…you feel so good in my arms. There was
a time when I was afraid I'd never hold you again."

Maria wrapped her arms around his waist and leaned
into his chest.

"Who knew all this would happen? I've been in Tulsa
nearly two weeks now and spent seven…"

"Eight," Bodie corrected.

"…eight days of that time in a hospital. I just want to
feel normal again."

He laid his cheek against her head, taking care not
to get close to the healing cuts, and closed his eyes.

"You feel pretty normal to me," he said.

She laughed softly. "I can't believe you're still making
passes at me. I look like a used target on turkey-shoot
day."

Bodie pulled back with a grin. "You do not." Then he frowned. "Have you ever been to a turkey-shoot?"

"I *won* a turkey-shoot."

His grin widened. "Seriously?"

"Seriously. About five years ago. I think I was all of nineteen. Horrified Bud. It was the one and only time I outshot him, but he's never lived it down."

Bodie laughed. "Like I said before…my folks are going to love you."

Maria tugged at his hand. "Come sit down in the living room with me. Tell me about them. I might actually want to meet them one of these days."

He rolled his eyes. "You can keep telling yourself this isn't serious, but you and I both know you'd be lying. I'm serious as a heart attack, Maria. I want you, woman. In my life. For the rest of my life."

Maria's heart jumped. That was a pretty serious vow for the short time they'd known each other, but she was in total agreement. He just didn't know it.

He led the way into the living room, then settled onto the sofa beside her. When he turned to face her, he reached for her hands.

"Here's the deal, love. Are you much of a gambler?"

Maria frowned. "As in cards and money?"

"Not particularly. I mean as in…taking chances when you feel like something is right. Like maybe with your horses."

"Oh. Yes, I guess I am. There have been horses that everyone told me couldn't be trained, but something in me knew that wasn't true. Between the two of us, we would always prove them wrong."

"Yeah. Like that. Gut instinct. Well, that's how I feel about you. Doesn't matter how long we've known each other. I just know we're a pair. I'll willingly wait as long as it takes for you to get into that mind-set, but I'm not willing to let you go."

"We've never even made out…let alone made love," Maria said.

He pretended a huge, heartfelt sigh. "If it hadn't been for that damned bomber, that situation would already have been rectified." Then he wiggled his eyebrows and grinned.

He was crazy, which she loved. But to be fair, there was something he needed to know. She rubbed her thumbs across his knuckles, then looked him straight in the eyes.

"I've dreamed about making love with you."

His eyes widened. "Was I good?"

She laughed. "Mind-blowing."

He shuddered. "Lord, woman. Don't put any more thoughts into my head than what I'm already dealing with."

"X-rated?" she asked.

"No way. What kind of a man do you think I am?" he said, then leaned forward. "Triple-X…at least."

Their foreheads touched.

She felt the heat from his body. There was an energy between them that was almost audible—like a low, urgent hum. She knew that making love with this man would be, at the least, explosive.

"Just get well, then you watch out," he whispered.

"Will you sleep with me tonight?"

He grunted, as if he'd just been punched, then drew back and stared into her eyes.

"I will lie with you. I will hold you. But tonight… nothing more."

She sighed. "How about tomorrow night?"

"Damn, woman. Are you trying to kill me here? I'm doing my best to be sensible. You just got out of the hospital."

Her voice trembled. "And I'm doing my best to remember what living is about."

He lifted a lock of her hair away from her forehead, then ran his finger down the side of her face to her lips. Now he understood.

"Because you came too close to dying, didn't you, baby?"

"I *know* I'm alive. But I want to *feel* it, too."

"I can make that happen," he said.

And just like that, he stood up, scooped her into his arms and carried her back to his bed, set her on the side of the mattress, then began taking off her clothes.

Maria's heart started to race, but when she was naked and he still hadn't removed anything but his shoes, she caught his hand.

"You next."

"No. Tonight is just for you."

Nineteen

Maria slowly eased herself back onto the mattress, then resisted the urge to pull up the sheets.

Bodie saw her reticence and stopped.

"If this feels wrong, I'll stop right now."

"No." She pulled him down beside her. "I just wish we'd done this before, when my body was all in one piece and one color."

"You're beautiful," he said softly, and kissed the hollow at the base of her throat, feeling the pulse of lifeblood beneath his lips.

"You're alive." He kissed the bruise on her shoulder, then the one above her right breast.

"You take my breath." His lips moved across her stomach, kissing every cut and every bruise that he saw.

"You stole my heart. Let me love you, Maria mine."

She shivered, but pulled him to her, giving him the access for which he asked.

"Close your eyes," he whispered, then swept his hand downward across her face.

She did as he requested, leaving herself blind and defenseless.

His breath was warm on her skin, but his kisses were scorching. By the time he got to her belly button, she was trembling.

Then he rose up on one elbow and looked down at her.

"Did I miss a place?" he asked.

She put a hand to her mouth.

He swooped.

Maria moaned, then cupped the back of his head with one hand and his shoulder with the other. She wanted him closer—deeper—forever. A coil of need was building in her belly as he parted her legs and found the nub between that was the beginning and end of detonation.

Maria's body arched against the pressure, which he obligingly increased. She moaned beneath her breath, as his fingers parted her feminine folds, then circled and stroked, circled and stroked, the tiny nub until it was hot and pulsing. She couldn't think, couldn't speak. She couldn't think to give back. There was no time for anything but remembering to draw her next breath. Then she blanked out to everything but the feeling.

Minute after earth-shattering minute, he took her up, then eased her down, bringing her to the brink of a climax so many times that her whole body was one solid ache.

"Bodie...Bodie...please," she whispered.

His answer was another kiss, taking the words right off her lips, and an increase in the pressure between her legs.

A sheen of sweat glistened on her skin. She was on fire from the inside out, and still she wanted more and more.

Ah, God. Let this feeling last forever.

And just when she thought it might, she shattered.

Abruptly.

Completely.

With a small, choking scream and the sensation that she was flying, she rode the bone-shattering spill all the way to the top and then, in a free fall, all the way down.

Bodie was shaking so hard his teeth were chattering. The need to be inside her was next to maddening. But it wasn't going to happen. Not tonight.

"Good, baby?" he asked softly.

"Yes...oh, my God...yes."

He nuzzled the side of her neck, right below her ear.

"Tell me how you feel."

"Alive. I feel alive."

Officer Nora Watts had shed the dark wig and the bandages hours ago, and was hanging out in her sweats behind closed curtains. This stakeout in Maria Slade's hotel room was a good gig and a welcome break from her normal job riding shotgun with her partner on Tulsa's south side.

She'd ordered steak and a baked potato, compliments of the Tulsa P.D., and while a nice glass of wine would have been good to go with it, she was still on duty. A big glass of sweet tea had been a suitable substitute.

When she heard thunder rumble overhead and then the sound of rain blowing against the windows, she hunkered down into the bed, thankful she wasn't out on patrol on a night like this. Satisfied and sleepy, she was thinking about turning off the TV and trying to sleep when someone knocked at the door.

She thought about alerting the cop on stakeout in the room next door, then changed her mind, grabbed the remote and hit Mute, reached for her gun, then quietly moved to the door on bare feet.

"Who's there?" she called out.

"Bellman. You have a message from someone in Montana. Shall I slip it under the door?"

"Just a minute," she said.

The woman she was impersonating was from Montana. Nothing seemed out of order. Her gun was in her hand, her finger on the trigger, as she stretched to look through the peephole.

Franklin's eyes were focused on the tiny hole in the door. From out in the hall, he could see nothing but a tiny hint of light. The moment the light was blocked, he knew right where Maria Slade was standing.

Confident that his shot would not be heard, he put the gun with the silencer up to the peephole and pulled the trigger.

At the same time he fired, a shot came from inside the room—a bullet shot through the door, slicing Franklin's side and then the wall behind him.

The shock of what had just happened was enough to stifle his scream of pain. But the sound of gunfire exploded in the hallway, which was exactly what he hadn't wanted to happen. Blood was already dripping through his fingers and onto the carpet as he bolted toward the elevator he'd wedged open. He pulled out the length of pipe he'd shoved in the door and punched L for Lobby, ripping off his undershirt as he rode and shoving it against the wound in his side. He could tell by feel that the bullet had only grazed him, but he was bleeding profusely.

His heart was racing as the car neared the lobby. He couldn't exit the elevator dripping blood, even if he was wearing a raincoat. Horrified that he was leaving his DNA all over the place, he came up with a quick change of plans as he rode. He stopped the car on the second floor, got out on the run and headed for the stairwell. By the time he reached the ground floor, he was shaking, but made himself walk in a calm, ordinary manner as he exited into a side hall, then left the hotel.

He'd stuffed the pipe into the top of one of the hiking boots he was wearing, the gun was in a shoulder holster under his raincoat, and he was walking as casually as he could out onto the street and then toward the parking area to his car, still holding the makeshift pressure bandage against his side.

He made it a point not to make eye contact with anyone, although he doubted his own mother would have recognized him. It was amazing what a wig and a little stage makeup could do.

His side was on fire as he got into the car, and his clothes were slowly being saturated with his blood. He drove cautiously through the rain-slickened streets, making sure he didn't get stopped for speeding. By the time he reached his house, he was trembling from blood loss and shock.

He pulled into the garage, waited until the remote-controlled door rolled down behind him, then staggered into his house. By the time he got to his bedroom, he was on the verge of passing out.

Cursing his continuing run of bad luck, he managed to clean up the wound, pack it with gauze, and then dig some antibiotics out of the medicine cabinet, left over from a sinus infection he'd had a couple of months ago. He downed three of them at one time, then began looking for painkillers. He found a couple of good ones left over from a root canal and swallowed them, as well. He didn't know if they would work, but going to a doctor was out of the question. Finally he fell into bed, telling himself that as soon as he rested, he would go back and clean up whatever blood he'd left behind downstairs and in the garage. His housekeeper came every other day, and since she'd been here today, he had a day's grace to get himself and the house back in order.

Confident he was safe, he closed his eyes and passed out.

The rain had passed over Tulsa on its way across the Oklahoma/Arkansas border. Sam was in his motor home. Although he was dozing in his recliner in front of the TV, he was having a hard time sleeping. After so many years of quiet at the lake, he was no longer used to the sounds of the city.

Inside the house, Maria had fallen asleep in Bodie's arms. Bodie was a light sleeper by nature, but now it felt as if every nerve in his body was on alert.

Every time the house creaked, the ice maker in the kitchen made a new batch or the clock chimed the hour, he would open his eyes with a jerk. Each time he quietly reassured himself that all was well, that his gun was on the table beside the bed and Maria was not running a fever, and he made himself relax. Common sense told him they were safe, but it was better to err on the side of caution.

Just as the digital clock registered 12:08 a.m., his cell phone began to ring.

The sound was rude and startling, and awakened him instantly. He grabbed it on the second ring, but not before it had awakened Maria, too.

"Sorry, baby," he said softly, rumpling her hair, then put the phone to his ear. "Hello?"

"Bodie. It's Dave. Are you all right?"

Bodie slipped his arm out from under Maria's neck and swung his legs to the floor.

"We're fine. What's wrong?"

"Nora Watts is dead."

Bodie inhaled sharply as he bolted to his feet.

"How the hell did it happen?"

"We don't know details, but we do know someone knocked on her door, and when she looked through the peephole, they put a gun up to the hole and pulled the trigger."

"Jesus…oh, Jesus," Bodie muttered, as he turned back toward Maria.

"What?" she asked.

He held up one finger and kept talking.

"Who found her?"

"The cop who was in the next room heard a shot and ran through the connecting door, but it was too late."

"He took her by surprise."

"That's the thing. Not entirely, he didn't. She had her weapon. She must have seen something when she looked through the peephole, because she got off a shot before she died. Her shot was the one her partner heard. We're guessing the killer had a silencer."

"Shit."

"Yeah. That bastard knows too many tricks. It's as if he knows what the police are looking for. We have security tape from that hall, but he was obviously disguised. No way he can be identified from that. However…thanks to Nora, we got his DNA. He bled like a stuck pig all the way out of the hotel. By the time the other cop got out in the hall, the elevator was already on the way down. He ran to the stairwell and somehow beat the car down to the lobby, but when the doors opened, no one was inside. We found blood on two, so we think the killer got off there and took the stairs down—probably right behind our guy. At least Nora didn't suffer. The bullet went straight through her eye and blew out the back of her head."

Bodie closed his eyes, picturing the fun-loving cop who pitched softball at the policemen's picnic every summer, remembering the way she'd been laughing when she left the hospital room. He felt sick for the loss—and guilty because he was relieved it wasn't Maria.

Dave cleared his throat. "Look, the lieutenant wanted us to give you a heads-up, because as soon as the story gets out, the killer will know he failed again."

"Isn't there some way to keep it quiet that it wasn't Maria?"

"No. That's not the way the chief wants to play it. He's up in arms, going to have a press conference in the morning, and Nora's family has already been notified."

"Dammit."

"Yeah," Dave echoed. "So Lieutenant Carver says stay safe and keep out of sight."

"Will do."

Bodie snapped the cell shut, then laid it on the table as he sat back down on the bed.

Maria had scooted to the side of the bed, and she put a hand on his thigh.

"What happened?"

"Nora Watts…the cop who was your decoy. She's dead."

"Oh, my God," Maria gasped, remembering the woman and the smile on her face as she'd left the hospital room. What was it she'd said? *I've got your back.* "She died because of me. Oh, my God…oh, my God. *She died because of me.*"

Bodie grabbed her. "No! She was a cop. A good cop. She died doing her job. And it wasn't because of you. It's because a killer is panicking. The good news is, Nora got a piece of him before she died. They've got his DNA. Hopefully we'll get a match."

But that didn't help Maria. Guilt swept through her in waves as she covered her face and sobbed.

Bodie groaned, then wrapped her in his arms.

Morning couldn't come too soon.

Morning was somber. Maria walked through the rooms as if Nora's body were laid out nearby. There was nothing Bodie could say to make things better for her. She just couldn't get over the weight of guilt.

Finally Bodie sat her down on the sofa and put her cell phone in her hand. His voice was stern. The usual glint in his eyes was missing.

"Call your sisters. Call Bud. Talk to them. Listen to them. Feel their love, baby…'cause you're sure not feeling mine."

Then he walked away.

The first call was to Bud. Then to Savannah, then finally to her older sister, Holly. And oddly enough, it was Holly who finally got through, and in a tone of voice she rarely ever used with anyone. When she lit into Maria, she was close to shouting.

"Maria! You haven't been listening to a thing I've been saying," Holly said. "You know what I believe. That we choose our lives before we're born, and that whatever awful things happen to us while we're on earth, they're things we've already chosen, either because we want to learn something more about ourselves, or because we need to teach something to someone else. You've heard me preach this all our lives, and you've always laughed. Well, stop laughing now and *think!* If I'm right, then your mother's death was preordained, along with everything that's happening to you, including that gorgeous man you hinted about, including the policewoman who died in the line of duty. It's happening everywhere all over the world right now. Soldiers are dying in wars. Children are dying from abuse and hunger. People are dying from diseases that can't be cured. What's happening to you is horrible, but don't let it beat you. You're alive because you're supposed to be! Stop feeling sorry for yourself and learn what you're supposed to learn from this, then let it go!"

Maria flinched. It was like a long-distance slap in the face, but a much-needed one.

"Okay. I get it," she said, and then wiped her eyes and blew her nose.

Holly sighed. "You should be in my shoes, honey. It looks like my mother's fears were right. I think my father was that serial killer all of St. Louis was looking for."

Maria gasped. "Oh, my God. Have you talked to him?"

"Lord no! I'm not playing cop. The St. Louis police are all over it, but I'm trying to stay out of the line of fire. It would be good if you tried to do the same."

Maria hiccupped on a sob, then blew her nose again.

"Okay. I love you, Holly. Thank you for being the best big sister ever."

Maria could hear the laughter in Holly's voice.

"I do what I can. Call me again soon."

"You, too," Maria said.

There was a click in her ear, and then the line went dead. She dropped the phone in her lap, and then leaned back and closed her eyes.

Bodie came back to check on her only after he could no longer hear her talking. He paused in the doorway to the living room. All he could see was the back of Maria's head. He wasn't sure if she was sleeping, but if she was, he didn't want to wake her.

"Stop tiptoeing around and come sit with me," she muttered.

He blinked, then did as he was told.

"How did you know I was in the doorway? I'm in my sock feet, and I wasn't making any noise."

"I don't know," she said. "Maybe I have good

mothering instincts. Maybe this proves my kids are never going to be able to put one over on me. Okay?"

Bodie slid an arm behind her neck and nuzzled the spot below her ear.

"Not 'your' kids—'our' kids, remember? Are you mad at me?"

Maria turned and crawled up into his lap, then tucked her head beneath his chin.

"No. You have very good instincts. I do listen to you. I guess I excel at guilt, okay?"

"Are you going to be able to be married to a cop and live with the knowledge that danger is a constant?"

She shrugged. "As my sister Holly just pointed out to me, people die every day, no matter how careful they are or what they're doing. When it's their time, it's their time."

Bodie pulled her close, reveling in the feel of her in his arms.

"Becky called while you were on the phone. She's coming over later. I didn't think you would mind."

"That will be great. Does Sam know…about Nora?"

"I told him."

Maria couldn't hold back a shiver. "What did he say?"

"That she must have been a damn fine cop to get off a shot anyway."

She sighed. "I guess that's a really good way to look at it, isn't it? That she was still doing her job when she took her last breath."

Bodie closed his eyes, unwilling for her to see his tears.

"Yeah, baby...that's exactly right. She was one damn fine cop, and the department is going to miss her."

Dave was at his desk the next afternoon, finishing up the paperwork on a hit-and-run, when his phone began to ring.

"Homicide. Booker speaking."

"I'm Sheriff Fraley out of Rogers County. I'm calling to update you on the status of Tom Jack Bailey, the man you wanted for questioning."

Dave sat up in his chair. "Great. Do you have him in custody?"

"We have him all right...or what's left of him."

Dave's expectations shifted. "What happened?"

"Well, judging by the bullet hole in Tom Jack's forehead, our best guess is someone shot him and tossed him in his own farm pond. Some neighbor kids snuck over the fence to go fishing. Thought they'd snagged the giant catfish known to inhabit said pond and pulled up a piece of Tom Jack, instead. They're pretty upset, as you can imagine. Anyway, he won't be doing any talking. Thought you'd want to know."

"Dammit," Dave said. "But thank you for letting me know. Does the M.E. already have the body?"

"Yeah. Hauled it off about an hour or so ago. Told him you'd be wanting a copy of the autopsy...when he gets around to it."

Dave grinned to himself. The sheriff did have a way of imparting information.

"Thank you for the call."

"No problem. Happy to help."

Dave hung up, then glanced toward the lieutenant's office, making sure he wasn't on the phone, and headed that way.

Sam was in Bodie's kitchen watching Becky take a cake out of the oven. Maria was on a stool near the counter, licking the spoon Becky had left sitting in the bowl of cake batter. Becky set the cake down on a rack to cool, then grinned when she saw what Maria was doing.

"Still have that sweet tooth, don't you, honey?"

Maria grinned. "It's chocolate. For that, no excuses are needed."

The front door slammed.

Sam stood abruptly and bolted out of the room.

Maria tilted her head slightly, then took another lick from the spoon. "It's just Bodie."

"How do you know?" Becky asked.

"I can tell by the sound of his walk."

Becky nodded knowingly. "You've got it bad, don't you?"

Maria looked startled, then almost blushed, but she was saved from answering when Bodie strode into the room with two sacks of groceries in his arms.

"Man...if I knew my house could smell this good when I come back, I'd leave more often."

Maria pointed. "Becky made a chocolate cake."

Bodie sat the sacks down on the cabinet, then swiped his thumb across Maria's nose.

"And my Maria is eating what's left over, isn't she? Did you save some for me?"

Maria eyed the last bit of batter, then extended the spoon toward his mouth.

"Open wide."

He obliged, rolling his eyes in mock delight as the batter hit his tongue. It made Maria laugh, which was all he was shooting for.

He gave her a quick kiss, noting the slight chocolate taste, and then began putting up the groceries.

Maria watched as a feeling of deep satisfaction swept through her. This was how she felt with her family back in Montana. Warm. Safe. Confident that she was loved.

It had never occurred to her that she could make a new family somewhere else and still feel the same contentment, but life here in Tulsa was proving her wrong. Sam and Becky were family to each other, and once she'd belonged to that family, too. Now she was in the act of reestablishing her place.

Bodie had his own branch of family on the Claremore ranch. She had yet to meet them, but she was eager to. She couldn't help but wonder if she would fit in there, as well.

Then he turned around and caught her staring, and the look that passed between them made her ache. She'd better figure out a way to fit into his family, because he was already the perfect fit in her heart. And right at that moment, she made a calculated decision. Tonight was the night. No more guff or playing the hero from Bodie Scott. She wanted him in her life, in her heart, and as deep between her legs as he could go. Then she shivered. The mere thought of how it would feel was making her hot.

Just to make him nervous, she smiled.

When he suddenly flinched and dropped the liter of pop he was holding, she grinned to herself, then looked away. Oh, yeah. He was way past ready, too.

The moment passed, and the cake cooled enough for the frosting to go on. Sam was in the living room watching TV. Bodie was in his office, and Becky was getting out plates to serve the cake, when Bodie's cell phone began to ring. Maria grabbed it from the counter and headed toward his office.

He had heard the ringing and was on his way down the hall when she met him halfway. He took the phone out of her hand, and at the same time slipped an arm around her shoulders and kissed her senseless.

Before she could take a breath, he'd flipped the phone open and answered, but he held her close and began doing a slow two-step to an imaginary song as he spoke.

"Hello?"

"It's me," Dave said. "They found Tom Jack Bailey... in pieces. He was in his own farm pond with a bullet hole in his head. Looks like whoever hired him to kill Maria was pissed off because he missed."

Bodie went suddenly still.

Maria could tell it wasn't good news.

"Dammit," Bodie said. "That's two dead hit men and still no clue as to who's the man behind the money."

Maria frowned. This must mean the bomber was dead and they'd found the body.

"No, not a hint," Dave said. "But we have one interesting bit of news I thought you might want to hear."

Bodie glanced down at Maria again, then kissed the tip of her nose.

She cupped his butt with her hands and slid beneath his arm until they were standing face-to-face. She smiled, knowing whoever Bodie was talking to had no idea that he was doing an admirable job of making out with her in the middle of their conversation.

Bodie's muscles tensed as his eyes narrowed. She was playing with fire and didn't know it.

"So what's the good news?" he muttered, as he turned and backed Maria against the wall.

She stifled a moan as he did a little bump and grind, then hid her face against his chest.

"You know that theory you had that Maria's father might be the one who killed Sally Blake?"

Bodie stilled. All his playfulness stopped.

Maria felt the shift in focus and knew something important was being said.

"What about it?" Bodie asked.

"On a hunch, I had the crime lab run the blood from Nora's killer to see if it matched that old DNA test you found in Sally Blake's things. Well, guess what, partner?

It's a match. The man Sally claimed was Mary's father is the same man who shot Nora and left a trail of his own blood as he ran."

"Son of a bitch," Bodie whispered, then looked down at Maria. How did a man get so fucked up that he was willing to off his own child? "That's huge. Have you guys found anything on the phone records of our two dead hit men? Like maybe the same number showing up on both?"

"Yeah. We already covered that. There are phone numbers on both we can't confirm because they're throw-aways. Whoever is behind this is smart. He knows what the cops look for. He knows how to hide his tracks."

"Except he didn't expect to bleed all over that hotel."

"Yeah, karma's a bitch," Dave said. "You guys take care."

"And you keep me in the loop," Bodie countered.

Dave grinned. "No problem. Oh. The guys wanted me to ask you to be sure and take lots of pictures. We're all interested in seeing the sights you're enjoying on your vacation."

"You tell the guys to go screw themselves. And when they're done…go find the killer. He'll know soon enough that Maria Slade isn't dead," Bodie drawled, then dropped the phone in his pocket and turned his attention back to Maria.

Maria was holding her breath. Something bad had

happened, and she was afraid to ask, especially after the way Bodie had signed off. But she had to know.

"What's wrong?"

"Oh…the guys at the office are just a bunch of clowns."

"So nothing's wrong?"

He sighed, then lowered his head until their foreheads were touching.

Maria could feel the warmth of his breath against her cheek. But something *was* wrong. She could feel it.

"Bodie?"

"Remember that DNA test we found in the baby book your mother made?"

"Yes."

"It matched the blood found in the hall outside the hotel room…your hotel room…where Nora was killed."

It took a few moments for reality to sink in, and when it did, Maria pulled out of his arms, needing space to absorb the blow from the truth.

"No," she finally said.

"Yes, baby. There's no mistake."

She started to shake. "This man. This Frankie who is my father and who wanted to put me in a sack and throw me in the river? Purposefully…knowingly…stood outside the door to what he believed was *my* room, put a gun to the peephole and pulled the trigger, thinking it was me?"

"Yes. I'm so sorry, baby."

Maria couldn't take a full breath. The air felt heavy.

Her body was frozen in place as shock spread through her. But another emotion was growing that made her feel as if she was about to split in two.

"Maria. Are you okay?"

She glared. "What the hell do you think?"

"I think you're not."

"Well, you'd be right," she snapped. "It seems that remark he made about throwing me in the river wasn't just bullshit after all."

Bodie's eyes narrowed. He'd been waiting for her to burst into tears. He hadn't been expecting anger.

Maria lifted her chin and doubled up her fists.

"So that son of a bitch wants me dead, does he? He must be a real fuckup! When it comes to everything related to my mother's murder, except for killing her, he hasn't been able to do anything right."

Sam heard all the shouting and came into the hall, almost as angry as Maria looked.

"What's happening?" he growled.

Maria turned, her eyes blazing. "My sperm donor is still trying to eradicate his little weed. I'm going to eat cake. Anyone want to join me?"

Ignoring the twinges of pain, she stomped down the hall and out of sight while the men stood and watched.

Confused, Sam turned to Bodie. To his surprise, the cop was grinning from ear to ear.

"What the hell just happened?" Sam asked.

"My Maria is getting well," Bodie said. "That cake sounds good. Want to join us?"

Sam threw up his hands. "What the hell. If it will get me some answers, I'll eat cake."

Twenty

Maria plowed through two pieces of chocolate cake so fast that Bodie thought she would choke. He was afraid to offer so much as a glass of milk for fear he would get it back in his face.

But it was a revealing time for him. At least he knew that in the years to come, if he ever made her mad, he would either need chocolate or would have to make himself scarce.

Becky and Sam had gotten the rundown on the news, and both were staggered by it. Becky couldn't look at Maria without wanting to burst into tears. The thought that a man could so coldly put a gun to what he thought was the face of his own flesh and blood and pull the trigger without a second thought was chilling.

They'd seen Maria's reaction and knew the last thing she needed was talk. Sam had taken his cake to his motor home, and Becky packed up a piece and went home.

Bodie stuck it out with Maria, eating his cake without

talking, then quietly getting up and putting his plate in the sink. Before he could turn around, she was behind him, sliding her arms around his waist and burying her face against his back.

"I wasn't mad at you."

His heart swelled as he covered her hands with his own.

"I know, baby."

He turned, then caught her gaze. The fire was still in her eyes, but the tension in her body was gone.

"This is hell," she said.

"We'll get through it together."

"Are we alone?"

He nodded.

"Lock the doors. I want to make love."

Bodie felt his heart stop, then kick back into rhythm in double time. He headed for the back door, turned the locks and took her by the hand, then led her into the hall and put a finger against her breast.

"You. In my bed."

He pivoted sharply, heading for the living room as Maria made a move toward his room, stripping off her clothes as she went.

By the time Bodie got back to the hall, he was running. The trail of clothing almost stopped him in his tracks, but he felt the challenge. She was still mad—as mad as a woman could be and not burst into flames. But she was channeling it into a need for sex. The most basic reminder of life.

He pulled his shirt over his head and started walking.

She was in the middle of the bed, flat on her back with her arms over her head. The thrust of her breasts was defiant. He felt like she'd just flipped him off.

A muscle jerked at the side of his jaw. It was the only hint of emotion.

He stripped where he stood. When he dropped his shorts, his erection was already an undeniable fact. He watched her eyes glaze and her lips grow slack, and imagined he could feel the heat from her body from where he was standing.

"Open your legs."

Maria shuddered. She heard him, but her body felt as if she'd shifted into slow motion. She felt her legs move almost of their own volition. When he started toward her, she moaned.

If he didn't hurry, she was going to climax without him.

"I need—"

"I know what you need," Bodie said, and slid between her legs so fast he was in her before she knew it.

She was slick and hot, and he felt her climax coming before his first thrust. Just to make things interesting, he hammered home the point that she wasn't the only one burning with a need to explode.

Maria's scream was at the back of her throat when he put his mouth over hers and swallowed the sound. She tried to hold on—to think, to move—but the rage of her passion took her by surprise. She thought she would die from the jolt and the force as her body betrayed her. It was over before it had begun. She was the vessel, and he was the means of filling her as the climax took her up and up and up, rolling through her body in wave upon wave of blood-rush.

When it peaked, she gave herself up to the fall, knowing that the little death that came with it would be worth the pain.

Moment after moment, her body shook and her heartbeat raced, and she rode the feeling back to sanity and reason. She had no sense of self, or of the fact that Bodie was still inside her, hard and pulsing, as yet unfulfilled. She couldn't see him for the haze of red before her eyes.

Had she died?

Was this heaven, or had she fallen into hell?

She did not know her hands were fisted in his hair, or that he was counting the racing beats of her pulse pounding at the base of her throat.

This wasn't sex.

It wasn't love.

It was a mating between two forces of equal power.

Then finally, finally, Bodie heard what he'd been listening for.

A sigh.

Her heart was silent. Her rage was spent.

And he was still inside her. Hard and focused. Waiting. Waiting. For her to open her eyes.

She took a slow, shaky breath, then looked up.

Bodie was covered in a sheen of pure sweat, born of restraint.

"Mine."

When he spoke, her heartbeat ricocheted once, then stilled. He hadn't asked. He'd informed. It was only fair that she acknowledge the fact.

"Yes."

"This is for you, so that you never forget."

Then he started to move, this time following his heart and not her heat, taking the time to wind her back up and then let her go—all over again. Only this time he went with her, spilling his seed with such force that he forgot to breathe.

Franklin Sheets was but a shadow of his former self. He hadn't been to the office in days, claiming illness, claiming migraines, claiming anything he could come up with to get his secretary off his back. He'd canceled appointments, rescheduled court dates, lost clients, made more enemies than he'd had before, and nothing mattered.

He'd lost the clear focus of the trial lawyer he had been. He was a walking, talking vehicle of revenge. And he was losing his grip on sanity.

He didn't remember that Sally was already dead. In his mind, the clone-like image of her daughter had turned into its own time machine, sending him twenty years into the past, reminding him of the mistake he had made in ever getting involved with such a slut.

He'd been tricked by her beauty, then caught up in the

hot rabbit sex. She was a good lay. No one could fault her for that. But the bitch couldn't read or write, and bedded others as readily as him. What the hell ever made her think they were a couple, he didn't know. Racked with a low-grade fever and unshaven, he thought of nothing but shutting Sally's mouth.

But he couldn't find her. Last time he'd seen her, she'd been with that cowboy cop. Which meant…since the woman he'd killed in Sally's hotel room had turned out not to be her, that the cowboy cop had been in on the bait and switch.

He already knew the cop's name from the dossier Ed Underwood had mailed.

Bodie Scott.

Detective Bodie Scott.

Homicide.

Murder.

Which was fitting, considering that was what he intended to commit.

But when he'd called the precinct—using an alias, of course—and asked to speak to him, he'd been told Scott was on vacation.

A lie.

Obviously.

But he'd let it slide.

He swiped a spoonful of mayonnaise across the bread he had out, then added the meat and cheese, stacked another mayonnaise-slathered slice of bread on top, and bit into it with animal-like force.

He glanced at the clock as he chewed. Nearly 7:00 p.m.

He took another bite, unaware of the blob of mayo hanging at the corner of his mouth, and scanned Ed Underwood's file, making a mental note of Homicide Detective Bodie Scott's home address.

The son of a bitch.

He was helping Sally hide.

So as soon as he finished eating, he was going to pay Scott a visit. If the lights were on, he was going to bet the rest of his life that was where the Tulsa P.D. had hidden her. Then he was going to take her out, her and the cop both, and end this bullshit once and for all.

He finished his food, swiped a napkin across his mouth, then moved toward his office. He needed his gun and silencer, a flashlight and some extra ammo, just in case. The only thing different this time around was the cop, so he would take him out first. Problem solved. Killing Sally would be easy. He'd already done it once before.

Sam couldn't sleep. Every nerve in his body was on edge. He'd walked the perimeter of Bodie's place twice and seen nothing to give him pause. The lights were on inside the house, but he didn't feel like talking, so he'd gone back into the motor home, but without bothering to turn on his own lights. Instead, he'd gone to the fridge, gotten himself a beer and then settled down in front of the windows in the dark to drink his beer with a good view of the street and the house.

* * *

With the help of his GPS, Franklin drove right to Bodie Scott's house, but he didn't stop. This first pass was a test run to check out the site. Seeing the lights on inside the house had been a confirmation that he was right. No way did the cop decide to go on vacation when he'd been lead detective on the reopened case.

What pissed off Franklin was that she'd been here all the time. If he'd only known, he wouldn't have wasted time with the hotel, and he wouldn't have gotten himself shot.

It was the same with a trial. Just when you thought you had it in the bag, there was always a surprise.

Yeah, life could be a bitch, and then it got worse.

It was always something.

But he knew how to take care of business. He'd proven that time and time again. He would fix this and then get his life right back on track. He *would*.

He took a second run past the house, going slower this time to verify the location of doors and windows, then turned at the corner for another run around the block, this time checking out the number of neighbors who were gone or in bed. The fewer witnesses reporting a disturbance, the easier it was to get away.

Sam knew that several of Bodie's neighbors had teenagers, which meant plenty of coming and going.

But he knew cars. And he'd picked up instantly on the fancy headlights and taillights of a Mercedes as it drove slowly past the house, and thought to himself that there was a car he'd always wanted to drive.

It wasn't until he saw it go past the second time, and even slower, that his instincts kicked in. It cost a bundle to drive a car like that. And it cost money to hire a killer, no matter how inept they were. Even if he was jumping to conclusions—even if it was nothing but a false alarm—he wouldn't let anything else happen to Mary on his watch. He reached for his cell phone.

Bodie and Maria were asleep in a tangle of arms and legs, exhausted from what had been a combination of love and war.

When his phone rang suddenly, Bodie woke with a jerk, startling Maria enough that she woke, too, then began trying to unwind herself from his arms.

She pointed to the bathroom as he grabbed the phone.

Bodie couldn't help noticing that she looked as good going as she did coming, then heard Sam's voice in his ear and remembered he hadn't said hello.

"Hey…Bodie! Bodie! You there?"

"Uh, yeah, sorry, Sam. I got distracted. What's up?"

"It may be nothing, or it may be something, but there's a Mercedes that's made two sweeps past your house, and if I was a betting man, I'd lay money that he's going to try for three."

Bodie flew out of bed, grabbing for his pants and looking for his gun.

"Where are you?" he asked.

"In the motor home, in the dark, watching."

"Don't turn on your lights, but if you get a chance, can you get out and maybe get on the blind side of the house, then watch to see if the car comes around again?"

"Yep."

"In case this is the real thing, if you see someone suspicious, don't try to approach him on your own. Remember, he's already killed twice this time around. I don't want you to be the third. Just call the police for me. I'll take care of us inside."

"I can do that. You just make sure nothing happens to Mary."

"Deal," Bodie said, and hung up, then headed for the bathroom.

Maria was about to step into the shower when he stopped her with a look. Her heart began to hammer.

"What?"

"It might be nothing, but Sam saw the same car, a Mercedes, circling the block too many times. I can guarantee it's not one of my neighbor's cars. That's out of our league in this neighborhood. Get dressed. I want you out of sight until I say it's okay."

"What if it's him? What if he found us?"

"I hope to hell it *is* him," Bodie muttered. "I want to see the bastard's face before I shoot."

Maria's eyes widened. "You're a cop. I thought you were supposed to arrest him."

"If I'm lucky, he'll shoot first. It'll give me a damned good reason to shoot back."

"I want a gun."

Once again, he was in awe of her spirit. Instead of cowering, she wanted to fight.

He remembered the turkey shoot. "I have a hunting rifle."

"Good. That's what I shoot best."

"I do not want you playing cop."

She nodded.

"It'll only be for your protection…just in case. Get dressed. I'll get the gun.

She flew out of the bathroom, then remembered that her clothes were scattered down the hall, so she got new ones out of the closet. Within moments, Bodie was back. He handed her a rifle and a box of ammunition.

"I'm thinking you'll know how to load this."

She eyed the weapon. "Sure do."

"Stay in this room. Stay on the floor and away from the windows."

He turned out the light in the bathroom, then grabbed her and kissed her—hard.

"Love you," he whispered.

"Love you more."

She was on the floor between the wall and the bed before he closed the door. She kept waiting for fear to set in. For her heart to thump and her palms to sweat. But it didn't happen. She felt calm. She felt secure. This was why she'd come. And if the killer was truly making a strike, one way or another, this would be over tonight.

* * *

Bodie had his cell on vibrate and was standing in the hall, just out of the glare of the living room lights. He'd turned on the television, upping the volume so that if the killer came up on the porch, he would assume his quarry was just inside, watching TV.

He hadn't heard from Sam again, but something in his gut told him this was the night. The killer had to be in a panic. They had his DNA. He had to assume Maria might have remembered enough of her past to put him away. He was obviously desperate to even be considering this move, but then again, he hadn't shown any restraint so far.

Bodie had his gun up, the safety off. Listening. Waiting. Watching for that one hint of motion, the tiniest indication that something was about to go down.

It was after the third sweep past the house that Franklin decided to make his move. He'd parked the car a couple of houses back and made his approach on foot. Dressed all in black, he felt part of the night as he slipped through the shadows between Bodie's house and his neighbor's. A part of him felt as if he was watching this unfold from outside himself, because this wasn't how he had chosen to live. This was the behavior of the people he represented. But he'd learned enough from all their stories to remember what to do.

Lesson number one. Check for dogs.

He'd found the house. No fence, which probably meant no dog, but he'd approached from a back alley, which was how he saw the big man standing at the front corner of the house, slightly hunched over and watching the street.

He froze.

Son of a bitch. They knew he was coming!

His heart started to pound.

How the fuck had they made him?

Then he made himself focus. If there was a guard out here, it figured that Sally was inside.

Thankful he'd had the foresight to bring the gun with the silencer, he took aim and fired. The pop was less than the sound of a breaking balloon. The man's body bucked, then made more noise hitting the ground than the gunshot that had taken him out.

Franklin waited, making sure the man was still down and that the shot hadn't alerted someone else. After a couple of minutes, he grinned.

One down. At least two to go.

Nothing was moving. Not inside the house. And as far as Bodie could tell, nothing outside, either. He was about to head outside and check on Sam when he thought he caught a glimpse of movement out on the porch. He tensed, watching the windows, then the door, listening for the sounds of someone circling the house, but the television was making too much noise. The very thing he'd used to indicate they were home was defeating his purpose.

All of a sudden he saw the doorknob turn. Once to

the left. Then once to the right. Testing, and finding it locked.

Shit. He wished he could tell Maria it was about to go down and she should get out of sight, but he had to trust that she was following his instructions.

His body tensed. His gaze was fixed on the doorknob as he took one slow, quiet step back, moving a little deeper into the shadows of the darkened hall as a knock sounded at the door.

He frowned. The killer was brazen enough to knock?

Then he remembered Nora. That was how the man had gotten her to the peephole. No way was he falling for that. He waited. A second knock followed.

Come on. Come on. Stop fooling around.

All of a sudden the door reverberated.

He's kicking in the door! Damn, I hope Sam already called the cops.

One more kick and the door flew inward.

Bodie caught a glimpse of a black-clad figure flying through the air, and then he fired. The intruder was already firing as he rolled. Pop. Pop. Pop.

Bodie ducked. The killer had a silencer! Something must have happened to Sam or he would be in here by now, which meant no one had called the police.

Shit. He'd lost Sam, and now he'd lost sight of the intruder.

All of a sudden the man came straight up from behind the sofa, popping off shot after shot straight at Bodie's hiding place. And then Bodie was on the floor, blood gushing from his shoulder. The bullet had gone through the wall and into his arm without stopping.

Get up. Get up. You can't let him get to Maria.

He rolled, switching his gun to his other hand. He wasn't a great shot with his left, but if he got close enough it wouldn't matter. He crawled down the hall and into the first bedroom, reloading as he went. Then he pushed himself up, using the wall as support, and waited, listening for footsteps and hoping his neighbors had heard enough to call the police.

The sound of shattering wood, followed by gunshots, was all Maria needed to hear to know that the battle had begun. She was on her knees behind the bed, watching the door and the faint beam of light beneath it, when a sensation of déjà vu suddenly rocked her back on her heels.

God, oh, God…just like before and that strip of light under the door.

Some of the gunshots sounded funny. Sort of a firecracker-popping noise. It hit her that he was using a silencer. She heard Bodie return fire, and then a loud, sudden thump before everything went silent. She thought she heard a groan, then a shuffling, crawling noise. Someone was hurt! What if it was Bodie?

This was crazy. This was hell. The worst night of her life was happening all over again, but she wasn't four anymore. And she wasn't helpless. She came up and out from behind the bed in one leap and, in bare feet, moved swiftly to the door. She waited, listening, and then heard the sound of footsteps coming up the hall.

When Bodie heard the thump from the bedroom next to him, he knew Maria was no longer hiding. He couldn't wait any longer. He stepped out from the doorway with his gun leveled and found himself standing face-to-face with the startled intruder.

A shot rang out.

They both dived for cover.

But Bodie knew a rifle shot when he heard it.

It was Maria.

Maria was in the hall, the rifle still on her shoulder, ready to fire again. The fact that Sam was nowhere in sight made her nervous, the blood on Bodie's shirt even more so. But it was the black-clad figure at the end of the hall on whom she focused.

The gun hung limply from his hand, as if he'd forgotten it was there, and the look of horror on his face was unmistakable.

Maria stepped out of the shadows into the light.

Franklin couldn't believe it. Sally was armed. He didn't know she knew how to shoot.

"You won't shoot me," he said.

Maria frowned. The man had to be crazy. Hell yes, she would shoot him—in a heartbeat.

"Drop your gun," she said.

She heard Bodie groan and then a shuffling noise behind her. "Bodie! Stay down."

She could hear him on his cell phone, calling 911, but her gaze was glued to the intruder.

"I said, drop your gun," she repeated.

All of a sudden Franklin flinched. Her words had reminded him that he was armed. He swung the gun up, but not quickly enough.

The blast from the hunting rifle took him off his feet and slid him down the hall.

Pain radiated through him like cracks in a broken windshield, spreading outward as the light in the hall began to dim. And then Sally was standing over him, that rifle up against his chest.

Blood was bubbling from the corner of his mouth as he tried to point up at her.

"Sally...didn' know...didn' know you could shoot."

"I'm not Sally," Maria said. "I'm Maria. And I'm not four—and you don't scare me anymore." Then she got down on one knee until they were staring face-to-face. "Just so you know...after you die, I will put your god-damned ashes in a sack and throw them off a bridge into the Arkansas River...just like a litter of unwanted pups."

Franklin shuddered. This wasn't Sally. He didn't know this woman at all.

"They won' let you.... You can't. They won't give you my ashes."

"Sure they will, Frankie. I'm your daughter. Your

blood kin. I can do whatever the hell I choose with your body, you worthless piece of shit."

Then she stood and, for a moment, the urge to kick him was so strong that she had to force herself to step away.

Franklin's eyes glazed over as she waited for him to take his last breath.

All of a sudden Bodie was behind her, taking the rifle out of her hand.

"Let go, Maria. Let go."

She swayed; then her fingers loosened.

The gun slipped from her to him without hitting the floor.

"He's not going to hurt anyone else. The police are coming. Hang on with me, baby."

She slipped an arm beneath his shoulder, but when she felt him stagger, she knew she couldn't keep him upright.

"You need to sit down."

"Yeah," he said, and slid onto the floor, the rifle still in his hand. They could hear the distant sound of sirens. If they hurried, maybe he wouldn't bleed to death.

"I've got this," he said. "Sam is outside somewhere… probably behind the house. He has to be hurt or he would be in here. See if you can find him."

She stopped in front of the gunman. Her father. "Is he dead yet?"

"Yeah. He's dead."

"Good," she said, and then ran through the house to the back door and out into the night.

But Bodie had lied. He could see the faint rise and fall of the man's chest. What was weird was, he knew him. Franklin Sheets. Hotshot criminal lawyer with an eye on the district attorney's job.

Surprise. Wasn't going to happen now.

"Hey, Sheets. Can you hear me?" Bodie said, and then scooted closer, wanting the man to see his face.

Franklin moaned. Someone was calling his name, but the pain in his chest was so bad. He just wanted to close his eyes until it went away.

"Sheets!" Bodie yelled, and kicked the bottom of Franklin's shoe.

The motion jarred Franklin into a few seconds of lucidity as he opened his eyes.

"Somebody call 911. I've been shot."

"I did, but you're gonna die before they get here."

Franklin moaned. This wasn't how he'd expected the night to end.

"She shot me."

"So did I. It's gonna be a race to see which bullet kills you, but I'm hoping it's mine."

Franklin blinked. Everything was turning into one solid blur as he began to mumble.

"You…sworn t'protect and serve."

"Except when you mess with what's mine," Bodie said softly. "At that point, all bets are off. You're a cold-blooded, snake-in-the-grass bastard who doesn't deserve so much as a flower laid on your grave. The day she tosses your ashes into the river, I'll be standing beside her watching them sink."

Franklin shivered. He could already feel the swirling water of the Arkansas pulling him down, pulling him under.

Epilogue

Sam was released from the hospital the same day Becky started her summer vacation. The bullet Franklin Sheets had fired had missed every vital organ, except for nicking a lung, which had collapsed. He'd been unconscious when Maria discovered his body, and was still out when they'd loaded both him and Bodie up and whisked them off to Saint Francis.

Finally he'd healed enough to be released. He and Becky hadn't lived under the same roof since they were both in their teens, but they were going to do it again now, at least for a while, despite every argument he could make.

She wasn't going to take her cruise down to Mexico as she'd planned earlier in the year. She was taking Sam back to his cabin at Lake Eufaula, and whether he liked it or not, she wasn't leaving until he was able to manage on his own.

Bodie's wound had been a through-and-through, and

he'd recovered much faster. And while he had yet to be cleared for full duty, he was at home on medical leave, enjoying his time with Maria and the fuss his family was making over the both of them.

It wasn't until his family had finally gone home and he had Maria back all to himself that he saw another side of the woman he loved.

What they hadn't talked much about, but what he knew was impending, was the dispensation of Franklin Sheets' estate. What surprised him then was Maria's immediate claim on his property as his only heir.

He would have expected her to want that kept under wraps, not set herself up to be quoted in the papers and mentioned for days on end in every media outlet in the state.

What he *had* expected, though, was her desire for revenge, which, once again, reminded him to never piss her off. He just couldn't have predicted how it would play out.

She'd kissed his mother goodbye with tears in her eyes, hugged his father and remarked again, for the umpteenth time, how much he and Bodie looked alike, and told them she couldn't wait for them to come back. She'd stood on the porch waving goodbye and holding his hand, and the moment they drove out of sight, she morphed back into a hard-ass.

She strode back into the house and was already on the phone with the lawyer she'd hired when he walked inside and closed the door.

From what he could glean from her side of the conversation, her legal connection to Franklin Sheets had finally been proven through up-to-date DNA. Franklin was unmarried. He had no other next of kin. The estate had to go through probate, but though he'd died without a will, no one else was making any kind of claim on his wealth except for the daughter he'd tried to kill.

Maria held up a finger at Bodie, as if to beg for a couple more minutes.

He sat down in the easy chair next to the sofa where she was sitting so he could watch her face.

"So…you have the full extent of my wishes recorded? Good. When can I come in and sign it?"

She jotted down a date and time, and then scooted forward on the edge of her seat.

"One more thing," she said. "About my father's ashes…when can I claim them?"

Bodie's eyes widened. Holy crap. She'd been serious.

"Tomorrow? Perfect. And you'll notify the crematorium? Thank you. You know where to send the bill."

She hung up, then sat for a moment without moving, without seeming to breathe.

"Maria?"

She jerked as if she'd forgotten he was there, then looked up, her expression still blank.

"Hmm?"

"Talk to me."

"Right." She tucked her hair behind her ear as she

gathered her thoughts. "Here's the deal. Franklin Sheets was a son of a bitch. We both know that. But he was my biological father, and I have a right to his estate."

"I don't care about any of that," Bodie said.

"Well, actually, neither do I. Or not the way you might think, anyway. I've made arrangements for everything to be liquidated. A foundation has been set up that will be run by a bank of lawyers, with all the earnings and benefits going to the John 3:16 Mission."

Bodie started to smile.

"Sheets would hate that."

"I know," she said, and then leaned forward, her elbows on her knees. "Tyrell already knows this, but there's a full-ride scholarship in his name for any college or trade school he chooses to go to. It was his willingness to tell what he knew that tipped the scales in our favor. I want him to know it was appreciated."

Bodie's smile turned into a full-fledged grin.

"He'll love that."

"I know."

"As for the devil's spawn, I get his ashes tomorrow at three o'clock. Will you go with me?"

"Yes, but you'll have to drive."

"I know. I just need you to navigate the way to the bridge. I want to find the deepest part of the Arkansas."

"You're really going to do it, aren't you?"

There wasn't a trace of anger, a twinge of fury, even a frown across her brow, when she answered.

"Yes. But not for me. For Mommy."

"Then I'm your man."

Maria looked at him then, her gaze fixed on the face of the man who was her heart.

"You were always my man. Even when I didn't know it."

Maria stood on the bridge, holding a burlap sack in one hand and the box bearing her father's ashes in the other. The wind that had been blowing earlier had suddenly calmed.

She opened the box and unceremoniously dumped the clump of gray, dusty ashes into the sack, then tossed the box in after them.

The sun had gone behind a cloud, as if God refused to waste daylight on what was left of this man.

Bodie's hand was on her back as she swung the sack over the side and sent it sailing.

End over end, then oddly flopping about, as a small puppy might have done in struggling to get out.

It finally settled on the water without a sound, floating along with the current. As they watched, the river water began soaking the coarsely woven burlap, causing it to sag, then slowly sink beneath the surface.

She stood without moving, without speaking, watching intently until the sack and its contents were gone.

At that moment the sun came out from behind its cloud, the rays hitting the water in such a way that it appeared as if a million tiny diamonds had just been tossed into the flow.

"Ready to go home?" Bodie asked.

Maria nodded.

They walked back along the bridge to where they'd parked, got in their car and drove away, while deep within the dark, muddy water, the sack and its pitiful contents went about the business of sinking into the ancient mud below.

* * * * *

A brand-new trilogy from
New York Times and *USA TODAY*
bestselling author

SHARON
SALA

that is sure to keep you
on the edge of your seat.

Available wherever
books are sold!

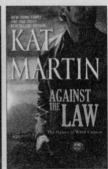

Start your Best Body today with these top 3 nutrition tips!

1. **SHOP THE PERIMETER OF THE GROCERY STORE:** The good stuff—fruits, veggies, lean proteins and dairy—always line the outer edges of the store. When you veer into the center aisles, you enter the temptation zone, where the unhealthy foods live.

2. **WATCH PORTION SIZES:** Most portion sizes in restaurants are nearly twice the size of a true serving and at home, it's easy to "clean your plate." Use these easy serving guidelines:
   - Protein: the palm of your hand
   - Grains or Fruit: a cup of your hand
   - Veggies: the palm of two open hands

3. **USE THE RAINBOW RULE FOR PRODUCE:** Your produce drawers should be filled with every color of fruits and vegetables. The greater the variety, the more vitamins and other nutrients you add to your diet.

Find these and many more helpful tips in

YOUR BEST BODY NOW

by

TOSCA RENO

WITH STACY BAKER

Bestselling Author of

THE EAT-CLEAN DIET®

Available wherever books are sold!

REQUEST YOUR FREE BOOKS!

2 FREE NOVELS
FROM THE SUSPENSE COLLECTION
PLUS 2 FREE GIFTS!

YES! Please send me 2 FREE novels from the Suspense Collection and my 2 FREE gifts (gifts are worth about $10). After receiving them, if I don't wish to receive any more books, I can return the shipping statement marked "cancel." If I don't cancel, I will receive 4 brand-new novels every month and be billed just $5.74 per book in the U.S. or $6.24 per book in Canada. That's a saving of at least 28% off the cover price. It's quite a bargain! Shipping and handling is just 50¢ per book in the U.S. and 75¢ per book in Canada.* I understand that accepting the 2 free books and gifts places me under no obligation to buy anything. I can always return a shipment and cancel at any time. Even if I never buy another book, the two free books and gifts are mine to keep forever.

191/391 MDN FDDH

Name	(PLEASE PRINT)	
Address		Apt. #
City	State/Prov.	Zip/Postal Code

Signature (if under 18, a parent or guardian must sign)

Mail to the **Reader Service:**
IN U.S.A.: P.O. Box 1867, Buffalo, NY 14240-1867
IN CANADA: P.O. Box 609, Fort Erie, Ontario L2A 5X3

Not valid for current subscribers to the Suspense Collection
or the Romance/Suspense Collection.

Want to try two free books from another line?
Call 1-800-873-8635 or visit www.ReaderService.com.

* Terms and prices subject to change without notice. Prices do not include applicable taxes. Sales tax applicable in N.Y. Canadian residents will be charged applicable taxes. Offer not valid in Quebec. This offer is limited to one order per household. All orders subject to credit approval. Credit or debit balances in a customer's account(s) may be offset by any other outstanding balance owed by or to the customer. Please allow 4 to 6 weeks for delivery. Offer available while quantities last.

Your Privacy—The Reader Service is committed to protecting your privacy. Our Privacy Policy is available online at www.ReaderService.com or upon request from the Reader Service.

We make a portion of our mailing list available to reputable third parties that offer products we believe may interest you. If you prefer that we not exchange your name with third parties, or if you wish to clarify or modify your communication preferences, please visit us at www.ReaderService.com/consumerschoice or write to us at Reader Service Preference Service, P.O. Box 9062, Buffalo, NY 14269. Include your complete name and address.

MSUS11

PRESENTING…THE SEVENTH ANNUAL
MORE THAN WORDS™ ANTHOLOGY

Five bestselling authors
Five real-life heroines

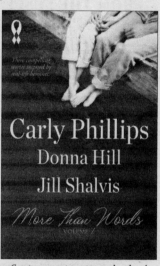

This year's Harlequin More Than Words award recipients have changed lives, one good deed at a time. To celebrate these real-life heroines, some of Harlequin's most acclaimed authors have honored the winners by writing stories inspired by these dedicated women. Within the pages of *More Than Words Volume 7*, you will find novellas written by Carly Phillips, Donna Hill and Jill Shalvis—and online at www.HarlequinMoreThanWords.com you can also access stories by Pamela Morsi and Meryl Sawyer.

Carly Phillips
Donna Hill
Jill Shalvis

More Than Words
VOLUME 7

Coming soon in print and online!

Visit
www.HarlequinMoreThanWords.com
to access your FREE ebooks and to nominate a real-life heroine in your community.

SHARON SALA

32802	SWEPT ASIDE	___ $7.99 U.S.	___ $9.99 CAN.
32792	TORN APART	___ $7.99 U.S.	___ $9.99 CAN.
32785	BLOWN AWAY	___ $7.99 U.S.	___ $9.99 CAN.
32677	THE RETURN	___ $7.99 U.S.	___ $8.99 CAN.
32633	THE WARRIOR	___ $7.99 U.S.	___ $7.99 CAN.

(limited quantities available)

TOTAL AMOUNT	$ _____
POSTAGE & HANDLING	$ _____
($1.00 for 1 book, 50¢ for each additional)	
APPLICABLE TAXES*	$ _____
TOTAL PAYABLE	$ _____

(check or money order—please do not send cash)

To order, complete this form and send it, along with a check or money order for the total above, payable to MIRA Books, to: **In the U.S.:** 3010 Walden Avenue, P.O. Box 9077, Buffalo, NY 14269-9077; **In Canada:** P.O. Box 636, Fort Erie, Ontario, L2A 5X3.

Name: _____
Address: _____ City: _____
State/Prov.: _____ Zip/Postal Code: _____
Account Number (if applicable): _____

075 CSAS

*New York residents remit applicable sales taxes.
*Canadian residents remit applicable GST and provincial taxes.

MIRA®

www.MIRABooks.com

MSS0211BL